A TAMING

"I'll help you," he offered, walking with her.

"That's fine with me. That's the least you can do after knocking me down." She was surprised that she actually found herself teasing him.

Jace gave a slight laugh. "What about you? You used your whip on me."

"Paybacks are tough, aren't they?"

"You have no idea," he agreed.

They were both smiling as they led the horses into the stable.

"Let me have a look at your hand," Sammie said.

"Why?"

"This will help you." She got a jar of salve and went over to where he was standing. "It works on the horses."

"So you use that whip on the horses a lot?" Jace asked.

"Only when I'm taming them or when they deserve it," she answered as she took his strong hand in hers to get a better look at the injury. She felt a shiver of awareness at that simple contact. She was startled by her reaction. No man had ever affected her this way before, and unsettled, she deliberately kept her gaze focused on the lash mark.

"Which one was I? Did I deserve it or were you trying to tame me?"

BOBBI SMITH

LAWLESS, TEXAS

LEISURE BOOKS NEW YORK CITY

A LEISURE BOOK®

August 2007

Dorchester Publishing Co., Inc.
200 Madison Avenue
New York, NY 10016

ISBN-10: 0-8439-5849-9
ISBN-13: 978-0-8439-5849-2

The name "Leisure Books" and the stylized "L" with design are trademarks of Dorchester Publishing Co., Inc.

Printed in the United States of America.

Visit us on the web at www.dorchesterpub.com.

DEDICATION

This book is dedicated to Donna and Jim Byerlotzer of the Midland Education Foundation in Midland, Texas, and to the real Mary Smith who won the bidding to "Be A Character in A Bobbi Smith Novel" at the fundraising auction that was held for the foundation last fall. Mary is the principal of Emerson Elementary School in Midland! Watch out for our Texas Tour coming this August!

I would also like to thank all my fans for their support. 2007 represents my 25th year of being a published author. Wow! I've been very blessed to be able to follow my dream of having a successful writing career. Thanks!

LAWLESS, TEXAS

Prologue

Texas, 1870s

Sarah Jenkins was smiling as she gazed out the window of the stagecoach at the vast Texas landscape. The stage would arrive in San Gabriel later that day, and she could hardly wait. Soon, very soon, she would be reunited with her fiancé, Jace. She had missed him terribly during the three weeks she'd been gone on this trip with her mother to visit relatives. Their wedding was less than a month away, and she was counting the days until they would never have to part again.

"You're smiling," Martha told her daughter with a smile of her own.

"We're almost home—" Sarah said.

"And Jace and your father will both be in town to meet us," Martha finished her thought.

"Do you think they missed us as much as we missed them?"

Martha laughed. "Where your father's concerned, I'm

sure he missed us more. He's been eating with the boys out in the bunkhouse since we've been gone."

"You're right about that." Sarah laughed, knowing how much her father enjoyed her mother's cooking.

"It's hard to believe that your wedding is coming up so soon—" Martha looked at her daughter lovingly.

"I know, but it's so exciting! I'm going to be Mrs. Jace Madison . . ."

"You got yourself a good one in Jace, Sarah," put in Andrew Norton, the other passenger and a friend from town.

Sarah grinned over at him sitting across from her in the stagecoach. "I know."

Hiding out on a rocky hillside farther up the stage route, the outlaws Vic Lawrence, Al Denton and Buck Carson were all watching and waiting for the stagecoach.

"It's due any time now," Vic told them. "Keep an eye out and be ready."

It was only a few minutes later that the stage came into view.

"There it is, boys!" Vic shouted. "Right on time! As soon as it gets within range, start shooting!"

Al and Buck were ready. A big payroll was being transported on this run, and they were looking forward to getting their share of it. They had some serious drinking and gambling to do.

The stage drew closer.

"All right! Let's go!" Vic ordered.

Vic led the way, and they charged down out of their hiding place, firing wildly at the stagecoach.

John, the stage driver, and Mark, the man riding shotgun, heard the sound of the gunfire and saw the gunmen coming.

"Get us out of here!" Mark shouted. He knew immediately that the outlaws meant trouble, and he began to return their fire.

John whipped the horses to a frenzied pace in his desperation to escape, knowing they were still a long way from the safety of San Gabriel.

Jarred by the sound of gunfire and the sudden lurch of the stage, the passengers realized something was wrong.

"It must be a holdup!" Andrew shouted.

"What are we going to do?" Martha asked, terrified.

"John's trying to make a run for it, so just hang on," Andrew advised as he drew his own gun and leaned out the window to return fire.

Sarah and Martha struggled desperately to stay in their seats as the stagecoach raced over the rocky road.

Though the driver was doing his best to outrun them, the outlaws closed in. Their gunfire proved accurate and deadly. Both John and Mark were shot and fell from the driver's bench, leaving the stage's team of horses completely out of control.

Andrew had to stop to reload his gun and when he did, one of the outlaws' bullets slammed into his chest, grievously wounding him. Sarah and Martha tried to get to him, but with the horses racing wildly across the uneven terrain, they were being thrown around within the stage and there was nothing they could do.

The outlaws were excited as they closed in. Everything was working out just the way they'd hoped. With the driver and the shotgun dead, the payroll was theirs for the taking.

Vic raced ahead and caught up with the runaway team. He leaned down to grab the reins and try to slow their pace.

Panicked as the horses were, though, they swerved sharply to get away from him. Their sudden move sent the stagecoach careening wildly. The team broke free just as the stage crashed into several large boulders and overturned.

The outlaws were surprised by the force of the wreck, but they didn't worry about it. The only thing they cared about was the strongbox. It had been thrown clear of the ruined stage, and they rushed to claim it. Gathering up the box, Vic shot the lock off. They opened the lid and smiled down at the sight of all the cash inside.

"Al, check on the passengers while we load this up," Vic ordered. "We don't need no witnesses."

The gunman made his way over to take a quick look at what was left of the stagecoach.

"There ain't nobody in there going to give us any trouble," he called out after witnessing the carnage.

"Good. Let's ride," Buck said, eager to enjoy his share of the money.

They mounted up, ready to head back to Los Rios. There was no law to speak of in Los Rios, and that was the way the gang liked it. They could do their celebrating there without any worries.

As they rode off, they gave no thought to the passengers who'd been killed. Nothing mattered but the good times they were going to have with the money they'd stolen.

Two days later, San Gabriel

Jace Madison was a solitary figure as he stood alone in the cemetery, staring down at Sarah's grave. Sweet, loving memories of Sarah played in his mind, haunting him. Anguish filled Jace as he finally faced and accepted the horrible truth—she truly was lost to him forever.

Never again would he hold her in his arms.

Never again would he know the thrill of her kiss.

The wedding they'd planned would never take place. Despair tore at him. She had been his love. They were to have spent the rest of their lives together, and now—now she had been taken from him in a tragic act of violence. The look in his eyes was a testament to the pain he was feeling as his grief overwhelmed him.

Jace drew a ragged breath. He was a man used to being in control, and he fought hard for that control now as dark, dangerous emotions filled him, but it eluded him. Bitterness and rage drove him as he turned away from the grave and went to mount up. He knew what he had to do, and he wouldn't rest until it was done.

Jace reined in before the sheriff's office. He dismounted and walked straight inside to find Tom Jenkins waiting there with Sheriff Daniels and several deputies.

Tom looked up at the man who was to have been his son-in-law. "You ready to ride?"

"I'm ready," Jace answered tersely.

"Let's go," Tom said, looking at the sheriff.

"Best we can figure, it was Vic Lawrence and some of his men. They probably headed for Los Rios."

Los Rios had a reputation as a dangerous, wild town, and they all knew the reputation had been earned.

"Let's go pay Los Rios a visit."

"Here are your badges," Sheriff Daniels said, handing Jace and Tom each a deputy's badge.

Both men were grim as they pinned the badges on their shirts. Iron-willed determination filled them. The killers were going to be brought to justice. They would see to it.

Jace had always been a rancher by trade. He'd never thought of himself as a lawman before, but nothing was going to stop him from finding the men who'd been responsible for Sarah's death.

Jace, Tom and the others left the office and mounted up. Moments later the posse rode out of San Gabriel in a cloud of dust.

Chapter One

"You boys ready to have a good time?" notorious gun-fighter Harley King asked his men as they rode into town late in the afternoon.

"You know it. We've got some serious celebrating to do," Al Denton said.

"Yes, we do," Jim Thomas and the others agreed.

It had been over a month since they'd last been in Lawless. They'd spent the past few weeks planning and carrying out a very successful stage robbery. Now they were ready to relax and enjoy themselves for a while.

"I wonder if Sheriff Anderson's moved on?" Al remarked with a grin, remembering their last encounter with the local lawman.

"If he's got any sense, he has," Jim said.

The sheriff had single-handedly tried to run them out of town during their last visit. Harley had gotten the draw on him and had pistol-whipped him severely. Harley believed Lawless was now his town.

"What do you say we find out?" Harley asked.

The gang leader didn't wait for them to respond. He spurred his horse to a breakneck speed and started to shout as he drew his gun and began firing wildly.

The rest of the gunmen followed Harley's lead. They raced down the dusty main street after him with their guns blazing, heading for their favorite saloon, the Tumbleweed.

The townspeople out on the streets heard them coming. They knew immediately it was the King Gang and ran for cover.

Down at the sheriff's office, Sheriff Anderson heard the sound of gunfire, too. He and the new deputy he'd hired, Charley Pierce, were just starting out the door to investigate when Slim Jones, who worked at the telegraph office, came running up.

"It's the King Gang, Sheriff! I just saw them! They're back!" Slim warned them.

The lawman stopped in his tracks.

"What are we going to do?" Charley asked, hesitating.

"I warned you this day would come, and it looks like it's here." Sheriff Anderson looked back at the deputy, his expression dark. "We're going to lock them up."

"But Sheriff—" Charley started to protest. It had been one thing to talk about arresting the outlaw gang. It was another to actually do it.

The lawman turned on his uneasy deputy. He'd vowed after his last encounter with Harley King and his gang that they would never set foot in Lawless again, and he'd meant it. It wasn't going to be easy ridding the town of their unwelcome presence, but keeping the peace was never easy. He challenged Charley, "If you're afraid to do your job, then hand over your badge right now."

Sheriff Anderson waited.

Charley didn't respond.

Satisfied that the deputy would back him up, he looked at Slim. "You coming with us?"

Slim was scared, but knew he couldn't let the two lawmen take on the entire outlaw gang alone. This was his town, too. "Yeah. I'm with you."

The sheriff grabbed a rifle and handed it to Slim. The three men started off toward the saloon where they knew they'd find Harley King and his men.

"I need a drink!" Harley declared loudly as he entered the Tumbleweed and holstered his gun.

Dennis, the bartender, had heard the commotion outside and feared it was the King Gang returning. Wanting to keep things as quiet as he could, he rushed to set out glasses for them.

"I thought it sounded like you were back in town. You wanting whiskey tonight?" he greeted them as they came up to the bar.

"Smart man," Harley said.

Dennis quickly poured the drinks, and the outlaws settled in for a long and raucous night.

As Sheriff Anderson, Charley and Slim neared the saloon, they split up. The sheriff sent Charley and Slim around back to help him get the upper hand over the gunslingers. Once he was sure they were in position, he made his move.

"Hold it right there, Harley King!" Sheriff Anderson was feeling close to desperate as he drew his gun and took a stand just inside the swinging saloon doors.

Harley had been about to take a drink when he heard the lawman. He slowly set down his tumbler of whiskey and turned to face his challenger. He smiled arrogantly. "Well, well, well, if it isn't Sheriff Anderson."

"Listen up! You and your boys are under arrest. Put your guns down on the bar—real slow," he ordered, eyeing the outlaws nervously.

"You can't just throw us law-abiding, peaceful citizens in jail," Harley said sarcastically.

"Oh, yes, I can," Sheriff Anderson declared, growing even more furious at the outlaw's arrogance.

Harley was not the least bit afraid of this man. He'd only let him live the last time because he'd thought the sheriff was too lily-livered to give them any real trouble. Harley realized now he might have been wrong.

"You think you're man enough to lock us up?" he asked.

"I know I am. Now, do what I told you. All of you! Put your guns on the bar."

Harley ignored his order. He turned his back on Anderson and took another drink, all the while watching his reflection in the mirror. He could see the outrage in the sheriff's expression and smiled to himself.

Dennis knew tensions were rising, and he could tell Sheriff Anderson wasn't going to back down. The last time there had been a confrontation between the two men, Harley had severely beaten the sheriff. Dennis wasn't going to let that happen again. Determined to try to help Anderson, he started to reach for the shotgun he kept safely stowed under the bar. He wondered where the sheriff's deputy was, but he didn't have time to worry about it. He just knew he couldn't let Sheriff Anderson try to handle these gunmen all alone.

"Don't," Al ordered in a low voice, anticipating the move the bartender was about to make.

Sheriff Anderson finally caught sight of Slim and Charley as they came to stand in the back doorway, and he knew the time had come to bring this confrontation to an end.

"I've got all the exits covered, King, so let's go." He had to prove to the outlaws that he meant business. "You're under arrest!"

Harley had had enough. He didn't know how many men the lawman had with him and he didn't care. Lawless was his town. It was time this sheriff learned that lesson once and for all.

Harley turned slowly. "Whatever you say, Sheriff."

Al and the other men knew exactly what Harley was up to.

"Now, boys!" Harley yelled.

The sheriff managed to get a few shots off before Harley's aim proved true. He shot the sheriff and watched in satisfaction as the lawman collapsed to the floor.

Slim and Charley had been ready when the shooting started. They fired several rounds and managed to scatter the outlaws, but when Charley saw the sheriff take a bullet, he lost his nerve and turned to flee.

"Where you goin'?" Slim demanded.

"You want to end up like the sheriff?" Charley was ready to run for his life.

"Aren't you going to stay here and fight?"

"Hell, no!"

"You can't just run off!"

"Watch me!" Charley was heading for the door to the alley.

"The sheriff's been shot! You're our deputy!"

"Not anymore, I'm not." The coward took off his badge.

"You can't let him get away with shooting Sheriff Anderson!"

"Then you go arrest him!" Charley said, throwing the badge at Slim. "I quit! You know damn good and well what will happen if we try to take them on—just the two of us! As far as I'm concerned, if Harley King wants this town, he can have it!"

The ex-deputy wasted no time running off.

Slim was horrified to discover what a coward Charley was, but he realized that alone, he had no chance of capturing the gunmen. He dropped the rifle and disappeared out the back door before the outlaws could catch up with him. Slim knew if there was ever going to be any hope that the townsfolk and neighboring ranchers could reclaim Lawless for their own, they were going to have to band together and find a way to drive the outlaws out.

Slim hurried to get his horse and then rode quickly out of town, heading for the Madison ranch. He had to let Will Madison know what had happened. Will was one of the biggest ranchers in the area, and Slim hoped he would have some idea of how to drive the deadly gunmen out of Lawless. Harley King and his men had proven they would stop at nothing to get their way.

Chapter Two

Los Rios, Texas

Sheriff Jace Madison was sitting at his desk in his office, enjoying the peace and quiet of the morning. Things were a lot different in Los Rios now from when he'd first taken on the sheriff's job some eighteen months before. His search for Sarah's killers had led him to Los Rios, and after bringing Vic Lawrence and Buck Carson to justice, he'd stayed on to help the townsfolk regain control of their town. With the assistance of his deputy, Grant Richards, he'd tamed the town. It hadn't brought Sarah back, but he'd felt good knowing others could live there safely now.

"Hey, Jace—"

Jace heard Grant's call and looked up to find the deputy coming through the office door.

"A telegram just came in for you."

With a look of surprise, Jace took the message from him and started to read it. His mood turned grim.

"Who's it from?" Grant asked, concerned. He knew from the change in Jace's expression that the news was not good.

"My Uncle Ben up in Lawless," he answered tersely.

"What's wrong?"

Jace looked up, his expression dark and troubled. "Harley King and his gang killed the sheriff, and the deputy quit and ran off. The gang's just about taken over the whole town."

"Sounds like Los Rios a few years ago," Grant remarked, remembering their early days there. It had been a deadly, bloody time, but they'd finally managed to restore law and order.

"According to my uncle, the folks in Lawless are scared—real scared," Jace went on.

"Why's he telling you all this?"

"He met with some of the townsfolk, and they're desperate to bring in a new sheriff. They heard the talk about what went on here in Los Rios, and they want me to come out there and clean up their town."

Both men fell silent for a long moment, thinking of what Jace would face if he agreed to take on the job. Life in Los Rios was comfortable now. The streets were quiet. As the sheriff, Jace had earned a reputation for dealing harshly with troublemakers, so gunmen made it a point to stay away.

"What are you going to do?"

"I don't know . . ."

Before Jace could say any more, the door to the office was thrown open and a young boy ran in.

"Sheriff Madison! Sheriff Madison! Come quick! Mrs. Thompkins's dog is digging up our yard again, and Ma says if you don't put an end to it, she's going to get her shotgun and stop that dog from digging once and for all!"

"Tell your ma I'll be right there," Jace assured him.

The boy hurried off.

Jace stood up, ready to handle the biggest dispute they'd had in town that day.

"The trouble here is a far cry from what's going on in Lawless," Grant remarked with a wry grin as he watched Jace go.

"Now," Jace agreed, but memories of those far more dangerous times still had the power to haunt him.

Leaving the telegram on his desk, Jace left the office to bring in the outlaw mutt. When he returned a short time later, having convinced the Thompkins family to keep their dog tied up on their own property, he found Grant still in the office.

"Anything happen while I was away?" Jace asked.

"Not a thing."

"I ran into the mayor on my way back," Jace told him as he sat back down at his desk.

"How soon are we heading for Lawless?" Grant had read the telegram while Jace was gone. He'd met Jace's uncle when he'd come to visit the sheriff the year before, and Grant realized the trouble in Lawless had to be real bad for him to have sent such a desperate wire. Knowing Jace as he did, Grant had no doubt his friend would be taking on the job.

"'We'?" Jace glanced at him. "I told the mayor you might be interested in taking over the sheriff's job here."

"I'll just have to let him know different." Grant's tone was firm.

"Are you sure you want to do this?"

"Who else will be around to watch your back if I don't go with you?" Grant responded with a grin. He understood full well what Jace would be facing with the Harley gang.

Jace nodded. "Thanks."

"Now, when did you tell the mayor you'd be leaving?"

"In the next day or two."

"Then I'd better go talk to him. You got any idea how we're going to handle things up there?"

"Not yet."

The two men shared a serious look as they got ready to face the challenge to come.

Lawless
Two weeks later

It was late in the morning when eighteen-year-old Sammie Preston left the stable she owned with her brother and made her way toward the general store to pick up the supplies they needed. She was glad to get away from work for a while, and she was even more delighted when she saw her friend Mary Smith headed in the same direction.

"Good morning, Mary," Sammie called out.

Mary stopped when she heard Sammie's voice, and she waited for her friend to catch up with her.

"Where are you going?" Mary asked, smiling in welcome.

"The general store. What about you?"

"The same. I've got a big order I have to take care of for the Tumbleweed." Mary showed her the lengthy list. At twenty-one, widowed with a small son to raise, Mary was supporting herself and her son by working as the cook at the saloon. There had been a time before she'd married when she'd been a schoolmarm, but married women weren't allowed to teach, so there had been no going back to that preferable, safer job when her husband, Johnny, had died.

"Good, that means we'll have some time to visit," Sammie said.

"I see you're working today," Mary remarked, eyeing the work pants, shirt and boots that were her friend's standard wear when she was at the stable. She remembered the days a few years earlier when life hadn't been so hard for Sammie and her brother Walt, when their family had owned a ranch and had seemed to be doing well enough. Inwardly, Mary sighed. She knew from her own experience with her husband's unexpected death of a fever the year before that, in an instant, your whole life could change—and not for the better. It was then that you learned what fortitude was. You had to have the courage and strength to make do with what you were handed. Sammie and Walt were doing just that now, and Mary was proud of them.

"I'm beginning to think there aren't any days when I'm not working," Sammie told her.

"I know what you mean," Mary agreed. Then, grinning, she added, "Of course, you could look at it as a good thing—"

"How's that?" Sammie was skeptical.

"We both have jobs."

Sammie couldn't help it. She started laughing and Mary joined in as they walked on toward the store.

"You know, I always have thought of myself as a bit of a tomboy and I do love horses," Sammie mused, looking down at what she was wearing. She could hardly wear anything else to do her job in the stable. "But there are some days—"

"I know what you mean, but think of it this way—since you love horses, working in the stable is the perfect calling for you, just like my job at the Tumbleweed is for me," Mary said, wanting to be positive. "I always liked to cook, so here I am, feeding a lot of hungry folks every day."

"And I know you're appreciated," Sammie said. "A lot of the men head straight for the Tumbleweed when they leave the stable."

Now, Mary really laughed. "I don't think my cooking is the real reason they hurry over to the saloon. I think Dennis and his liquor, not to mention Lilly and Candy, are much bigger draws than I am."

"You mean they don't tell you how much they like your meals?" Sammie asked. "I hear a lot of wonderful comments about your cooking. Trust me, they may not say it to you, but they're thinking it."

"Well, thank you. It's always nice to know you're appreciated."

"Yes, it is," Sammie agreed, opening the door of the general store so they could go inside.

Eloise Peters was not happy to be stuck living in Lawless, let alone working in her father's general store. Having gone back East to school, she believed she deserved a better life than this. She wanted to wear the latest fashions and travel. She wanted to attend balls and socialize with civilized people. While she'd been away, she'd tried her best to find a gentleman to marry, but with no success. So here she was, back in Lawless, and totally miserable.

Her parents were happy living here; certainly her father did make decent money running the only general store in town, but she despised the place. To her, Lawless was little more than a hellhole. The only ray of hope in her entire situation was Hank Madison, the son of a successful local rancher. He was her best prospect for a husband, and she was trying to think of a way to get him to the altar. He was as close to rich as anyone around there, and he wasn't all that bad-looking for a rancher.

The bell over the store's main door rang, distracting Eloise from her thoughts of Hank and how to entice him into marriage. It was all Eloise could do not to groan as she heard the customer enter the store.

She didn't want to wait on anyone.

She wanted all the people of Lawless to just go away and leave her alone.

Glancing toward the front of the store, Eloise almost did groan out loud when she saw who'd just come in. It was Sammie Preston and her friend Mary Smith.

Eloise gritted her teeth; she had no choice but to go see what they wanted. Of the two, the petite, redheaded Mary was the easier to deal with, Eloise thought, but not by a lot. Mary worked at one of the saloons in town. That alone was enough to disgust Eloise. True, Mary was only the cook and she dressed like a cook, but still, Eloise thought haughtily, a true lady did not go near a saloon, let alone work in one.

And then there was Sammie.

Sammie, who dressed like a boy and acted like one most of the time. Her family had lost their ranch during a severe drought several years before, and, desperate to make a living, her widowed father had bought the only stable in town. He had since passed away, and Sammie now worked at the stable right alongside her brother. Her occupation was obvious just from looking at her and the clothes she was wearing—her soiled work pants, shirt and boots. She had stuffed her blond hair up under her hat just to keep it out of her way, and there was the unmistakable smell of the stable about her—it was an odor that definitely would never be confused with lavender water.

Eloise suppressed a shudder as she plastered a tight smile on her face and went to greet them.

"Good afternoon, ladies." She was definitely using the term lightly. She made a point of scornfully looking Sammie up and down as she always did.

Sammie was used to Eloise's haughty ways. She told herself she didn't really care what the spoiled, rich girl thought. "Hello, Eloise."

"Hello, Eloise," Mary added cheerfully.

"How can I help you today?"

"I have a whole list here of things I need for the saloon kitchen," Mary said, taking out the paper from her reticule.

"Well, come on up to the counter and let me see what I can do for you." Eloise led the way.

Mary followed her, leaving Sammie behind.

Sammie knew it would take some time for Eloise to fill Mary's order, so she decided to look around the store. Sammie wandered around for a while and was finally drawn to the area where bolts of material were displayed. The more she worked at the stable, the more she was finding that she missed having the opportunity to dress up in a feminine way.

But that didn't really matter.

Times had been so hard for her family, she had no choice but to keep working just to survive.

And she and Walt had survived.

It wasn't an easy life, but they were finally managing to make a living now. Of course, owning and running the stable was nothing like ranching. They'd loved their ranch, and sometimes she wondered if they would ever really get over losing it. That was why she and Walt despised their former neighbor, rancher Ben Madison. It had been during the drought that Ben had refused to let them water their stock on his land. Her father had been completely shocked, for up until then they'd gotten along. Ben Madison had even gone so far as to order his men to shoot anyone or any stock that tried to get to his water supply. The Prestons had lost everything. Her father never got over the loss before his death.

Sammie pushed her dark thoughts aside, determined to cheer herself up. When she saw a bolt of light blue satin, she couldn't resist the urge to run her hands over the silky material. She stood there touching the cloth, imagining how beautiful a gown made out of this material would look.

Eloise was at the counter working, but she caught sight of Sammie touching the satin and knew she had to take action. She excused herself from Mary for a moment and hurried back to where Sammie was standing. Without pause, Eloise reached out and took the bolt of satin from her.

"Here, let me have that. Did you want to buy some?" she asked, looking the material over as she smoothed it back down.

"No, I was just looking. It's beautiful material," Sammie answered. She would have loved having a gown made of the satin, but she knew it wasn't going to happen any time soon.

"Yes, it is," Eloise agreed, and silently added "and we want to keep it that way" as she put it back with the other bolts of cloth. "I'll be finished with Mary's order in a few minutes, and then I'll be able to help you."

Sammie noticed how Eloise had inspected the material before she'd put it back and resented her implication. She'd made sure to wash up thoroughly before she'd left the stable, so there was no way she'd gotten any dirt or marks on the satin. The other girl was arrogant and never missed the opportunity to try to make herself look better than other people. Sammie wished she didn't have to deal with her, but since this was the only general store in town, she had no choice.

A short time later, Eloise was ready to wait on Sammie.

Sammie handed her the list of things she needed, and then looked over at Mary, who was lingering there, waiting for her to finish so they could leave together.

"With any luck, this won't take long," Sammie told her.

"That's all right. Trust me, I'm in no hurry to get back to the saloon."

"I understand. I'm not excited about heading back to the stable, either."

They stood there, making small talk and enjoying their time together. They both worked so hard, it wasn't often that they got to be with each other anymore; they wanted to take full advantage of this moment.

Chapter Three

It was late afternoon as Jace and Grant rode down the hot, dusty main street of town. It had been a long trek, but they'd finally made it. They were in Lawless, the town whose reputation matched its name.

Not wanting to draw any undue attention to themselves, Jace and Grant deliberately kept their pace slow as they looked around to get a feel for the place. They rode past the deserted sheriff's office, a small hotel and the general store. A few people on the street were going about their business. Nothing seemed out of the ordinary. Jace knew, though, that looks could be deceiving, so he didn't let his guard down for even a moment. The King Gang had already proven how deadly they were, and he and Grant had to be ready for anything.

Jace spotted the Tumbleweed saloon up ahead. Past experience had taught him you could learn a lot about a town by just listening to the talk that went on in the saloons, so he decided to start there. He had to admit, too, that the prospect of having a drink sounded real good.

"You ready for a drink?" He looked over at Grant. Knowing his friend as well as he did, he figured it wouldn't take much encouragement to get him to agree.

"As long as you're buying," Grant countered with a grin. He'd seen the Tumbleweed up ahead, too, and was definitely ready for some refreshment after the long miles they'd traveled.

They headed for the saloon.

"I am not looking forward to going back to work," Mary told Sammie, thinking ahead to the drunken cowboys she'd have to deal with that night. "It would be much more fun to spend the rest of the day with you."

"I wish there was some way we could sneak off, but then we'd both get in trouble."

"Yes, we would."

They heard the sound of horses passing by, and Mary glanced out the window to see two heavily armed strangers riding slowly down the street.

"Sammie, who are those men?" she asked nervously.

Sammie glanced outside as they rode past, and she was as startled as Mary at the sight of the two gunmen. One of them, in particular, drew her attention. He was dressed all in black. Tall and lean, with several days' growth of beard, he was wearing his hat pulled low over his eyes to shield his features from clear view. But even though she couldn't see his face clearly, there was an aura of danger about him, and a shiver of awareness trembled through her. She looked at the other man and found he was equally intimidating. Even so, there was something about the first man that mesmerized her.

"I don't know. I've never seen them before, and I'm sure I would have remembered them if I had. They look like trouble," Sammie answered warily, a sense of unease filling her.

"And that's just what we don't need." Mary was worried. "We've already got enough trouble here in town with the King Gang around and the sheriff dead. We don't need any more gunmen riding in."

"Did you say there are more gunmen riding in?" Eloise asked as she returned, carrying one of the boxes filled with Sammie's order. She set the box down on the counter and hurried over to look out the window with Mary and Sammie. "Oh, my. You're right, they do look like trouble." It wasn't often Eloise agreed with anything Sammie said, but this time she did.

"I was hoping it was going to be quiet for a while since Harley and his men rode out last week, but now I'm not so sure," Mary said, frowning.

"I was hoping that, too," Sammie agreed, knowing how hard her friend's job was when the gunmen got drunk and things got wild in the saloon.

"Look—they're going to the Tumbleweed," Eloise pointed out, watching the two in fascination.

Mary moved in closer to the window to watch as the strangers reined in before the saloon. They dismounted and tied up their horses, then stood there for a minute taking a look around town.

"If they stay in the Tumbleweed long enough, I should be able to find out who they are tonight," Mary said.

"I wonder if they're outlaws?" Eloise said.

"From the looks of things, I'd say they are," Sammie added.

"It's such a shame that things have turned out this way in town. I'm beginning to wonder if we'll ever be safe again," Mary said sadly. "Maybe we should all just pack up and move on."

"I'm not going anywhere." Sammie bristled at the thought of running away from the outlaws. "This is my home. The King Gang isn't going to chase me off."

"But what else can we do? We're no match for the likes of killers like Harley King."

"And just look what happened to the sheriff," Eloise said nervously.

"I've heard talk around town that some of the ranchers are banding together, trying to find a new sheriff," Sammie told them.

"I heard the talk, too, but with the terrible reputation Lawless has got now, what lawman in his right mind would want the job?" Mary put in.

"If they ever do find anybody, he's going to have to be meaner than the outlaws and faster on the draw—if he plans to stay alive." Sammie didn't know if a man like that even existed.

"I hope they find somebody—and fast. Some days it gets real rough down at the Tumbleweed." Mary looked tense for a moment as she remembered some of her encounters with the gunmen over the past few months, and then her expression brightened. "I just had a thought— maybe a Ranger will catch up with Harley and his men while they're committing some crime, and they won't ever come back."

"I like the way you think," Sammie told her, "but with

the luck we've been having around here lately, I wouldn't count on it."

"We'll pray it happens, how's that?"

"Right now, I think that's about all we can do."

Eloise said nothing more, but hurried off to get the last of Sammie's order. After paying her, Sammie and Mary left the store. Sammie walked Mary down to the alley behind the saloon, where her friend hurried off to work in the kitchen, then Sammie headed for the stable.

Once they'd left the store, Eloise merely sat down on the stool behind the counter and wished for the day to be over so she wouldn't have to wait on people any longer.

Jace led the way into the Tumbleweed. He and Grant stopped just inside the swinging doors to take a look around. Several men were drinking at the bar, and a raucous card game was going on at a table in the back. Two scantily dressed saloon girls moved around the room, waiting on customers seated at the other tables. A few of the men looked up when Jace and Grant came in, but none of them paid much attention. Jace was glad as he led the way to the bar. He wanted to keep a low profile for now.

"What'll it be?" the barkeep asked, coming to wait on them.

"Whiskey," Jace answered.

"And you?"

"The same," Grant told him.

"Coming right up." The barkeep wasted no time in pouring two glasses of the potent liquor and shoving them across the bar.

"Thanks." Jace paid him, then picked up his glass and took a deep drink.

The barkeep eyed them with interest as he asked, "You two are new in these parts, aren't you?"

"We just rode in."

"I'm real good at recognizing folks, and I didn't reckon I'd seen you around before. My name's Dennis, by the way."

"I'm Jace."

"And I'm Grant."

"Nice to meet you boys. You just passing through or are you planning to stay on for a while?"

"Don't know just yet." Jace was deliberately vague. The barkeep would find out who he was soon enough.

"Dennis! We're needing more drinks down here!" one of the men at the far end of the bar yelled.

"Yeah, yeah. I'm coming." The barkeep looked back at the newcomers before heading off. "You two need anything else right now?"

"You serve food?"

"Sure do. Mary!" he bellowed, moving off to wait on the other customers. "Mary will be out in a minute. She's our cook. She'll take care of you."

Jace and Grant had no idea who Mary was, but they soon found out when a petite, red-haired beauty appeared in the back doorway. She was a far cry from the other working girls in the Tumbleweed, for she was modestly dressed in a shirtwaist dress and apron, and she carried a cast-iron frying pan in her hand as she looked toward the bartender.

"What do you need, Dennis?" Mary called out.

"Jace and Grant there are wanting some food," Dennis answered, pointing out the two strangers standing at the bar.

Mary glanced their way and went still for a moment. The men Dennis had pointed out were the same two she and Sammie had seen riding into town just minutes earlier. Determined not to let her unease show, she managed a tight smile as she started across the saloon to take their order.

Chapter Four

Ned Ballantine was a low-life drifter who had been in town for a few days; most of that time he'd spent in the Tumbleweed enjoying the liquor and the women. He'd already had some fun with the other two bar girls, but the redheaded one named Mary had eluded him. As she walked by his table on her way to the bar, Ned decided it was time to find out what was under that prim little dress and apron she was wearing. Snaring her around the waist, he hauled her down onto his lap.

"Let me go!" Mary had been so intent on watching the two strangers standing at the bar that she'd forgotten about Ned. She struggled to break away from his vile touch.

"Why, little darlin', don't go fighting me. I hear you're a real good cook, so I want you to cook up somethin' hot just for me. What do you say?" he asked, enjoying the way she was wiggling against him as she fought to get away.

"Get your hands off of me!" she ordered, giving him

one last chance to behave himself before she used her secret weapon on him.

From past experience, the other customers in the saloon knew better than to mess with Mary. They were watching with open interest as they waited for her to make her renowned move.

"We could have a real good time together," Ned said with a leering grin as he began to grope her. "I sure do like what I'm finding underneath this apron."

"Ned, I wouldn't do that—" one of the other men sitting at his table warned, knowing what was going to happen next.

Jace and Grant had been looking on, too, watching the scene develop. When the drunk started to molest the young woman, they both stepped away from the bar, ready to go to her aid, but they quickly found out that Mary the cook was more than able to take care of herself.

This wasn't the first time Mary had been molested by one of the drunks in the saloon, and she'd learned early on just how to handle them. With skill and accuracy, she brandished her cast-iron frying pan, beaning the obnoxious Ned on the head as hard as she could.

"Owwww!" he cried out, shoving her away from him to hold his head.

Mary jumped up and quickly backed away, holding her frying pan up in front of her her like a lethal weapon. "Next time you'll know to keep your hands off of me!"

"Why, you little!" Ned began cursing her.

He started to get up and go after Mary, but one of the other men who was sitting at the table with him grabbed his arm.

"Don't do it, Ned," the man advised. "Why waste your time on her when we got pretty little Lilly to entertain us?"

The man nodded in the direction of the buxom blonde bargirl who was heading their way.

Though his head was still throbbing, Ned took one look at Lilly and backed down from his confrontation with the cook.

"You're right about that," he agreed, leering at the saloon girl in the low-cut dress. Though he was still furious, what Lilly was offering distracted him from Mary and what she had done to him—for the time being.

Mary was relieved and grateful for Lilly's help distracting the man who'd grabbed her. Drunks like this one could sometimes cause real trouble in the Tumbleweed, and she knew she'd have to thank the other girl later when she got the chance.

Mary went on toward the bar to take the strangers' meal orders; as she approached she was able to get her first good look at them. She was surprised when they both tipped their hats to her. The sense of danger she'd felt about them earlier eased a little, and she realized, even as trail-weary as they were, they were the best-looking men she'd seen in Lawless in a long time. Both men were dark-haired, tall, lean, broad-shouldered, and ruggedly handsome. They were definitely an improvement on the quality of men that had been hanging around town lately.

"I'd say you are a well-armed young lady," Grant said with a grin, eyeing her and her cast-iron skillet with respect.

"Sometimes, you just have to be ready for trouble,"

Mary answered. "What can I get you boys tonight? We've got stew or fried steak."

"Fried steak will do just fine for me," Jace answered, looking forward to the hot meal.

"I'll take the steak, too," Grant added.

"You did a real fine job of handling your 'friend' there," Jace complimented her, impressed.

"'Friend' isn't exactly what I'd call him," she said, anger still edging her voice. "I do work here at the Tumbleweed, but I work here as a cook. That's all."

"I think he may have finally figured that out," Jace said, noticing how the drunk was busying himself with the dancehall girl.

Mary glanced that way, too, and finally relaxed a little. She managed a half-smile. "I hope so. Why don't you go find yourselves a table, and I'll bring your food out to you just as soon as it's ready?"

She headed back to the kitchen to start fixing their meals.

Jace and Grant picked up their drinks and went to sit at a table off to the side. They positioned themselves with their backs to the wall, so they could keep an eye on what was going on. So far, the saloon was reasonably quiet. They'd seen no sign of Harley King or his men, and they wondered what the outlaw was up to.

It wasn't long before Mary brought them their meals. They were just digging into their food, enjoying the good cooking, when the saloon girl named Candy made her way to their table.

"I see you both got real big appetites," Candy purred seductively. "You hungry for anything besides food, cowboys?"

She came to stand at Jace's side of the table and leaned down close to him to give him an unobstructed view of her full cleavage.

Jace smiled up at the shapely blonde, enjoying the view. She was a temptation, but he had other things on his mind. "Not tonight."

"What about you?" She looked at Grant, giving him an inviting smile.

Grant just shook his head.

"That's too bad. I would have showed you a real good time." She moved off to strut her stuff in front of the other men.

"It sure isn't very exciting around here with Harley gone," Lilly remarked as Candy passed by. She was making the rounds of the tables, having finished her time with Ned.

"The money ain't here, that's for sure, but I don't really mind having a quiet night or two."

"Enjoy it while you can. He said they'd be back in a week or so. When they show up, things will get back to normal."

Candy wasn't sure "normal" with Harley King and his men was anything to look forward to, but she did need the cash. This was her livelihood.

Ned had bided his time, enjoying himself with Lilly, but all the while he'd been with her, the cook named Mary had been on his mind. Anger still burned inside him, and his head still ached. No woman ever told him no or humiliated him. He didn't know who this Mary thought she was, but he was going to teach her a lesson she wouldn't ever forget. He knew the kitchen had an entrance from the alleyway, so he pushed back his chair and got up to leave.

"Where you going?" one of the other men at the table asked.

"I've got some unfinished business to take care of."

The other men didn't give his early departure a thought. They didn't care what he did. They just kept drinking and enjoying themselves.

Ned knew he had to come up with a plan. It was still light, and he had to wait until it got dark before he could take any action. He left the saloon to check out the alley. After finding an out-of-the-way place to keep watch, he settled in to wait, looking forward to the revenge to come.

Jace and Grant lingered on at the saloon for a time. They'd hoped to listen in on some conversations and find out what was really going on in town, but the only important thing they heard was one saloon girl remarking that the King Gang had ridden out and wouldn't be back for a while.

Jace was pleased by this news. Their absence would give him the time he needed to get his plans in order. He was determined to reclaim this town for its law-abiding citizens. He glanced around the crowded saloon and wondered how many of those drinking at the bar fit that description. He would be finding out soon enough, that was for sure.

As evening drew near, they finally decided it was time to stable their horses and check into the hotel.

"First thing in the morning, we'll ride out to my uncle's ranch and let him know we're here. I don't want to trust anyone in town until we know exactly what's going on," Jace told Grant as they left the Tumbleweed and stood outside for a moment.

"Sounds good. You know, for all the talking going on in there tonight, Lilly was the only one who mentioned Harley."

"Makes me think there might be more to the gang than just the men who ride with him."

"I suppose we're going to find out," Grant said with a pained grin.

"The sooner the better."

Candy made her way back into the kitchen area to talk with Mary for a few minutes before Mary went home for the night.

"Who were those two new fellas named Jace and Grant?" Mary asked.

"I don't know, but they sure were good-looking."

"You noticed that, too, did you?"

They shared a smile as they thought of the strangers who'd graced the Tumbleweed with their presence that night.

"They're definitely different from our usual crowd, that's for sure," Candy said thoughtfully.

"I wonder what they're doing here? When I saw them riding in earlier, I thought they looked mean, like they were part of the gang."

"I think your first impression was wrong."

"I hope so."

"Did you know they actually were going to help you with Ned?"

Mary was surprised by the news. "They were?"

"They were on their way over when you took care of Ned yourself."

"If I see them again, I'll have to thank them."

"Let's hope they stay around for a while. Men like those two are rare, real rare in Lawless."

They talked a little while longer, then Mary closed down the kitchen and left for the night.

Ned was ready when Mary came out the back door and started down the alley. He was glad to see she wasn't carrying her skillet with her. She was definitely going to pay for having used it on him earlier. Ned waited until she was far enough away from the door that no one would be able to hear her if she screamed, then he made his move. Reaching out, he quickly grabbed her by the arm and jerked her savagely back against him.

Mary was caught off guard by Ned's assault and managed only one cry for help before he clamped his hand over her mouth.

"You think you can get away with treating me like that, bitch?" he snarled.

She fought with all her might as he started to drag her off, deeper into the shadows, but had no success against his overpowering strength. She feared for her very life.

Jace and Grant had taken rooms at the hotel and were on their way toward the livery to stable their horses when Jace stopped.

"Did you hear that?"

There had been no mistaking the sound of a woman's scream.

"Yeah, it sounded like it came from around back."

Both men drew their guns.

"Cover the far end of the alley, Grant. I'll take this end," Jace ordered.

They split up, ready for trouble.

Jace made it into the alley first. He heard a noise back behind the saloon and as he closed in, he spotted Ned in the shadows with a struggling woman in his arms. He was reasonably certain the woman wasn't there willingly and decided to confront the drunk.

"What's going on?" Jace asked as he moved closer, gun in hand.

Ned was furious that someone had found them. He continued to force Mary farther back down the alley as he called out, "Nothing." Then he threatened Mary in a low voice, "You better keep your mouth shut if you know what's good for you."

"Hold it right there!" Jace ordered, following them and squaring off against the drunk. He sensed that something was wrong, and he wanted the drunk to know in no uncertain terms that he meant business.

The last thing he expected was the blow that struck him in the next moment.

Out of nowhere, the savage lash of a whip hit Jace's gun hand in a slashing attack that sent his gun flying from his grip.

Chapter Five

"Don't move!" Sammie yelled at the gunman. When she'd heard someone scream in the alley behind the stable, she'd realized someone was in trouble, so she'd grabbed her whip and rushed outside into the darkened passageway to find what looked like a robbery taking place.

Jace didn't know who was issuing the orders, and he didn't care. He just reacted instantly, turning and launching himself at the man who'd attacked him with the whip. Jace tackled him to the ground and was surprised to find how small he was. In fact, he seemed kind of soft, almost like a youth, but Jace had no time to think about it. He tore the whip from his attacker's grip and went to retrieve his own gun.

Jace grabbed his weapon and looked up in time to see Ned throw Mary harshly aside and then take off running, drawing his sidearm as he went.

"Are you all right?" Jace asked as he kept an eye on where Ned was heading.

"I—I think so." Mary answered in a trembling voice. She'd always considered herself a strong woman, but she was deeply shaken by the assault.

Reassured that she hadn't been seriously hurt, Jace took off after Ned, who'd already disappeared into the night.

It took Sammie a moment to recover from the stranger's unexpected attack. Her hat had been knocked off and her hair had come unbound. She felt confused by all that had happened. The stranger had come after her, but then, once he'd disarmed her, he'd stopped to ask Mary if she was all right. Sammie got to her feet and rushed to where Mary was trying to get up.

"Mary, what was going on out here?" she asked, taking her friend by the arm to help her to her feet.

Mary started to explain, but as she tried to put her weight on her right ankle, she cried out in pain. She fought back tears as she clung to Sammie.

"My ankle—" she gasped, trying to find her balance.

Sammie put an arm around her friend's waist to help support her. "Let's get you out of here. Do you think you can make it home?"

"I don't know. Maybe, if we go slow." She was limping heavily.

Together, they started away from the alley.

"Who was the man who hurt you?" Sammie asked.

"I was heading home and that drunk named Ned was waiting here for me." She told Sammie what he'd done earlier in the saloon. "I don't know what would have happened to me if you and Jace hadn't come along."

"Jace?"

"The man you used the whip on. He was trying to help me."

"Oh—"

"His name is Jace. He must have heard me scream, too, because he showed up out of nowhere—"

"When I first arrived and saw him standing there with his gun drawn, I didn't see you at all. I just thought he was robbing somebody."

"Thank God you were using your whip and not your gun," Mary said. She knew what a good shot her friend was and was horrified by the thought of what might have happened.

"Me, too," Sammie admitted. "Wasn't he one of the men we saw riding into town earlier?"

"Yes. He and his friend had dinner at the saloon tonight."

"I wonder if he'll catch up with Ned . . ."

Sammie looked back down the alley. "I hope so."

Just then, they heard the sound of gunshots coming from the direction the men had run, and a tremor of fear ran through them both.

"I hope Jace is all right," Mary said anxiously.

Sammie quickened their pace as best she could, ready to get Mary to safety.

Jace had been cautious while he was pursuing Ned. He'd stayed up against the buildings and moved as quietly as possible. He'd learned long ago not to rush blindly into any confrontation, especially if he didn't know the lay of the land, and Lawless was still unfamiliar territory to him.

Jace had neared the end of the alley in time to see Ned

dart out from where he'd been hiding. Seeing Ned silhou-etted against the dimly lit street had given Jace the chance he needed. "Hold it!"

At the sound of his call, Ned had turned and fired wildly in Jace's direction.

Grant was in position and waiting. Ned's shots missed Jace, and while the drunk was focused on his partner, Grant snuck up on him from behind. Grant wasted no time. He hit Ned on the head with his gun.

Ned groaned as he collapsed facedown on the ground. Between this unexpected attack and Mary's earlier as-sault with the frying pan, he was in agony.

Jace came running up to find that Grant had things well under control.

"Is this who you were looking for?" Grant asked.

"You figured that out, did you?" Jace returned with a slight grin, glad their strategy had worked.

"I thought he might be the one you were after."

"That's why I keep you on the payroll," Jace said wryly.

"What payroll?"

"We'll talk about that later," he countered.

"What happened back there?" Grant asked, looking down the deserted alley in the direction from which Jace had come.

Jace quickly told him about the man's attack on Mary.

"He didn't hurt her, did he?"

"No. She seemed all right when I left her. Let's get him locked up, then one of us can go check on her."

"All right." Having spoken with Mary in the saloon, Grant believed she was a good woman who didn't deserve to be accosted by a drunk.

Grant disarmed Ned and gave Jace the gun. As Grant

handed the weapon over, he noticed the bloody mark on Jace's hand. "What happened to you?"

"Nothing," he denied quickly. "Let's take him in."

Grant grabbed Ned by the collar and hauled him to his feet.

"Let's go," he ordered. He shoved the staggering man ahead of them as they moved off down the street toward the jail.

Ned looked at the two men in total confusion. He recognized them as the strangers he'd noticed in the Tumbleweed, but he had no idea why they'd bothered to come to Mary's rescue. "Who are you?"

"My name's Madison. Jace Madison," Jace answered. "I'm the new sheriff in town."

"What?" Ned responded in a shocked tone.

"You heard him," Grant said. "He's Sheriff Madison, and I'm Deputy Richards."

"But this is Lawless. There ain't no sheriff in Lawless—"

"There is now," Jace said.

The people of Lawless were used to hearing gunfire during the night, and generally they ignored it, but the shooting had sounded close to the stable, and Walt Preston was worried—especially since he knew Sammie was over there working alone. Carrying a shotgun with him, he left the house and hurried out to see what was going on. Walt went inside to find Mary sitting on a bale of hay with Sammie helping her take off her shoe.

"What happened?" he asked.

"I'm glad you're here." Sammie went on to quickly explain about the drunk's assault. "Mary sprained her ankle."

"It looks like it," he agreed, kneeling down to examine

her leg. "Do you know who was doing the shooting?"

"No, when we heard the gunfire start up, I just got Mary in here as fast as I could."

"I'm worried about Jace," Mary told them.

After her own encounter with the man named Jace, Sammie had a feeling he could take care of himself, but she didn't say anything.

"Who's Jace?" Walt asked.

Mary and Sammie told him about the new man in town.

"I'll go check on things and see what I can find out."

"Do you want me to go with you?" Sammie offered.

"No. You stay in here with Mary. I'll be right back."

"Be careful."

"I will."

Walt was a man on a mission as he headed out into the alley with his shotgun, but he soon returned.

"It's quiet. I didn't find anything."

"I wonder where they went?" Mary worried.

"I don't know, and, right now, I don't care," Sammie said. "All that matters is you're safe."

Mary looked up at her with heartfelt emotion shining in her eyes. "Thanks, Sammie."

Sammie gave her a hug. "We need to get you home so you can soak your ankle."

Mary's house was on the other side of town. It wasn't too far, but injured as her friend was, Sammie thought it best that she not try to walk home. Her brother readied a horse and lifted Mary up into the saddle for the trip.

"I'll take her. You stay here," Walt told his sister. They'd already found out the hard way that it was a wild night in town, even with the King Gang gone, and he didn't want to put her at any more risk.

Sammie was relieved that no one had been seriously injured. Ned was a mean drunk, and he had obviously been planning to rape Mary. Sammie started back to work, but even as she forked hay into the stalls, she found the man named Jace slipping back into her thoughts, and she wondered what had happened to him and to Ned. She wondered, too, how his hand was.

The door to the abandoned sheriff's office wasn't locked, so Jace and Grant walked right in with Ned. The main room was a decent size. There was a lamp on the desk, and they were lucky enough to find a match so they could light it. The room had a desk and two chairs along with an empty gun rack on one wall. There was a jail cell in the back, and off to the side there appeared to be a small sleeping room.

Grant kept a gun on Ned, while Jace searched the desk drawers for the keys to the jail cell.

"Let's see what the cell looks like," Jace said. He led the way into the back room and was satisfied to find the cell was windowless and furnished with only a cot and a washstand. "He won't be getting out of here."

Grant shoved Ned inside, and Jace locked him in.

Ned turned on them, cursing vilely.

"I don't want to hear a word out of you the rest of the night," Jace ordered in a tone that let the prisoner know he meant business.

Ned glared at the two men as they went back into the outer office and closed the door behind them. Silently, he vowed that one day he would get his hands on Mary and make her pay for all the trouble she'd caused him, and he'd get even with these two, too.

Jace looked over at Grant as he tossed the keys on the

desk. "I got a feeling that taking down the rest of the troublemakers in Lawless isn't going to be as easy as handling Ned."

"What do you want to do with him in the morning?"

"We'll let him go, as long as he promises to stay away from Mary. I'm hoping he learned his lesson tonight."

"She did wield that cast-iron frying pan like she knew what she was doing," Grant said with a grin, thinking of the feisty, red-haired beauty. "Too bad she wasn't carrying it in the alley."

"I doubt she would have needed any help if she had been. I sure wouldn't want to take her on," Jace agreed.

"You know, if things get rough around here, you might consider hiring her on as a deputy. She's fast on the draw."

"If you think you can't handle your job and you're going to need the help, I'll consider it," Jace countered, smiling at the thought. "Right now, though, I'm going to walk back over and make sure Mary got out of the alley safely. I'll take the horses to the stable while I'm at it."

"I'll be waiting right here for you," Grant said as he went to look in the small room off to the side of the office. "At least one of us has got a place to sleep here."

The small narrow bed didn't look like the most comfortable place to spend the night, but they'd been stuck in worse places.

"I don't think Ned had any friends here in town who might come looking for him, but just in case, lock the door after I leave. We don't need any surprises tonight."

Grant did just that as Jace left, then he settled in at the desk to await word on Mary.

Chapter Six

"I got Mary all settled," Walt told Sammie when he returned to the stable a short time later. "She should be fine in a day or two."

"Thank heaven," Sammie said, feeling relieved.

"Mary was lucky you heard her scream. Things could have turned out real ugly if you hadn't shown up when you did."

"Me and that man named Jace—"

They didn't even want to think about what might have happened to their friend if Ned had managed to take her away.

"Any sign of Ned while I was gone?"

"No, but I wonder who was doing the shooting we heard."

"I don't know and I don't care as long as they stay away from here."

"I just wonder why Jace got involved. When Mary and I saw him ride into town with another man earlier today, we thought they were part of the King Gang. The two of them looked like trouble, but then Jace tried to help Mary. None of Harley King's men would have done that. They'd have been the ones going after her."

"There's no telling what he was thinking, and we may never find out. Let's just hope this Jace took care of Ned," Walt said, then he gave his sister a half-grin. "Mary told me you used your whip on him. Maybe he didn't come back because he figured it was smarter to stay away from you."

Walt knew how strong-willed and determined Sammie was. When it came to using a gun or a whip, she was any man's equal. Their father had known they lived in dangerous times, and he'd insisted she learn how to take care of herself. Walt felt sorry for any man who underestimated Sammie and tried to tangle with her.

"I had to do something. I heard the scream and ran outside to find Jace holding his gun on someone. I thought he was one of the outlaws. I thought he was robbing somebody. I didn't even know Mary had been the one yelling or that Ned was involved until after I'd disarmed Jace."

"Well, it's just good that things turned out the way they did. Maybe we'll find out tomorrow what really went on back there. For now, it's getting late, and I think we've had enough excitement for the night."

"Me too," Sammie agreed, taking the horse's reins from him. "I'll take care of him and be along shortly."

"You need any help?"

"No, I'll be fine."

Nodding, Walt left her to close down the stable for the night.

Alone again, Sammie's thoughts turned to the tall, dangerously handsome stranger as she took care of Walt's horse. She'd had run-ins with some of the gunmen in town before, but very few of them had been as fast to react as Jace. The move he'd made on her had been impressive. She was still aching from being knocked down that way, but she knew he must be sore, too. She found herself wondering how his hand was faring. She wondered, too, if she'd ever see him again. A part of her hoped she would.

After finishing with the horse, Sammie went to wash up a bit. The feminine part of her longed to soak in a hot bath, but that would come later. Right now, she had to settle for a quick scrub-down before going home. Taking off her hat, she freed her untamed mass of pale curls from confinement. Rolling up her sleeves, she unbuttoned a few buttons at the neckline of her shirt and started to wash. She wanted to cleanse herself of as much of the day's grime as she could.

Jace returned to the darkened alley and was glad to find no sign of Mary or her friend there. He checked in at the saloon, to see if the bartender had seen the women. Dennis was surprised to learn what had happened. He told Jace that those who'd been drinking in the saloon had heard the gunplay, but hadn't concerned themselves, since it was a common occurrence. After learning that Mary hadn't returned to the saloon for help, Jace felt confident she'd made it safely away. Satisfied, he got the horses and headed over to the stable to put them up for the night.

Since it was getting late, Jace wasn't sure if anybody

would still be there working. He was glad when he saw that a lantern was burning inside. He tied the horses up out front and went to stand in the doorway. He looked around the dimly lighted interior.

"Anybody here?" he called out.

"Yeah, what do you need?"

Jace frowned slightly when he heard the gruff response from the back of the building. The voice sounded vaguely familiar for some reason. "I've got two horses—"

He stopped in mid-sentence as he found himself staring at the woman who'd just come out of the back stall and was walking toward him, wiping her forearms and throat with a towel as she came. There was no mistaking she was female, in spite of the men's clothing she was wearing—the pants that fit her shapely, long-legged figure, the work shirt that was unbuttoned just enough to reveal the beginning swell of her breasts. Her long blond hair fell loosely around her shoulders in a tumble of untamed curls.

And then Jace realized . . .

She was the same person who'd used the whip to knock his gun out of his hand. She was the same person he'd thought was a boy when he'd knocked him down during the earlier confrontation over Mary.

As Jace stared at the woman walking toward him now, though, he wondered how he could have been so wrong about her.

"You're a girl." As he stated the obvious, guilt filled him for having treated her so roughly earlier.

Sammie was startled to find that it was Jace standing there in the doorway, looking so tall and broad-shouldered and lean and handsome. An unexpected jolt of physical awareness shot through her as she eyed him up and down. He was an imposing presence, and having already seen him in action, she knew he was a man to be reckoned with. Realizing her shirt was partially unbuttoned, she felt a bit vulnerable and decided to use sarcasm to defend herself.

"You're a real observant fella, there, Jace," she said. "Are you always this sharp?"

"I try."

"How sharp were you at catching the bad guy?" Sammie challenged.

"We got him."

"'We'?"

"My friend Grant helped me."

"What did you do with Ned? Where is he?" She was worried for her friend's safety.

"Don't worry. We took care of him. He won't be bothering anybody any more tonight."

"Good," Sammie said, relieved. She had no idea what the two men had done with Ned, and she wasn't going to ask. Mary wasn't in danger, and that was all that mattered.

"By the way, how did you learn my name?" Jace asked.

"Mary told me."

"How is she?" he asked.

"She hurt her ankle. It'll be sore for a while, but she should be all right. Thank you for helping her."

"I was just glad I got there in time."

"So am I—and so is Mary."

Jace realized then that he didn't know her name and asked, "I take it you're a Preston?"

"So, you're not only sharp, you know how to read, too," she quipped, knowing the big sign out front read "Preston's Stable."

"That's right. I can read," he countered, finding himself half-grinning at her in spite of himself.

It was the first time she'd actually seen him smile and the change in him was breathtaking. The dangerous edge about him vanished, and he looked even more handsome—if that were possible. Her heartbeat quickened in response and she smiled back at him. "I'm Sammie Preston. My brother Walt and I own and run this place."

"Your name is Sammie?" He was genuinely surprised that a woman as lovely as she was would have such a masculine name.

"Samantha, really," she was quick to explain, "but nobody's called me that since I was in school."

"Well, Sammie, are you all right? I didn't hurt you too badly when I tackled you earlier, did I?"

"No, I'm fine," she lied. Dealing with men every day, she knew she had to be strong. She would not whine, no matter how sore she really was. She countered, "How's your hand?"

At her question, his smile broadened, and he flexed his hand a little.

"It's been better," Jace answered. "You sure know how to handle your whip."

"A girl's got to know how to protect herself in a town like Lawless."

"Maybe you should teach your friend Mary how to use one."

"Mary doesn't need a whip. She just needs to carry her skillet with her all the time."

"You're right about that. I saw her in action in the

Tumbleweed. She used the skillet on Ned earlier tonight, and I'm sure he was wanting some revenge, waiting for her in the alley like that."

Again, she wondered why Jace had acted so gallantly in coming to Mary's aid. "Jace, do you mind if I ask you a question?"

"What?"

"Why did you try to save Mary? A lot of the men in Lawless make it a point to look the other way when there's any kind of trouble going on. It doesn't matter whether there's a woman involved or not."

Jace had been wondering how much to reveal to Sammie, and he decided he might as well tell her the truth.

"It's my job," he said seriously.

"Your job?" She frowned in confusion. "What are you talking about?"

"I'm the new sheriff of Lawless."

Sammie was caught completely off guard by his claim. She'd heard some quiet talk around town that a few of the ranchers had been trying to find a new lawman, but she hadn't heard that they'd had any luck. "You're the new sheriff? Who hired you?"

"I got a wire from some ranchers in the area wanting to know if I was interested in taking on the job."

"Did they tell you Harley King and his gang have turned Lawless into a living hell?"

"They did. That's why Grant and I are here. We brought law and order to Los Rios a few years back, and now we're going to clean up Lawless."

Sammie noticed that Jace's eyes had hardened as he spoke, and she knew he was serious about taking back the town for its citizens. She also knew her first impression of him had been true—he was a dangerous man, and Harley King and his men were in for real trouble when they returned. She was glad Jace was on the townspeople's side, and she was determined to do all she could to help him. "It's not going to be easy."

"It never is." He was grim, thinking of what lay ahead. Dealing with Ned had been nothing compared to taking down the cold-blooded killers who ran with Harley. "Are there many folks in town willing to work with us and stand up to these gunmen?"

"I am."

"But you're a woman."

"I stood up to you, didn't I?" She drew herself up angrily, refusing to let him dismiss her this way.

"Yes, you did." He admired her fearlessness, confronting him. "And you'll never hear that from me again."

"Good. That means my first impression of you was right."

"How's that?"

"You are sharp."

He smiled.

"Grant and I are going to need all the help we can get if we're going to rid Lawless of these killers."

"You can count on me."

"How many other folks feel the way you do?"

"My brother—I know Mary will do anything she can to help. There's the owner of the general store." She was thoughtful as she tried to think of all the people who would be willing to put themselves at risk confronting the gunmen. "I'd say there are probably at least ten people here in town you can count on, and then the ranchers who sent for you."

"From the sound of the telegram my uncle sent to me, I didn't think there would be anybody willing to help here in town."

"Who's your uncle?" She was surprised by the news that he had relatives in the area.

"My last name is Madison. My uncle is—"

"Ben Madison," she finished for him, tensing inwardly as she waited for his answer. There had been bad blood between her family and the Madisons for a long time.

"That's right. He owns the Circle M. Do you know him?"

"Oh, yeah, I know him and his son, Hank," Sammie answered. Jace's connection to them troubled her deeply, but she also realized that Jace had already proven himself to be a far better man than either his uncle or cousin by coming to Mary's aid. Dealing with the fact that he was a Madison wouldn't be easy for her, but that didn't matter. Saving Lawless mattered, and she would to do whatever she could to help him. "Did Ben send you word about what happened to our last sheriff?"

"He did. That's why I'm here."

"Do you really think you can stop the King Gang?"

"Yes."

Sammie wanted to believe that.

"We'll need to set up a meeting with the townspeople I know we can trust," she told him.

"I'll do that after I meet with my uncle. I plan to ride out to the Circle M tomorrow and let him know Grant and I are here."

"Who else knows you've taken the job?"

"So far, only Ned."

"Well, be careful who you talk to. There's no way of knowing who might be working with Harley King on the sly."

"I appreciate the warning." Jace had suspected he and Grant would have to be on guard and watch their backs every minute in Lawless, and Sammie's statement had just confirmed his hunch.

"I'll get your horses now." Sammie started to move past him toward the hitching rail outside.

"I'll help you," he offered, walking with her.

"That's fine with me. That's the least you can do after knocking me down." She was surprised that she actually found herself teasing him.

Jace gave a slight laugh. "What about you? You used your whip on me."

"Paybacks are tough, aren't they?"

"You have no idea," he agreed.

They were both smiling as they led the horses into the stable.

"Let me have a look at your hand," Sammie said, when they'd finished with the horses. She'd noticed that Jace was favoring it slightly, and she knew exactly what he needed to help heal the lash mark.

"Why?"

"This will help you." She got a jar of salve and went over to where he was standing. "It works on the horses."

"So you use that whip on the horses a lot?" Jace asked.

"Only when I'm taming them or when they deserve it," she answered as she took his strong hand in hers to get a better look at the injury. She felt a shiver of awareness at that simple contact. She was startled by her reaction. No man had ever affected her this way before, and, unsettled, she deliberately kept her gaze focused on the lash mark.

"Which one was I? Did I deserve it or were you trying to tame me?"

His quip got to her. Sammie looked up at Jace, laughing.

Jace found himself laughing, too, and he realized he hadn't laughed this easily in all the years since Sarah's death. As his gaze met Sammie's, he was mesmerized by the way she affected him and by the innocence he saw mirrored in the depths of her green-eyed gaze. He was discovering that Sammie was nothing like any other woman he'd ever known. She was just about any man's equal, and yet there was no doubt, despite the way she dressed, that she was a woman—all woman.

"You definitely didn't deserve it, and, as far as taming you goes, I think you're going to need to be wild if you're going to have any luck taming this town," she countered.

"So I'm safe? You're not going to use your whip on me again?"

"That's right."

Sammie was aware of the intensity of Jace's regard, and she forced herself to look away, concentrating, instead, on tending to his hand. Very carefully, she rubbed the soothing salve into his skin.

"There. It should be feeling better by morning."

"Thanks." Jace deliberately moved away, needing to put some distance between them. "Can you get the word out and set up the meeting?"

"I'll start working on it first thing tomorrow."

"Good. I'll see you then." Jace turned to leave.

"Jace—"

He stopped and looked back at her.

"I'm glad you're here."

"So am I." As he turned and walked away, he was surprised to find that he meant it. He wanted to make this town safe for her.

Sammie watched Jace go. He was a solitary figure as he moved off into the night, and she found herself wondering how he'd come to be a lawman and why he'd chosen this dangerous way of life. She knew he was going to have his work cut out for him, taking on Harley King and his gang of killers, but she had a feeling that if anyone could bring Harley down, it would be Jace Madison.

The knowledge that Jace was related to Ben and Hank Madison still troubled Sammie. She knew that her father never would have approved of her helping Jace. He had harbored a real hatred for Ben Madison, and he wouldn't have accepted anyone related to him. The families had been feuding for years, but she knew she had to put that hatred behind her now and do whatever was necessary to bring true peace back to Lawless. She just hoped her brother could accept Jace, too.

Nothing was more important than saving their town.

Jace kept a lookout for trouble on his way back to the sheriff's office. He was glad the town seemed calm. He only wished it would stay this way, but that wasn't going to happen.

Sammie slipped into his thoughts again as he walked through the darkened streets, and he realized she was a very special woman. Not only was she pretty, but she was smart and spirited, too. He'd never had any female stand up to him the way she had, and he found he respected her for it.

As Jace neared the sheriff's office, he forced all thoughts of Sammie aside.

He hadn't gotten involved with any woman since losing Sarah, and he planned to keep it that way.

He had no time for any distractions in his life.

He had a job to do, and that job was making this town safe again.

Chapter Seven

Grant had been watching for Jace from the sheriff's office and quickly let him in.

"It's still quiet in here," Jace said, surprised. He'd expected the drunk to give them more trouble.

"I think our friend back there passed out," Grant told him. "He stopped shouting a while ago, and I've been enjoying the peace ever since. What did you find out? Is the girl all right?"

"Which girl?" Jace countered.

"What are you talking about?" Grant was confused.

At his puzzled look, Jace told him the truth about Sammie.

Grant chuckled in surprise. "That's the first time I've ever heard of you losing out to a female. If this Sammie is that good with a whip, think what she might have done to you if she'd had a gun."

"Yeah, yeah." Jace didn't even want to think about that. "The good news is she's on our side now."

He went on to explain how, once he got back from his trip to his uncle's ranch, they would meet with the folks from town who were interested in helping them fight the King Gang.

"What about Mary? How is she?"

"From what Sammie told me, she injured her ankle, but other than that she's all right."

"I'm glad we showed up when we did. This has been a pretty lively first night in Lawless. Think what it's going to be like when Harley and his men show up again," Grant said.

"It's going to be just like Los Rios was when we took over there a few years ago," Jace said, remembering their early days in that wild town.

Jace's mood turned grim at the memory of his first trek into Los Rios. It had been during his days of riding with the posse from San Gabriel in search of Sarah's killers. The posse had been trying to track the outlaws for weeks, but had turned up nothing. Most of the members of the posse had quit and had gone back home, but he and Sarah's father and a few others had never given up. They'd kept after the gunmen, and ultimately, their determination had paid off. They'd finally managed to corner Vic Lawrence and Buck Carson in the wild, notorious town of Los Rios. There was no law there to help them, so they'd been on their own. The outlaws had refused to go down without a fight, and the shoot-out that had followed had been a bloody one. Jace and the others had ultimately won out and had taken the two wounded killers back to San Gabriel, where they'd stood trial and were hanged for their crimes.

At that time, the people of Los Rios had been living in terror of the various gangs of murderous gunmen who'd overrun the town. The good citizens of Los Rios had seen Jace in action. They knew what he was capable of, and they had banded together to ask him to come back and be their sheriff.

Jace had never planned to be a lawman, but he knew he had no future, no life left in San Gabriel without Sarah. He'd taken the job, and it was there that he and Grant had first met up. They had been working together ever since.

"We've got our work cut out for us, that's for sure," Grant said, wishing he could forget the ugliness of those early days in Los Rios. Taming that town hadn't been easy, and he knew Lawless might prove to be even worse.

"Yes, we do, so why don't you head on back to the hotel and get some sleep?" Jace suggested. "You're going to need the rest."

"What about you?"

"I'll stay here tonight and keep an eye on things."

"Are you sure you don't want me to stay, too?" Grant found the prospect of sleeping in a clean, comfortable bed tempting, but he didn't want to leave Jace alone at the jail on their first night in Lawless.

"I'll be all right. Go on, but get back here early. I want to head out to my uncle's ranch first thing."

"What are we going to do about Ned?" Grant nodded toward the jail cell in the back room.

"We'll decide when we see how he's behaving in the morning. I have a feeling he's just a mean, stupid drunk. Once he's sober, he may see the error of his ways."

"I'll see you in the morning."

"Enjoy your night."

Grant was smiling as he started off to the hotel. "I will. You don't have to worry about that."

Once Grant had gone, Jace locked the door and took a look around the shabby, dirty, run-down, sparsely furnished office. He checked out the small sleeping room off to the side and decided that, though the narrow bed was none too clean, at least it would offer a little more comfort than the wooden desk chair. Jace settled in as best he could, knowing it was going to be a long night.

"Let me out of here!"

Jace heard Ned's shout and wearily opened his eyes to find it was growing light outside. It had been quiet all night, but that time of good fortune had now come to an end. Jace got up slowly and went to deal with his prisoner. He opened the door and found Ned glaring at him with bloodshot eyes.

"Good morning, Ned."

Ned cursed him. "I don't know who you think you are, but you got no right to keep me locked up this way!"

"I have every right to keep you off the streets. Last night you attacked an innocent woman and—"

"Innocent? Mary works in the saloon! She ain't nothing but a slut! She's the cause of all this! Once I get my hands on her, I'm going to—"

"Are you threatening Mary again?"

"You're damned right I am! The no-good—"

The look Jace gave him stopped Ned in mid-sentence.

"In that case, you're going to stay right here locked up for a long time," Jace said in a cold, unyielding tone.

"You can't keep me here!" Ned was furious, but he was also on edge as he began to wonder just who he was dealing with.

"Oh, yes, I can." Jace looked him straight in the eye. "My name is Jace Madison, but you can call me Sheriff

Madison. Like I told you last night, I'm the new law in this town, and you're going to learn what that means."

Jace turned and walked out, shutting the door behind him.

Ned watched him go in disbelief.

A short time later, Grant showed up to find a tired-looking Jace sitting at the desk.

"How did your night go?" Grant asked.

"About like I expected."

"Did you get some sleep?"

"Not as much as you did, but it doesn't matter. I've got to get out to the Circle M and let my uncle know we're here. Keep Ned locked up. He's still threatening to go after Mary."

"I'll make sure he doesn't go anywhere."

"Good. When I get back, we'll set up a meeting with the people here in town who are willing to cooperate with us. We've got to have a plan in place before King and his men show up."

"I'll be waiting right here for you. How late do you think you'll be?"

"If everything goes the way I hope, I should be back by mid-afternoon."

Jace left Grant then and went to the stable to get his horse. He was hoping to run into Sammie again, and he found he was disappointed when he met her brother and learned she wasn't working that morning.

Sammie hadn't slept well all night. Concerns about Mary had left her tossing and turning through the long dark hours, so she got up just after dawn to go check on her friend. She had no doubt it was going to be hard for Mary to be laid up with Jonathan to watch, so she wanted to help out if she could.

"Sammie, what are you doing here?" Mary asked, surprised to find her friend knocking on her door at such an early hour.

"I was worrying about you, and I wanted to make sure you and Jonathan were all right."

Mary smiled, touched by Sammie's concern. "Come on in. Jonathan was up at the crack of dawn, so I'm fixing him some breakfast."

"Did you get any rest last night?" Sammie asked, following her inside.

"Not much. My ankle was throbbing."

Her answer didn't surprise Sammie, for she had seen the dark circles under Mary's eyes and noticed how she was favoring her injured leg as she returned to the kitchen to finish preparing Jonathan's food.

The toddler was in his high chair, and he smiled brightly at the sight of Sammie following his mother into the room.

"Sammie!" Jonathan squealed.

"Good morning, little love," Sammie crooned, going to kiss him on the cheek and give him a hug.

"I think you just made his whole day." Mary laughed. She knew how much her son adored Sammie.

"Why don't you go on back to bed, and I'll take care of Jonathan for a while?" Sammie volunteered, sitting down at the kitchen table as Mary dished up the eggs she'd fried.

"You're kind to offer, but you know as well as I do that I can't afford to take any time off work," Mary answered, joining Sammie at the table with her son. "I've got to get ready and head down to the Tumbleweed."

"But your ankle—"

"Lying around doing nothing isn't going to make that much difference. I have a child to feed, and he does like his food. Don't you, sweetie?" Her tone turned childish as she concentrated on feeding the two-year-old a bite of his breakfast.

Sammie couldn't help smiling as she watched the two of them. Jonathan was Mary's whole life now. "I wanted to tell you, I found out what all the gunfire was about last night."

"You did? What was it? What happened?" Mary looked up from feeding Jonathan.

Sammie explained how Jace and Grant had overpowered the drunk and locked him up at the jail. She also told Mary the news that Jace was the new sheriff in Lawless and Grant was his deputy.

"I don't believe it," Mary said, sounding surprised that anyone would dare to take on the King Gang.

"It's surprising, that's for sure," Sammie agreed.

"Well, Jace and his friend—what did you say the deputy's name was?"

"Grant. Grant Richards."

"They are definitely the answer to my prayers. Thank God they're here, and thank God they showed up when they did last night. I almost feel like they were my guardian angels."

"Their timing was good."

"Just like yours," Mary said, smiling at her.

Sammie gave her a quick hug.

"How many people in town know about Jace and Grant taking over in place of Sheriff Anderson?"

"Not many that I know of. I told Jace we could set up a meeting with all the folks who are willing to help them fight Harley's gang." She paused. "There is one thing I forgot to tell you."

"What is it?" Mary asked.

"It's about Jace."

"What about him?" There was a note of puzzlement in Mary's voice.

"His last name is Madison." Sammie looked up at Mary as she said, "He's Ben Madison's nephew."

"Are you serious?" It was obvious that Mary was shocked by the revelation. The bad blood between the Prestons and the Madisons was legendary in the area.

"Yes. I was shocked, too, but just judging from the way Jace helped you, I think it's safe to say he's nothing like his relatives."

"You're right," Mary said. "I can't imagine Ben or Hank putting themselves at risk for anyone else— especially not a lowly cook from the saloon." She paused before going on. "But what about you and your brother? Are you going to be able to deal with him, knowing he's a Madison? Are you really going to be able to trust him?"

"I'll do whatever I have to do to save our town, and if that means cooperating with a Madison, then that's what I'll have to do."

"What about Walt?"

"It won't be easy for him. He's as hard-headed as they come, but hopefully he'll understand what needs to be done."

They shared a look of understanding.

Desperate times called for desperate measures.

They talked for a little while longer, discussing the wisdom of Mary trying to go to work that morning.

"I'm hoping Dennis will help me out some today," Mary explained.

"You just make sure that he does. They don't have anybody to replace you, and if your ankle gets worse from standing on it too much, you'll be really laid up."

"I'll tell him, but whether he'll listen to me or not is another thing. He's a man, you know."

"You just let me know if he gives you any trouble. I'll handle him."

"You think you can take on Dennis just like you did Jace?" Mary asked, a humorous twinkle in her eyes as she imagined that confrontation.

Sammie laughed. "If he needs handling that way, I can do it. You just say the word."

"I think that kind of 'handling' might get me fired."

"All right, if you need me to go easy on him, I will."

"I appreciate that. Like I said, I've got to keep food on the table."

At that moment, Jonathan began to fuss, wanting more to eat, and Mary quickly obliged.

"Seriously, if you need any help with anything, let me know," Sammie said as she stood up to go.

"I will," Mary promised, "and Sammie?"

Their gazes met.

"Thanks."

Chapter Eight

"Hey, Ben! There's a rider coming in!" one of the Circle M ranch hands yelled to the boss.

Ben Madison had been working stock in the corral, and he quit what he was doing to see who was riding in. He wasn't expecting any trouble, but these days, he never knew what might be going on in town. As soon as the rider drew close enough, any concerns he'd had vanished.

"Boys, it looks like things are about to get better around here," he announced as he went to welcome his nephew.

Jace spotted Ben right away, standing with the ranch hands. His uncle was a tall, heavy-set man with a head of silver hair that set him apart in any crowd. Jace reined in before him.

"I see you got my telegram," Ben said, smiling up at Jace.

"Yes, I did," Jace answered as he dismounted and went to shake hands with his uncle. "I got into Lawless yesterday. My deputy, Grant Richards, rode in with me, too."

Ben had heard tales of Jace's deputy. "That's some real good news. Where is Grant? Why didn't he ride out with you?"

"We had some trouble in town last night. He's at the sheriff's office, taking care of that right now."

"Bad trouble?"

"Nothing we couldn't handle."

Ben was relieved. He looked over at his ranch hands. "Boys, this is my nephew, Jace."

The ranch hands had heard Ben talk about how he hoped Jace would come to Lawless and clean up the town, just like he'd cleaned up Los Rios. They welcomed him to the ranch.

"Where's Aunt Catherine and Hank?" Jace asked, looking around.

"They're up at the house. Come on. I know they'll be as glad to see you as I am." Ben led the way.

Jace walked with him as the ranch hands went back to work.

The sprawling, impressive Circle M ranch house and the well-kept surrounding outbuildings were a testament to Ben's driving ambition to make the ranch a success. Jace's father had often said that Ben was the kind of man who would do whatever he had to in order to succeed.

Ben led the way inside and called out for his wife and son.

"What, Pa?" came Hank's answering shout from somewhere in the back of the house.

"Get your ma, Hank! Jace is here!" Ben announced.

Catherine and Hank hurried to the front of the house to find Jace and Ben already settled in the parlor. It had been a long time since they'd last been together and the reunion was a warm one.

"Why, Jace, it's so good to see you again," Catherine said, going to give him a welcoming hug.

"It's good to see you, Aunt Catherine," he told her.

Hank was watching his cousin. He'd heard all the talk about what a good lawman Jace was, and it was obvious, just by the serious look of him and the way he wore his gun, that Jace was a man to be reckoned with.

"Jace." Hank reached out to shake hands. "Welcome to the Circle M."

"Glad to be here," Jace replied, noting the close resemblance between Hank and his father.

"Sit down, Jace, we've got some catching up to do," Ben directed.

They spoke for a while longer and enjoyed the refreshments Catherine served before getting down to discussing the trouble in town.

"We're desperate," his uncle began. "A lot of folks were ready to pack up and leave for good after the King Gang killed Sheriff Anderson. We've tried to keep Lawless respectable for years, but now the gunmen think they can come here and hide out and be safe from the law."

Jace understood their fears. "From what Grant and I were able to find out, the King Gang rode out last week. No one we talked to knew where they were going or when they'd be back, so it was relatively quiet in town last night."

"But you said you had some kind of trouble?"

"You know Mary, the cook at the Tumbleweed?"

"Yes," Ben answered worriedly. "Did something happen to her? Is she all right?"

"When she was on her way home after she got off work, one of the drunks tried to attack her in the alley. Grant and I got there before anything too bad happened. Sammie Preston showed up, too."

"So you've had dealings with the Prestons already, have you?" Ben asked tersely.

"Just Sammie. Why?" Jace was puzzled by his reaction.

"The Prestons—that family is nothing but trouble. Stay away from them and don't trust them. Don't trust them at all," Ben warned.

Jace was surprised by the hatred he heard in his uncle's voice. "Sammie seemed straightforward enough. She even offered to get together the townsfolk who are willing to help us bring down the gang, so I could meet with them and plan what we're going to do."

"Listen to my pa. He's right about the Prestons. They may seem nice, but be careful around them," Hank told him. "There's bad blood between us."

Jace always trusted his instincts when he was dealing with people. That was the way he'd managed to stay alive all these years, and he had sensed nothing conniving or underhanded about Sammie. "What caused the trouble between you?"

"They ran into hard times and lost their ranch some years back. They blamed us. I guess they couldn't deal with our success. Don't turn your back on them," Ben explained.

"I'll keep that in mind. What do you know about Harley King and his men?"

"He has at least four gunmen riding with him; sometimes there are more. They're all cold-blooded killers. Sheriff Anderson and his deputy tried to run King out of town, but they were no match for the gang. You're going to need more than one deputy working with you, if you plan to face him down."

Jace looked at his cousin. "How good are you with a gun?"

"I'm good. I'm real good," Hank answered confidently.

"You ever think of wearing a badge?" Jace challenged his cousin.

"You need another deputy, you got one."

"Good." Jace was looking for men he could trust. He caught a glimpse of fear that shone in his aunt's eyes, but knew there was more to fear from not going after the gunfighters than from confronting them. "Can you ride back to town with me today?"

"Let me pack up what I need, and I'll be ready to ride," Hank told him. He went to get his things.

"I'll go with you, too," Ben said, then he looked at Catherine. "Have some of the hands ride out to the neighboring ranches and tell them that Jace has shown up and is taking the sheriff's job."

"I will. They'll be glad to hear it."

"What we're facing here in Lawless is not going to be easy—dealing with killers like Harley King never is," Jace said.

"Just be careful, Jace," his aunt cautioned.

"We will be. I've got Grant and now Hank to back me up, and whoever else I can find in town."

A short time later, Jace, Ben and Hank were on their way to Lawless.

"So you've already had a run-in with Sammie Preston, have you?" Hank asked as they rode along. He'd had trouble with Sammie in the past and truly despised her and her brother. "I'm not surprised. She always seems to be in the middle of everything, causing trouble."

"Actually, Sammie wasn't causing any trouble last night. She was trying to help Mary."

Hank ignored what Jace had said, and asked snidely, "Could you tell she was a girl when you first saw her?"

"No. I didn't find that out until later."

Hank was chuckling derisively. "You're not the only one who's thought she was a boy, and to tell you the truth, I don't think she knows how to be a girl. She acts more like a man than some of the men in town."

"She's tough. I'll give her that, but then, living in a place like Lawless and dealing with the people around here, she has to be. I saw how good she is at using that whip of hers. She knows how to crack it, that's for sure." He'd listened to his cousin's opinions, but he knew Hank was wrong. Sammie was very much a woman, and a beautiful one at that.

"She's good with a gun, too, so watch yourself around her. Like Pa said, the Madisons and the Prestons don't get along at all."

"What started all the trouble between you?"

Everyone in town knew the story behind their hatred for one another. Ben decided to tell Jace everything that had happened so he'd understand.

"Some time back, the Prestons owned the ranch north of us," he began. "There was a severe drought one year, and we barely had enough water for our own stock, let alone theirs. When their water dried up, they tried to run their herd onto the Circle M, so we had to drive them off. Times were hard then, real hard. By the time the drought finally ended, they'd lost everything and they blamed me."

Jace could understand the anger his uncle's actions had aroused in his neighbors. It was a harsh decision to refuse a neighbor help in a time of need. Obviously it was true that Ben was the type of man who did what he must to survive.

"For the sake of the town, you need to try to forget your past trouble with the Prestons. We all have to work together to make Lawless safe again."

"Tell the Prestons that and see what they say," Hank sneered.

Jace fell silent, considering the problems he was facing. They not only had a threat from the outside, but there was also trouble within the town. Straightening things out in Lawless was going to be even harder than he'd first thought.

It was early afternoon when Grant closed the sheriff's office and headed over to the Tumbleweed to get some lunch for himself and Ned. The shock of being kept locked up this long had silenced Ned, and Grant was glad. There were bigger things to worry about than a hungover mean drunk.

Dennis looked up from where he was wiping down the bar when Grant came into the saloon. Jace had told him what had happened the night before when he'd come in looking for Mary after the showdown in the alley, and he'd heard the whole story today from Mary herself.

"Afternoon," Grant said as he went to stand at the bar.

"Good to see you, friend," Dennis greeted him. "What'll it be?"

"It's too early for any drinking," Grant told him. "I was just wondering if you're serving food today?"

"We sure are. Mary's in back right now."

"She showed up for work?" Grant asked, surprised.

"She can't wait the tables, but she can still cook. Just let her know what you want, and she'll fix it up for you."

Grant went to the back of the saloon and looked through the doorway to the kitchen to find Mary working hard at the stove. The aroma of the fresh-baked apple pie on the side table and the stew she was stirring were tantalizing.

"It sure smells good in here," he commented.

Mary was startled by the sound of his voice so close by, and she turned quickly to find Grant standing in the doorway watching her.

"Oh! Hello, Grant." She smiled brightly at him.

"Hello, Mary. Looks like you've been hard at work for quite a while already today. Jace told me how you hurt your ankle, so I thought you might be taking the day off to rest up."

"I couldn't. I had something real special I had to do." Mary went to pick up the pie, which was now cool enough to touch. "I had to make this for you and Jace." She handed him the dessert. "I wanted to thank you for what you did for me last night. I don't even want to think about what might have happened to me if the two of you hadn't shown up when you did." She looked up at the handsome deputy, her gaze meeting his. "Thank you."

Grant saw the depth of her emotions in her eyes, and he smiled down at her. "I'm glad we were able to get there in time—especially since the reward is such a good one."

"Now, you know you have to share it with Jace."

"I was afraid you were going to say that." He was still grinning. "I'm just glad you're all right."

"So am I. My ankle's still sore, but Dennis is going to help me today, so I won't have to do too much walking."

"Good."

"Sammie told me why you and Jace came to Lawless, and I'm glad you're here. We need you."

"We'll do our best."

"I know you will."

"We're keeping Ned locked up for now. He's not the smartest man in town, that's for sure."

"Thank you. He sure was angry last night. I don't know what he might try to do next."

"I hope he's learned his lesson."

"That would be good," Mary said, relieved. "Now, what can I do for you?"

"I need two servings of your stew to take back to the jail with me."

"I can do that." She quickly prepared the food and put it in a basket along with the pie.

"Thanks," Grant said as he took the basket from her. He started to leave, then glanced back to find her watching him. "I'll see you later."

He stopped at the bar to pay Dennis.

"I ain't charging you," the bartender told him. "This is on me. I'd have bought you a drink, too, if you'd been a drinking man today."

Grant smiled. "I'll come back later for the drink—how's that?"

"You're on. I'll be here."

Chapter Nine

Jace, Ben and Hank rode into Lawless and reined in out-side the sheriff's office. Grant saw them and went out to meet them as they dismounted.

"Glad you're back," Grant told Jace.

"How have things been here?"

"It's been nice and quiet. Just the way it should be."

"This is my Uncle Ben and my cousin, Hank Madison. Ben and Hank, this is Grant Richards, my deputy."

The men shook hands, sizing each other up.

"Hank has decided to work with us as another deputy," Jace went on.

"Good. We can use the help."

Jace looked at his uncle and cousin. "Why don't you wait here with Grant while I go see about setting up the meeting?"

"That sounds fine," Ben answered.

They knew Jace was going to see Sammie Preston, and they were more than happy to let him go by himself.

"How's Ned doing?" Jace asked Grant before leaving.

"He's still squawking."

"He's not real smart, is he?"

"You got that right."

The three men went into the jail while Jace headed for the stable.

Sammie was hot, tired and dirty. But she was accustomed to it.

It had become a way of life for her.

There were just some days like today, though, when she really longed to be doing any other job besides cleaning out the stalls. Well, almost any other job. Bad cook that she was, Sammie knew nobody in their right mind would hire her to make food, and she sure didn't want to work as a saloon girl and have to deal with all those drunks every night. Of course, she would never consider taking a job like that, but it would be nice every now and then to dress up in something besides her usual work clothes.

For a moment, Sammie imagined herself wearing the kind of dress the dance hall girls wore—and then reality returned and she pictured herself trying to clean out one of the stalls wearing it.

Jace reached the stable entrance and looked in to see Sammie standing there in her soiled work clothes, her hair stuffed up under her hat, looking much as she had at the moment of their first encounter—except for her smile. The smile lit up her features, and he saw again the beautiful woman that she was.

"You're smiling," Jace said, alerting her to his presence. He wondered what had made her smile.

"Oh, hello." She was a little embarrassed that Jace had found her looking her absolute worst.

"You must have been thinking about something good."

"Honestly, I was just trying to picture myself in a different line of work." She looked down at herself. "It was a nice fantasy while it lasted."

"You looked like you were enjoying it."

"I was, but it's back to reality now." She grew serious and asked, "Now that you're back, are you ready to meet with the folks here in town tonight?"

"Yes. How soon do you think you can get them together?"

"I already talked to most of them, and they're eager to meet you. We can hold the meeting at the church."

"What time?"

"I should be able to get everybody there by eight-thirty."

"I'll be there."

Jace left her to her work as he returned to the sheriff's office to deal with his own. He still had Ned to consider.

Sammie stood in the middle of the stable a moment longer, thinking of all she had to do before the meeting that night, and then she went back to mucking out stalls. There was one thing she knew for certain—if she didn't do the work, it wouldn't get done, and she had to have the stalls cleaned out before she could do anything else.

"It's all set," Jace told Grant, Ben and Hank when he got back.

"It'll be interesting to see who shows up and to find out how willing they are to work with you," Ben remarked, remembering how terrified the townsfolk had been after the last sheriff was shot down.

"Does Lawless have a mayor?" Jace asked.

"Tom Harrison, the undertaker in town, tried to take charge and run things for a while. When the King Gang got so violent, he just gave up, like everybody else."

"We'll see what we can do about changing that tonight." Jace started over to the desk and noticed the partially eaten apple pie sitting on the desktop. "Where did the pie come from?"

Grant smiled. "Mary made it to thank us for helping her last night. She gave it to me when I went over to the Tumbleweed to get lunch, and I have to tell you, that pie is one fine reward."

"I can see that by how much is missing," Jace chuckled. He opened one of the desk drawers and took out the badges he'd found stowed there the previous night. "Here. It's time to get official about things."

He handed Grant and Hank each a deputy's badge and took the sheriff's badge for himself. They were silent as they pinned the silver stars on their shirts.

"And now I need to have a talk with Ned," Jace said, his mood turning even more serious as he made his way back to the jail cell.

Grant had no idea what Jace planned to do. He just hoped whatever the sheriff said would work. They had enough trouble in Lawless without having to worry about men like Ned.

Ned looked up from where he was sitting on the hard cot. He looked miserable and angry, but he kept his mouth shut for the time being.

"You sober now?" Jace asked.

"You know I am," he answered tersely.

"Good, because I don't like dealing with stupid drunks." Jace was deliberately trying to anger the man. He wanted to test him. He wanted to make sure Ned had his temper under control before they went any further. "Are you done being a stupid drunk?"

Ned's expression hardened. "Yes."

"Are you ready to get out of here?"

"Yes."

"There are conditions to your release."

"What are you talking about?"

"I'm going to let you walk out of here if you agree to two things."

"And if I don't?" Ned challenged.

"Then you won't be walking anywhere for quite a while."

Ned got up and went to stand close to the cell bars, glaring at Jace.

"Well?" Jace prodded. "What will it be? Are you getting out of here or are you staying?"

"What do I have to do?" he ground out.

"First, no liquor. If you go into the Tumbleweed or any other saloon in town, sarsaparilla is as strong as you get to drink while you're in Lawless." Jace could see the anger building within Ned, but he went on, "And when I release you, you're going straight over to see Mary Smith and apologize."

"I ain't apologizing to that—" Ned started to argue.

"Those are the terms," Jace said firmly, cutting him off. "If you refuse to do what I've ordered, you're staying right here until we can find a judge to—"

"All right," Ned said in disgust, just wanting to get out

of the jail. Apologizing was going to be humiliating, but sitting in jail was worse. He'd do what was necessary to get himself free, and then he'd get out of town. He had no reason to stay on in Lawless. There was nothing there for him.

"Grant, have you got the keys?" Jace called out.

"Right here," Grant said, handing them over.

"Ned's agreed to give up liquor while he's in town and he's going over to the Tumbleweed right now to apologize to Mary Smith. I want you to go with him and make sure he does what he's told me he's going to do."

"I'll do it," Ned snarled.

"That's right. You will, and Deputy Richards here will be your witness. I expect to hear all about it when he gets back," Jace said as he unlocked the cell door and let Ned out.

"Let's go," Grant ordered.

Ned walked out a free man at last. "Where's my gun?"

"You'll get your gun back after you've apologized to the cook," Jace dictated. "I'll keep it right here for you, nice and safe."

Ned didn't waste any time leaving the jail. He paid no attention to the third man in the office as he walked out. He just wanted to be free. He made his way down the street straight to the Tumbleweed, leaving Grant to follow.

Dennis saw Ned come in and wasn't sure what to think. He almost reached for the shotgun he kept under the bar until he saw Grant come in after him.

The other men who were in the saloon drinking looked up, too, expecting trouble.

"Afternoon, Grant. What can I do for you?" Dennis

asked, keeping a wary eye on Ned as the two men came to stand at the bar.

"Our friend here would like a drink," Grant said.

Ned was silent.

"Tell him what you're drinking now, Ned," he prodded.

"I'll have a sarsaparilla," Ned finally responded.

A roar of laughter tore through the Tumbleweed when the others heard what he ordered.

Ned's jaw locked in anger, but he didn't look around. He just stood there waiting for the bartender to set the drink before him.

"Drink up," Grant encouraged, enjoying the man's misery. "This is all he'll be getting here from now on, Dennis."

"All right," the barkeep answered.

Ned did as he was told, taking a deep drink of the sarsaparilla just to silence Grant. "There. Are you satisfied?"

"Not yet," he answered. "Let me see if I can find the cook for you."

"What do you want with Mary?" Dennis demanded protectively. He did not want Mary in harm's way again.

"You'll see," Grant told him.

"She's in back, I think," the bartender offered, edging closer to his shotgun just in case he needed it.

Grant went to the back of the saloon and looked in the kitchen door. He was glad to see that Mary was still there.

"Mary? Could you come out here for a moment?"

Mary had been cooking up a dinner for several of the men out front, and she was surprised by the interruption. "Why, Grant, what are you doing here?"

"You'll see. There's someone who wants to talk to you."

"All right."

Mary gave the food she was cooking one last quick stir to make sure it didn't burn, then, after wiping her hands on a towel, she limped over to see what Grant wanted.

"Got any more apple pies back there?" he asked with a grin.

"No, that was a special treat," she replied, giving him a quick smile as she joined him in the doorway. It was then that she saw Ned standing at the bar, and she stopped right where she was. Panic seized her, and she was ready to flee at the sight of him. "I don't want to go out there—"

She started to turn away, to go back to the haven of her kitchen, but Grant took her by the arm, stopping her flight.

"Trust me. I'm not going to let anything happen to you." He wanted to comfort her and let her know she was protected.

Trembling, Mary looked up at Grant. Their gazes met, and, in that instant, she saw the fierceness of his determination in his gaze. Her fear eased and she gave herself over into his keeping.

"All right."

Mary was still a little hesitant, but she allowed Grant to draw her out into the saloon. They moved slowly across the room, for she was favoring her ankle, and eventually joined Ned at the bar.

"Ned, there's someone here I know you want to speak with," Grant began.

"Yeah," he answered, not really looking at either Grant or Mary.

"Her name is Mary Smith."

"I know that," he said in disgust.

"I figured you did." Grant looked down at Mary, whose confusion was showing in her expression. "Isn't there something you'd like to say to her?"

Ned stayed right where he was, staring down at the half-empty glass of sarsaparilla sitting on the bar in front of him.

His hesitation annoyed Grant.

"I'm talking to you," Grant stated in a cold tone. "There were two conditions to your release from jail, and we're all waiting for you to do what you've been ordered to do. Now, if you don't see fit to apologize to the lady right here in front of everybody, I'll have to take you right back and lock you up again."

Grant had deliberately spoken loud enough so everyone in the saloon could hear him. The other men stopped talking to listen, waiting to see just what the usually rowdy, troublemaking Ned would do.

"Well?" Grant goaded again.

Ned was humiliated, but knew he had no other way out. He didn't doubt for a minute that the deputy would do exactly what he said, and, unarmed as he was, he didn't stand a chance of getting away if he tried to run. In a jerky move, he lifted his glass of sarsaparilla and downed it in one long drink. The sarsaparilla did nothing to embolden him, as whiskey would have, but having no alternative, he put the empty glass back down and looked straight at Mary.

"Sorry."

"What? I didn't hear you," Grant pressed, "and I'm not sure Mary did, either."

"I said I was sorry," Ned ground out, glaring at the cook, who stood close by the deputy's side.

"You ever going to do anything like that to her again?" Grant demanded.

"Hell, no—"

"What did you say?" Grant took a menacing step toward him. "You don't use that kind of language around a lady."

"Lady? She ain't no—"

"Watch what you're saying, friend." Grant spoke in a low, cold, threatening tone.

"Sorry," Ned said, quickly backing down. "I meant to say that I have no intention of getting drunk and acting up any more in Lawless, and I'm sorry if I hurt you the other night." He glanced at Mary, humiliated and embarrassed and enraged.

Mary was taken by surprise at the apology, and she wondered what Jace and Grant had done to get Ned to grovel before her this way. "You did."

"Like I said, I'm sorry. It won't happen again."

"You're right. It won't, because I'm going to be watching you real careful from now on." There was no mistaking the very real threat in Grant's tone. "Now, get on out of the Tumbleweed. I don't want to see you around here anymore."

Ned started to go.

"Don't you think you'd better pay for your sarsaparilla?" Dennis demanded sarcastically. "I'd hate to have to get Deputy Richards to arrest you again."

In utter disgust, Ned turned back and tossed a coin on the bar. He stalked out, knowing that all eyes were upon him. He couldn't get out of Lawless fast enough. He would just go back to the jail to get his gun and then he would leave.

"I can't believe you got him to apologize to me," Mary

said, looking up at Grant with open admiration. "Thank you."

"I'm just doing my job, ma'am," he said, grinning down at her. "Actually, it was Jace's idea."

He was glad the confrontation had gone so smoothly. In the back of his mind, though, he knew handling a drunk like Ned was nothing compared to facing down men like Harley King and his gang.

Mary started back to the kitchen to check on the food she'd left cooking on the stove. Grant watched her go, and he could tell just by watching how badly her ankle was still hurting her. He was glad Ned had apologized for the injury, but an apology still didn't take away her pain.

"You ready for that drink I promised you earlier?" Dennis offered Grant.

"Yes, I am," Grant answered, joining Dennis at the bar.

Grant kept watch over Mary until she had made her way untouched through the saloon and back into the kitchen. Satisfied that the other men had gotten the message, he relaxed and enjoyed the whiskey the barkeep set before him.

Chapter Ten

Once Sammie had finished her work in the stable, she quickly got the word out about the meeting to those she knew she could trust, and then went home to get cleaned up. Sammie longed for a long, hot bath, but had no time. After scrubbing off the day's grime, she dressed in clean work clothes and returned to the stable to get Walt.

"What are you doing going over to church dressed like that?" Walt asked, surprised she wasn't wearing a dress. It was one thing for her to wear pants at the stable, it was another to wear them to church.

"We've got to keep this meeting quiet," Sammie told him. "If anybody around town saw me wearing a dress tonight, they might think something strange was going on."

"You're right. I hadn't thought about that," Walt agreed. "I guess we'd better get over there."

Reverend Davidson was watching for those Sammie had told him would be attending, and he opened the back door to let them in.

"Is anybody here yet?" Sammie asked.

"Mary's here with Jonathan," the preacher told them.

Sammie and Walt went to chat with Mary and her son in the meeting room while they waited for the others to show up.

It wasn't long before Jim Peters, the owner of the general store, arrived, along with Slim Jones, Doc Malloy and Tom Harrison, the undertaker. April Kelly, the laundress and seamstress in town, showed up a few minutes later with Charlie Wilson, the hotel owner.

They had all settled in at the table when Ben and Hank came in, followed by Jace and Grant.

"Good, you're here," Sammie said.

She was actually looking past the Madisons at Jace and Grant, but her brother didn't realize it.

Walt glanced over at her, clearly disgusted by her comment. "You're glad the Madisons are here?"

Those at the meeting were just as surprised by her comment as her brother. It was common knowledge that the families despised each other. Just having both of them in attendance at this meeting was unusual. They usually cut a wide path around each other.

"This meeting is about saving our town," Sammie answered tersely. "Nothing else."

Reverend Davidson went to welcome the two new men. After all the introductions were made, they joined the others seated at the table.

"I understand you have some promising news for us," the reverend said once everyone was seated.

"Yes, we do." Ben spoke up, taking charge as he always did in his usual domineering way. "We all know Harley King and his men have got to be stopped. Sheriff Anderson tried to bring them in, and it cost him his life. When that happened, I knew we were in really bad trouble, and that's when I thought of my nephew Jace. I'm sure you've all heard about how wild Los Rios used to be a few years back." He looked around the table and read their expressions as they remembered the talk about that terrible town. "Well, Jace and his deputy, Grant Richards, are the two men who brought law and order to Los Rios."

A murmur of surprise went through the room, and the group eyed the two newcomers with open respect and admiration.

"I sent a wire to Jace asking him for his help in taking our town back from the King Gang. I didn't know if he'd agree to take on the job or not, but he and Grant rode in yesterday, and as you can see, we've got ourselves a new sheriff and deputy."

A murmur of approval went through the room, but Walt was clearly agitated by Ben's arrogant approach to deciding who the new lawman would be.

"I just want to know who gave you the right to pick our new sheriff?" Walt demanded.

Ben's expression was filled with loathing as he looked at the younger man. "Sheriff Anderson's tombstone gave me the right. Lawless is in bad shape. We've got money to hire a new sheriff and deputies, and we need the best lawmen we can get. We need men who can deal with killers like Harley King, and as far as I'm concerned, Jace and Grant are the only ones smart enough to take them down."

"That's right, Walt," Hank put in, deliberately provoking the other man. "I didn't see you pinning on that sheriff's badge after Sheriff Anderson was shot."

"Neither did you—" Walt returned hotly.

"I can always use another deputy, if you're interested," Jace interrupted, looking at Walt.

"All right." Walt accepted the challenge, not trusting the Madisons to have so much authority in Lawless. "You just hired yourself another deputy."

"Good," Jace said. "Show up at the sheriff's office tomorrow, and we'll discuss your duties."

Walt's offer surprised Sammie, but it made her proud of him. She thought it was a shame girls couldn't be deputies, too. She would have been glad to take on the job.

Jace went on, his tone deadly serious. "If we're going to save your town, I'm going to need more than just these three deputies. I'll need everyone in town to work with us. We have to figure out how we're going to outsmart Harley King when he gets back. We've got to come up with a plan so we can be ready to act on it when the time comes. That's why I wanted to meet with you here tonight. Grant and I need to know who's with us. We need to know who we can count on when things get tough."

"I think everybody here is willing to do whatever you need us to do," the reverend told him. "Isn't that right?"

"I was there when Sheriff Anderson was killed. I'll do whatever I can for you," Slim said.

"Thank you." Jace could imagine how hard it had been for him to witness the sheriff's murder.

The rest of the people at the meeting spoke up, too, committing themselves to the dangerous job that lay ahead of them.

Jace looked at those gathered at the table. "Good. As dangerous as these killers are, it's going to take the whole town of Lawless working together to bring them to justice. Are you ready to do it?"

"We're ready," said Tom Harrison, the undertaker. He'd seen far too much death and destruction these last months.

"Yes, we are," Mary said from where she was sitting, holding a very sleepy Jonathan on her lap.

"We know how these gunmen work, so we know the day is going to come when we will need you to back us up," Jace advised. "We'll be in contact with all of you as things develop. If you have any ideas ahead of time on how to bring the outlaws down, we'll be glad to listen."

"Are you planning just to gun them down as soon as they ride back into town?" Reverend Davidson asked.

"Only if they force us to," Jace answered. "I'm a man of the law. I believe the killers should be arrested and put on trial."

"But we don't have a judge," Doc Malloy put in.

"Don't worry about that. Once we get the gang behind bars, Jace will find us a judge," Grant reassured them.

"Good." The reverend was glad to know that the new sheriff was a civilized man.

"Is there anything in particular you want us to do right now?" April Kelly, the laundress, asked. "I don't know how much help I can be to you, but I'll do whatever you ask if it means making Lawless safe to walk the streets again."

"That goes for me, too," Mary added.

"I appreciate that," Jace told both women. "For right now, just listen to what's being said around town and keep an eye out for anything unusual. If you see or hear anything you think is strange, let one of us know right away. And if you hear any talk about Harley King, let us know that, too. Sometimes the smallest hint of trouble can be a big help to us."

"We will," Mary promised and April nodded.

"When Harley and his men do return, we're going to need all the backup we can get to face them down, so arm yourselves and be ready."

"One other thing," the reverend added. "I think it's important that we find a way to let the rest of the folks know that it's official—that Lawless does have a new sheriff and deputies."

"How can we best handle that?" Jace asked.

Ben quickly spoke up. "Reverend, tomorrow's Friday. Why don't you organize a social here at church for tomorrow night? You could introduce Jace and Grant and let them meet everyone."

"That's a fine idea, Ben. We'll do it. Plan on being here at six-thirty tomorrow evening."

They talked for a little while longer before calling it a night. Reverend Davidson closed the meeting with a blessing and a prayer that Lawless would once again be a town of peace and prosperity.

As everyone started to leave, Jace called his uncle and cousin aside to talk with them privately.

"What is it?" Ben asked.

Jace looked at them seriously. "I know we talked earlier about the bad blood between you and the Prestons. I just want to make sure it won't affect anything we do while we're working to bring down the King Gang."

"Talk to the Prestons," Ben said coldly. "They're the ones who are holding the grudge."

"I plan on doing just that." He looked at Hank. "As deputies, you and Walt are going to be working together, watching each other's backs. There's no time for any rivalry between you."

"Tell him that," Hank said dismissively.

"No, I'm telling you," Jace said harshly, staring his cousin straight in the eye. "You have to make this work."

Jace had a feeling this ongoing feud was ultimately going to cause trouble, but for now he had to focus on stopping the killers.

Hank looked disgusted, but said nothing more. He just turned and walked out of the church.

"Are you staying in town tonight or heading back to the ranch?" Jace asked his uncle.

"Your Aunt Catherine won't be a happy woman if she misses this social," Ben said. "I'll ride out in the morning and bring her back to town."

"Well, then, since you're not leaving tonight, what do you say I buy you a drink?" Jace offered.

"I'd say that sounds good right now."

"What sounds good?" Grant asked as he sought Jace out.

"We're going to the Tumbleweed. You want to join us?"

"No, I was just coming over to tell you, since it's so late, I'm going to see Mary home."

"Good idea," Jace agreed. Both men hoped Ned had learned his lesson, but it didn't hurt to be cautious.

"Are you staying at the jail again tonight?" Grant asked.

"I might as well. That's going to be home for me from now on."

"Since we're going to be here for a while, I'll need to

find somewhere else to stay besides the hotel, but I'll worry about that later. Right now, I'm going to take care of Mary. I'll see you in the morning."

"First thing."

Chapter Eleven

Grant left Jace and Ben to join Mary, who was speaking with Sammie and Walt.

"I'm proud of you for stepping up that way, Walt. You'll make a good deputy. Why, you might end up being as good as Grant here one of these days," Mary added, smiling up at Grant in welcome.

"I'm going to try," Walt said earnestly.

"Mary, since it's late, Jace and I thought it would be best if I walked you home tonight," Grant said.

"Why, thank you. I appreciate it," she replied. Jonathan was almost asleep in her arms.

"You mind if we walk with you part of the way?" Walt asked Grant, wanting to learn more about his new job as a deputy.

"Not at all," Grant replied. Then he looked at Mary and asked, "Are you ready to go?"

"Yes, and Jonathan is, too," she answered with a smile.

Grant thought about offering to carry her son for her,

but realized if they did run into any trouble, he needed to be able to act quickly, and that wouldn't be possible if he were holding a sleeping child.

"Sammie, are you finished here?" Walt asked.

"I wanted to talk to Jace for a moment. If you want to go on with Grant and Mary, I'll be along shortly."

"All right, I'll see you at home," Walt told her.

Grant held the door for Mary as they left the church. He and Walt followed her out.

Sammie looked over to where Jace was deep in conversation with his uncle. As she was watching him, he glanced her way. Across the room, their gazes met, and Jace gave her a slight nod before turning back to his uncle.

"Uncle Ben, why don't you find Hank and meet me over at the Tumbleweed? I need to speak to a few people here before I head out."

"I'll do that. We'll be waiting for you."

Ben left to find his son, and Jace went over to see Sammie just as Reverend Davidson approached her, too. Everyone else had already gone and they were the only ones left.

"Thank you for arranging this meeting. I think it went very well," Jace said.

"I admire your courage, Jace," the minister said. "I'll be praying for your success here in town."

"I appreciate it, Reverend." He knew they would need all the prayers they could get.

"Is there anything else I can do for you tonight?" Reverend Davidson asked.

"No, I just wanted to talk to Sammie before I left."

"Well, I'm going to retire for the night. Sammie, will you close up for me when you go?"

"I will, and thanks for letting us meet here."

"Any time you need my help, you just let me know," Reverend Davidson said. "Good night."

When the minister had gone, Jace looked at Sammie.

"It sounds like we've got some good people backing us up here in town," he said.

She looked up at him and saw his serious, determined expression. Having listened to him tonight, she truly was convinced that he was the man for the job. "They are good people, and, believe me, they're as glad as I am that you and Grant are here."

"We'll do our best for you."

"I know you will," she said.

Jace glanced at Sammie, giving her a smile. "I like the confidence you have in me."

"I've seen you in action. I know what you can do," she returned with a grin.

"I impressed you that much, did I?"

"You're going to be the best sheriff this town has ever had."

"I've only been on the job for a day. How can you be so sure?"

"I can tell. I'm a real good judge of character."

As she said it, her gaze met his, and they stood there, staring at one another, caught up in the intimacy of the moment.

Jace couldn't help himself. He reached out and drew Sammie to him, claiming her lips in a tender, yet demanding kiss. Sammie responded eagerly, lifting her arms to link them around his neck. She had been kissed by a few boys in town, but no one's kiss had ever thrilled her as Jace's did. Jace felt her response and deepened the kiss as his own desire began to burn within him. He held her close, savoring her nearness.

The embrace was an awakening for them both, and the power of it drove Jace to break off the kiss and push Sammie from him. She was breathless and a bit lost as she stood there staring up at him.

"We'd better go," Jace said.

"I know."

"What do you need to do here to close up for Reverend Davidson?"

At the mention of the minister, Sammie was jarred back to full awareness of where she was and what she'd been doing, and she found herself a bit embarrassed. "I just have to put out the lamp and make sure the door's shut tight. That's all."

Jace obliged, putting the lamp out and returning to walk with Sammie to the door. He held the door for her as they left.

"Did you bring your whip with you tonight?" he asked once they were outside.

"No, why?"

"I'll walk you home then." It was a statement, not an offer.

Not that Sammie would have argued. She wasn't about to discourage him. She wanted to be with Jace for as long as she could.

When they reached her house, they paused in the street outside.

"Good night," Jace bid her as they stopped at the end of the walkway.

She smiled up at him. "Good night."

Jace stayed there, watching until she was safely inside.

Only then did he head over to the Tumbleweed to meet up with his uncle and cousin.

Grant stayed alert as he, Mary and Walt made their way through the dark, quiet streets of Lawless. He was glad that the town seemed to be quiet that night. He and Walt discussed the duties of being a deputy, and he was glad Walt seemed to be enthusiastic about his new position. When they reached Walt and Sammie's home, Walt parted company with them.

Mary nestled Jonathan close as they continued on. She cast a quick glance up at Grant and knew there was something special about this tall, darkly handsome, very serious man. She'd recognized it the first time she'd seen him, and, now, walking with him this way, she felt safe and secure for the first time in ages. Mary remembered how she'd thought he and Jace were her guardian angels, and she was beginning to believe more and more that she'd been right.

"Where are you and Jace staying?" Mary asked.

"Jace has taken up living at the jail, and I've got a room over at the hotel," he told her.

"Celia Miller, the elderly lady who watches Jonathan for me while I'm working, runs a rooming house. You might want to think about renting a room from her. She's a good cook and includes two meals a day in the cost of the rooms."

"I may do that, but I'm not worried about the meals. I already know where to get the best meals in Lawless," he said with a smile.

"Did you enjoy the pie?" she asked.

"Oh, yeah," Grant answered. "It was delicious."

"Good. I'm glad you liked it."

"You are one fine cook."

"I'm lucky I had the skill to fall back on. After my husband, Johnny, died, I had to find a way to support myself and Jonathan."

"How long ago did he pass away?"

"It's been almost a year and a half since the fever took him." There was a note of sadness in her voice.

"It must have been hard for you with a new baby and all."

"It was terrible, but I'm thankful I have Jonathan. He's my life now." She smiled down at her son. "How did you end up being a lawman? Did you always know you wanted to be one?"

Grant chuckled at her question. "No. My family has a farm up in Kansas, but I didn't want to be a farmer. I thought I could make a living gambling. I was fast on the draw, so I figured if I built up a reputation, no one would challenge me."

"What happened?"

"A few years back, before I met Jace, I had a run-in with a very wise older lawman who convinced me to change my ways."

Mary had a feeling that there was a lot more to the story and hoped one day she'd hear it.

"Have you ever been sorry that you gave up that other way of life?" She wondered what was truly in his heart.

"I'll always be a gambling man," Grant admitted. "Taking chances is what life is all about, and right now, I'm betting that Jace and I can figure out how to bring down Harley King and make things peaceful around here again."

"I hope you win your bet."

"So do I."

"When did you meet Jace?"

"I heard talk about him a few years back and decided to ride up to Los Rios and see if he wanted some help."

"You are a gambling man, aren't you? Riding into a wild town like that all by yourself?" Mary admired his bravery.

"It worked out. Los Rios is a real quiet town now."

"Let's hope things go as well here in Lawless."

"We're going to do our best."

Mary looked up at him, meeting his dark-eyed gaze. "Just remember, Harley King is not just an outlaw. He's a cold-blooded killer."

"I'll remember that," he promised seriously.

They reached her small home, and Grant opened the door for her so she could get inside without waking her son.

"I'll be right back," she told him in a soft voice.

He waited on the porch while she went inside to put Jonathan down in his bed for the night.

When Mary returned a short time later, she found Grant standing with his back to the house staring out across the dark, quiet streets of town. He hadn't heard her return, so she took a moment just to study him. He was tall, lean and powerfully built, and she had been drawn to him from the first time she'd seen him. Mary hadn't felt these emotions in so long, she was a little confused by them. All she knew was that she wanted to be near Grant right now.

"Thank you for seeing me home," she said, going to stand by his side. The night was dark and warm, and a part of her wasn't willing to let him leave yet.

"It was my pleasure, Mary."

Grant gazed down at her in the glow of the soft lamplight coming from inside, and he realized just how much he had enjoyed being in her company. She was a rare and lovely young woman, who, in spite of all the hardships she'd had to endure, still found a way to see the goodness in life.

Grant found himself drawn to Mary. He was tempted to take her in his arms and kiss her, but he fought against the impulse. She was a good woman, and he didn't want to put her reputation at risk. The thought surprised him. It was the first time in as long as he could remember that he'd been concerned about a woman's reputation. As the thought of kissing her lingered, he wondered, too, if she kept her frying pan there at home. That thought made him smile wryly to himself.

Mary had been watching him closely, studying his compelling, handsome features. He'd seemed so serious that she was surprised when he suddenly started grinning. "You're smiling."

"I just had a thought . . ." It wasn't often that he found himself in situations like this, and he was trying to decide whether to be honest with her or not.

"What?"

"Well, I have to tell you," he began, turning to face her and lifting one hand to touch her cheek. "I wanted to kiss you."

"You did?" Her heartbeat quickened at his words, and a shiver of sensual awareness trembled through her at the gentle touch of his hand.

"Oh, yeah," he replied, still struggling against the impulse to take her in his arms.

In a daring moment that was totally unlike her usually quiet self, she asked, "Why didn't you?"

"I didn't want to put your reputation at risk."

"And that made you smile?" She was a bit confused.

"No, what made me smile was the thought that, along

with putting your reputation at risk, you might have a frying pan hidden somewhere close by." Grant was grinning when he finished.

Mary found herself smiling up at him in the darkness. She told him in a soft voice, "I don't."

Her unspoken invitation was more than he could resist. Alone there in the sweet heat of the night, Grant drew her away from the lamplight and into the shadows. He took her in his arms and kissed her.

For a moment, Mary held herself a bit stiffly. For so long now, she hadn't felt like a real woman. She'd almost been dead inside, but as Grant's lips moved over hers, Mary felt herself come alive. His kiss evoked sweet, hungry feelings deep within her, and she surrendered to the need to be in his embrace.

Grant felt the change in her, and he deepened the kiss. He drew her even closer, and they clung together. Her kiss was every bit as exciting as Grant had thought it would be. He wanted to crush her against him, to keep her there in his arms, but despite his heated desire, he knew he had to end the embrace. It took a lot of willpower, but he managed to end the kiss and set her away from him.

"I'm glad you didn't have a frying pan," he told her, smiling.

"Even if I had had one, I wouldn't have used it," Mary said softly.

He was tempted to take her back into his arms again, but he knew he shouldn't. "You go on inside now."

"Will I see you tomorrow?" she asked. She wanted him to stay, but knew it wasn't proper.

"Are you working tomorrow?"

"I'll be cooking."

"Then I'll be there," he promised. "I'll see you at the Tumbleweed and at the social tomorrow night."

"Yes, you will," she returned, eager at the thought.

"I'd better be going," Grant said reluctantly. "Good night."

Mary's eyes were twinkling as she told him, "Yes, it was a good night—a very good night."

Grant bent down and kissed her once more, softly, then left the porch.

Mary watched him until he had disappeared into the darkness and then went inside. As she sought the comfort of her lonely bed, images of the handsome deputy and his exciting kiss played in her mind, and she found herself looking forward to seeing him the following day.

Grant knew Jace and the others would probably still be at the Tumbleweed, and he considered joining them there for one last drink, but decided against it. He went on back to the hotel, wanting to get a good night's sleep instead.

Grant let himself into his room, but didn't bother to light the lamp on the nightstand. He went to look out the window at the deserted street below, appreciating how quiet things were in town this evening. Grant had a feeling it wouldn't be long until the outlaw and his gang of killers returned, and when they did, he knew things were definitely going to change.

As he bedded down for the night, his thoughts were on Mary and her son—and how he and Jace were going to keep them safe. He realized then that if he took a room at the boarding house, he might be closer to Mary just in case any kind of serious trouble did develop in town.

Grant decided to look into it the following day.

Chapter Twelve

Ben and Hank and several other men were standing at the bar in the Tumbleweed drinking when Jace walked in.

"Evenin', Sheriff," Dennis greeted him, eyeing the badge on Jace's shirt. "Looks like the law really is back in town."

"Evenin', Dennis," Jace returned as he joined his uncle and cousin at the bar. "I take it you know what's going on?"

"I heard the talk about your taking over for Sheriff Anderson and bringing your deputy with you, and now I just found out that Hank here is joining up with you, too," the bartender answered as he looked over at Hank.

"Hank is one of my new deputies and so is Walt Preston," Jace told him.

"So there's going to be four of you now."

"That's right. It's going to take some serious work to clean up this town, and we're ready to get started," Jace added.

"Well, I'll drink to that. How 'bout it? What do you say, boys?" Dennis shouted to the other men drinking in the bar. "The next round is on me in celebration of our new sheriff and his deputies."

It was obvious from their startled expressions that some of those in the saloon hadn't heard the news, but, happy about it or not, they weren't about to turn down free drinks.

Jace grinned and went along with the bartender's celebration. After getting his own drink, he took the time to speak to the other men in the bar as he made his way to sit at a table in the back with Ben and Hank.

"Looks like the word is out," Jace remarked drolly as he took a deep drink of his whiskey.

"You're right about that. By tomorrow, everybody will have heard you're the new sheriff of Lawless," Ben said.

"Yeah, we won't even need the social to spread the word," Hank added. "At least now we're ready for the King Gang."

"We're as ready as we'll ever be," Jace cautioned him. "But you can never be too ready to deal with someone like Harley King. Remember that."

"Listen to your cousin," Ben advised his son. "Jace is right. He's been at this for some time now, so you'd do well to heed what he says."

Hank took a drink of his whiskey as he studied Jace thoughtfully. He had heard the story behind Jace's becoming a lawman, but he'd always wondered why Jace had stayed at it after he'd caught up with the outlaws who'd robbed the stage and killed his fiancée. He decided now was as good a time as any to find out.

"Jace," Hank began, "why do you want to put your life on the line here in Lawless? Why do you care? You could go back to your old life. You could go back to ranching. You don't have to be a lawman."

Jace had been asked that question many times over the

years, and as he looked at his cousin sitting across the table from him, he knew no matter how he tried to explain it, Hank wouldn't understand. "I could quit, but there's nothing to go back to."

"You caught up with Lawrence and Carson, didn't you? You got your revenge. They were hanged, weren't they?"

"Yes." His answer was cold and emotionless. At the time, it had felt good to know the outlaws had paid for their crimes, but, even so, their deaths hadn't brought Sarah back. "Lawrence and Carson were hanged, but there are other men still out there who are just as vicious as they were, and some of them, like Harley King, are even more cold-blooded. They need to be stopped before any more innocent people suffer, and I enjoy stopping them."

Jace met Hank's gaze as he said the last words, and, in that moment, Hank realized just what a formidable, determined man Jace truly was. His respect for his cousin grew even more.

"So this is your life now," Ben added.

Jace nodded. "There's a satisfaction in knowing a town is safe for decent people to go about their business without having to fear for their lives."

"I'll bet there were a lot of folks in Los Rios who were sad to see you leave," his uncle said.

"They understood, and they were grateful for what Grant and I managed to accomplish. Let's just hope we're as successful here as we were in Los Rios."

"You will be."

"Keep thinking that way."

Ben changed the topic then. "Did Grant say earlier that you spent last night at the jail?"

"That's right. We had Ned locked up, and I wanted to

make sure nothing happened overnight. There's a small room off to the side of the office. I'll be satisfied staying there. Is that where Sheriff Anderson lived?"

"No. The townsfolk provided him with a house, but after Harley and his men shot him down, those outlaws took it over. I wouldn't want you to try to live there, not with them coming back at any time."

"That's fine. I've got all the room I need at the jail."

"What about you, son? Have you thought about where you'll be staying while you're in town?"

"I hadn't thought past tonight," Hank admitted.

"Where's Grant staying?" Ben asked.

"Right now at the hotel."

"Maybe you can check with Grant in the morning and take rooms at one of the boardinghouses," Ben suggested.

"That would be better than staying at the hotel," Hank agreed.

They went on to speak of other things, but took care not to make any mention of their earlier private meeting. Though it might be common knowledge now that the law was back in town, the other folks in town didn't need to know everything they had planned in their effort to bring civilization back to Lawless.

Jace quit drinking after one whiskey. He couldn't let his guard down tonight, and he wanted to make sure he wasn't going to be feeling the effects of the liquor in the morning. He had too much work to do in getting ready for what was to come when Harley returned.

They stayed at the saloon for a while longer before calling it a night.

The stable was closed up and dark as they passed by on their way to the hotel. Jace stared at the Preston name on the sign and considered asking Hank how he was going to manage working with Walt, but he decided to wait. He knew it was going to be up to him to make sure the two men learned to trust and rely on each other. It wasn't going to be easy, considering how tense things were between the two families, but he would worry about that tomorrow. Right now, he was looking forward to getting some rest. Trying to sleep with Ned locked up in back the night before hadn't been easy.

Sammie sat at the kitchen table, lost in thought. A great deal had been accomplished at the meeting that night. She was pleased with the way things had turned out, but she was also worried about her brother. She had never expected him to step up and take a job as a deputy.

"What are you thinking about?" Walt asked as he came into the room and saw her troubled expression.

Sammie looked up him. "I was thinking about you."

"Me?" Walt looked surprised as he sat down across from her. "Why were you thinking about me?"

"I'm worried about you being a deputy," she told him. "I'm worried something might happen to you."

"Jace and Grant need my help," he said seriously.

Sammie appreciated her brother's courage, but she was still troubled. "What about Hank?"

"What about him?"

"Are you going to be able to work with him?"

Walt's expression darkened at the thought. "I don't think Hank will try to cause any trouble between us as long as Jace is running things. I know Jace is a Madison, too, but he's nothing like Ben and Hank."

"Even with Jace running the show, there are going to

be times when you're going to have to deal with Hank on your own. You're going to have to learn to trust him if you're serious about being a deputy."

Walt looked grim as he realized the long-standing hatred between the families would be hard to completely put aside. "Somehow, I'll do it. I've got confidence in Jace and Grant. After listening to them tonight, I have no doubt they're as good as everybody says they are. If anybody can find a way to bring peace to this town, it will be them."

Sammie looked out the window into the darkness. Some people saw the night as comforting, but with all the violence in Lawless lately, the darkness left Sammie uneasy. "I just wish Harley and his men would never come back."

"You can keep wishing that all you want, but it's not going to change anything. They'll be back, and when they show up, it's going to be bad. They made it real clear that they consider Lawless their town when they killed Sheriff Anderson."

"Do you think they'll be showing up soon?"

"It's hard to say, and not knowing just makes the waiting that much worse. The last time they left, they were gone for over two weeks. We just have to be ready for them whenever they do show up."

They fell silent for a moment, dreading the confrontation to come. It would be bloody, there was no doubt about that.

"I guess we'd better get some sleep while we can. There's no telling what the new day is going to bring," Sammie said, getting up from the table. Then, just to let her brother know she was proud of him, she went over and kissed him on the cheek. "Who would ever have thought that I'd have a lawman in the family?"

Walt grinned at her, and then jokingly ordered, "That's right. I'm Deputy Preston now. You'd better remember that, little girl. I'm the law around here. What I say goes, and I say it's time to call it a night."

She laughed at him. "All right. I'll follow your orders this time, but only because I'm tired and I have to get up early in the morning. If you're going to be working as a deputy, I'm going to have to do more work at the stable."

They went off to their own rooms to get what rest they could.

Though Sammie was exhausted, sleep did not come right away for her. She lay in bed, her mind racing as she relived all that had happened during the last two days. She would never have dreamed that the two men she and Mary had seen riding into town looking like dangerous gunfighters would turn out to be brave men who were going to try to save the town.

An image of Jace played in her thoughts, and the sweet memory of his kiss stayed with her. She'd never been so attracted to a man before. He was different from any man she'd ever known, and she found herself wondering about his past, about how he'd come to be a lawman. It was obvious he was good at what he did. He'd tamed Los Rios, and everyone knew what a dangerous town that had been a few years back. She just hoped it wasn't too late for him to save Lawless.

Remembering that Reverend Davidson had told them to pray for their town to be peaceful again, she did just that, adding an extra prayer for her brother to find a way to get along with Hank. She finally drifted off to sleep, looking forward to the social the following night, when she would get to see Jace again.

Ned was still angry as he bedded down by his small camp-fire miles from Lawless. The humiliation he'd suffered at the hands of the new lawmen in town had left him filled with rage. Driven by the need for revenge, he lay staring up at the night sky, trying to think of a way to get even with them. Ned knew he was no match for Madison and Richards in a shootout, but he believed there had to be some way he could pay all of them back—the two law-men and the cook.

His dark spirits brightened as he thought of the day when Harley King would return to Lawless. The outlaw and his men would be able to take care of that new sher-iff and deputy in no time. He was sure of it. He just wished there was some way he could warn Harley ahead of time about what lay in wait for him, so he and his gang could sneak up on the lawmen and surprise them. Unfor-tunately, there was no telling where Harley was or when he'd be coming back.

As Ned lay there, he fantasized about getting his re-venge. He pictured himself meeting up with Harley and warning him about what had happened in town. He imagined Harley thanking him for his help and inviting him to join his gang. That thought made Ned smile—being in with the King Gang. He could see himself, gun in hand, riding into Lawless with the other outlaws. He wanted to strike terror in the hearts and souls of all those who'd humiliated him.

The fantasy was a good one, but the thought of really trying to deal with Harley unnerved Ned.

He was not a brave man.

He never had been.

And Harley King was a frightening killer.

Sleep was long in coming for Ned that night.

Harley King and his gang, Al Denton, Ken Hogan, Ed Thomas and Pete Sanders, were all relaxing as they sat around a small, low-burning campfire. The stage robbery they'd planned had gone off without a hitch. None of them had been shot. They had the money, and their reputation as one of the most dangerous gangs around was growing. They believed they'd made a clean, fast getaway. As far as they'd been able to tell, nobody was on their trail.

Life was good.

"Here, boys," Harley said, reaching into his saddlebag to pull out a bottle of whiskey. "I brought this along for a special occasion. I think we all deserve a drink to celebrate, don't you?"

"Yeah!" Al Denton agreed. He grabbed the offered bottle from Harley and took a deep swallow. It was potent and burned all the way down.

Pete took the bottle from Al and took a swig before passing it on to Ken and Ed. Soon the bottle was close to empty, and they were all feeling good.

"You got anything else planned for us to do before we head back to Lawless?" Al asked Harley. He knew it wasn't unusual for them to pull off several jobs while they were out.

"Not this time. I figured we'd just go back to town and enjoy ourselves for a while. With Sheriff Anderson dead, we can do whatever we want."

The thought of partying all night long in the Tumbleweed with the saloon girls made them all smile. They liked Lilly and Candy, the two beauties who worked there.

"Too bad we gotta take the roundabout way back," Al complained. They were taking the longer route to Lawless so they could make sure no one was after them. "I'd like to be with Candy right now."

"You're not the only one," Ed put in.

"I know what you mean," Pete added. "Candy and Lilly sure know how to please a man."

"And knowing those two girls, I'm sure they'll be watching and waiting for you—and your money—when we get there," Harley said.

"That's fine with me," Ken said, smiling.

"That's right," Ed remarked. "Those girls earn their money. They're worth every cent we pay them."

"And then some." Pete was smiling, too, remembering his last passionate encounter with Candy. "And I'm looking forward to having my meals there again. That Mary is a good cook."

"You're right about that. I wouldn't mind eating one of her dinners right now," Harley agreed. He was fond of the hot, home-cooked meals served at the saloon.

"You can have the cooking, Harley. I'm after something hotter than food," Ken said, laughing.

"I'm hungry," Ed put in, "but it ain't for Mary's cooking. I'm wanting a taste of Candy, and I don't mean the confectionery kind!"

They were all laughing.

"Well, you boys just keep on dreaming about those pretty girls, because it's going to be a while before we get to town," Harley told them.

"I'm gonna keep that Lilly up all night pleasuring me when we get back," Ed replied.

"Yeah, I got a powerful itch for them girls to scratch," Ken said.

They all laughed, looking forward to the day when they would ride into Lawless. They were going to make their way straight to the Tumbleweed saloon and start celebrating their return.

Chapter Thirteen

Time was running out, but Sammie was almost ready. She'd been at the stable working for most of the day and then had hurried home late that afternoon to dress for the social. It had taken some work, but she'd managed to transform herself. For the first time tonight, Jace would get to see her as Samantha, and not as Sammie the stable hand. It wasn't often she got to dress this way, and as she studied her image in her bedroom mirror, she was pleased with the results. Once a week, she wore a prim dress for church services, but dressing up like this for a social occasion was an uncommon pleasure for Sammie.

She was wearing her hair down and loose about her shoulders in a cascade of golden curls, held back by just a simple ribbon. Her rose-colored dress was modestly cut with delicate lace trim at the neckline. It was a far cry from her usual pants and shirts, and she was glad.

She wanted to feel like a lady tonight.

Jace was going to be at the social.

Sammie was smiling as she turned away from the mirror. She was eager to see what his reaction was going to be when he saw her dressed this way for the first time.

A knock at the front door interrupted her thoughts, and Sammie hurried downstairs to find Mary there, carrying Jonathan and a basket of food.

"You're right on time," Sammie told her friend as she invited her in. She found the delicious aroma drifting up from the basket enticing. "You fixed fried chicken, didn't you?"

"Of course, you know I would have gotten in trouble with Reverend Davidson if I hadn't."

They both laughed, knowing how much the reverend enjoyed her chicken.

"Tonight is so special. It's been too long since we've had fun this way."

"Or got to dress up. Just look at you! You look gorgeous," Mary told her as she set the basket aside and put Jonathan down to let him toddle around while they visited for a minute. With the jobs they both had, it was a special occasion when they got to act like real ladies.

"So do you," Sammie said, smiling.

It had been a long time since Sammie had seen Mary take such care with her appearance. After the long months of mourning had ended, Mary had shown little interest in how she dressed, but tonight, that had all changed. She was wearing her hair done up in a more sophisticated style and the dress she had on was a rich dark green that complemented her coloring.

Sammie remembered how Grant had walked Mary home the night before, and she found herself wondering if the other new man in town had anything to do with this change in her friend. Whatever or whoever had caused it, Sammie knew it was for the good. Mary was still a young, pretty woman, and, widowed though she was, she still had the rest of her life ahead of her.

"Why, thank you. Every now and then it's fun to dress up."

"I was thinking the same thing," Sammie agreed. "Are you ready to start over to the church?"

"If you are. Where's Walt? Isn't he going with us?" Mary had expected Sammie's brother to be going with them.

"He had to meet with Jace and Grant at the jail earlier this afternoon, and I haven't seen him since. They must be teaching him how to be a deputy. It's going to be interesting to see how this works out."

"Walt will do a good job."

"I know. He's got an iron will about him. Anything he sets his mind to, he can do. He's always been that way."

"He sounds just like his sister, I think."

They both laughed.

"Well, since he's not here, we might as well go to the social without him. It's after six."

"That's fine."

Sammie looked down at her friend's son adoringly. "Besides, we don't need my brother to escort us. We've got a date. We've got Jonathan."

With Mary carrying Jonathan and Sammie carrying the food she was donating to the dinner, they started off toward the church, looking forward to enjoying the evening to come.

As Sammie caught sight of the cross atop the steeple in the distance, she looked over at her friend.

"I hope my prayers work," she said.

"What have you been praying for?"

"Peace in town, just like Reverend Davidson suggested. The last thing we need is for the King Gang to show up tonight—or anytime soon."

"Let's hope God was listening to you."

"Oh, He always listens," Sammie said with a half-smile. "It's just that sometimes His answer to my prayers has been 'no.'"

"You've had that problem, too, have you?" Mary had to smile. "Well, for tonight, I'm going to believe His answer is 'yes.'"

They neared the church and could see that people had already started to arrive.

"It's been so dangerous in town. I think everybody's been afraid to come out and socialize, but it looks like a good number of people have already shown up tonight," Mary remarked.

"Jace has already begun to make a difference," Sammie said, confident it was the talk about his presence that had helped. "This is going to be fun."

Up ahead, they could see that lanterns had been strung up in an area behind the church, and tables and chairs had been arranged so everyone could settle in and enjoy themselves. Larger tables had been set up near the church so the ladies of the congregation could serve up the food that had been donated for the festivities. There hadn't been time to put up any more decorations, but that didn't matter. What mattered tonight was the joy of being together.

Sammie and Mary were heading toward the serving tables to drop off the food Mary had brought along when Reverend Davidson saw them and hurried over to welcome them.

"Ladies, it's so good to see you tonight," he said, smiling warmly. He looked down at the basket they had with them, and then glanced back up at Mary. "Is that your—?"

"Fried chicken," Mary answered quickly.

"You knew what I was going to ask, did you?" He was chuckling.

"I was thinking of you the whole time I was frying it up, Reverend," she said with a grin.

"And I'll be thinking of you when I'm enjoying every bite."

"I'm just glad I could help in some way."

"Everybody's pitched in. It looks like we got the word out just fine," the preacher said, gesturing toward the bountiful display of delicious foods that was being set out on the tables by the ladies. There was barbeque, corn bread and biscuits, along with several dishes of green beans, peas and corn. The dessert array was already impressive with mouthwatering peach cobblers and April Kelly's famous lemon cake. "It's going to be the perfect dinner once your fried chicken is up there."

They all laughed.

"It's wonderful that so many people decided to come," Sammie said.

"We needed this. We needed to feel a part of the community again, to have a sense of belonging," he said. "It's been quite a while since we've felt safe enough to hold a gathering."

"And we owe all this to our new lawmen," Mary pointed out. "It looks like Jace and Grant truly are the men who can bring this town together."

"Speaking of Jace and Grant—have you seen them yet tonight?" Sammie asked the reverend.

"No, but I'm sure they'll be showing up soon. Once they get here, I'll take them around and introduce them and then we can all relax and have a good time."

"It sounds like it's going to be a wonderful night," Mary said. "If there's anything you need us to do, just let us know."

They moved off to mingle with the other people who'd already arrived.

Eloise Peters was sitting at a table with her parents when she saw Sammie with Mary and Jonathan.

"Mother, can you believe it?" she whispered in a scandalized tone. "Look at Sammie! She actually dressed like a girl tonight!"

"You be nice," Dee scolded her daughter.

"I was just pointing out the obvious," Eloise said huffily, smoothing the skirt of her gown. She'd taken great care with her appearance this evening, for she knew she was finally going to get the opportunity to meet the two new lawmen who'd come to town. So far, she'd heard only good things about them, the best things being that they were both handsome and single. She'd caught sight of them walking around town several times, but hadn't had the chance to speak with either yet. Tonight was going to be the night.

"Sammie! Mary! Come join us," Jim called out, unaware of the subject of the terse, whispered dialogue between his wife and daughter.

Sammie liked and respected Jim and Dee, but she wasn't about to spend any time socializing with Eloise.

Mary knew her friend well and understood her hesitation to join the Peters family at their table.

"I know what you're thinking, but you're going to have to keep smiling," Mary advised Sammie as they started over to the table to exchange pleasantries.

"I'll try," Sammie reassured her friend, "but I make no guarantees."

"You're a strong woman. I know you can do it," Mary kidded her.

"And I'm dressed like a lady tonight, so I have to act like one, right?"

"That's right. You wouldn't want your brother, the new deputy, to arrest you for acting up and causing trouble at the social, would you?"

"He's already started threatening to arrest me at home," Sammie countered, smiling. "I don't need to hear it from you, too."

They both laughed as they reached the table and sat down with the Peters family.

"Sammie, you look very pretty tonight," Dee complimented her. "Your dress is lovely."

Sammie smiled at her. "Thank you. Going to a social is definitely different from working in the stable."

"And it's a lot more fun," Dee added.

"There's no doubt about that."

"I can't believe we're actually having a social, can you?" Eloise put in.

"It's wonderful, isn't it?" Mary agreed, cuddling Jonathan on her lap. "Getting to visit with everybody like we used to . . ."

"Yes, it is," Dee agreed. "It's been so hard lately. I've been so frightened. I was beginning to feel like a prisoner in my own home."

"Things are going to get better now," Jim said, "thanks

to Ben Madison. He's the one who brought Jace and Grant to town."

"If anyone can make Lawless safe again, it will be Jace and Grant," Mary agreed.

"I heard how they saved you from that terrible drunk their first night in town," Eloise said.

"Yes, they did, and I'll forever be grateful to them. They're good men."

"I can't wait to meet them," Eloise cooed. Just from what little she'd heard in the gossip around town, she knew the newcomers had to be an improvement over most of the other men in Lawless.

"They'll be along soon, I'm sure," her father put in. "The whole point of the social was for everyone to meet our new sheriff and deputy and get acquainted with them."

Just as he finished speaking, Reverend Davidson appeared by the food tables with Jace and Grant, followed by Walt and Hank. Jace and Grant stood with the minister while Walt and Hank stood off to the side, apart from each other.

"Good evening, everybody," the reverend called out, drawing everyone's attention.

As soon as the crowd had quieted, he began.

"We're here to welcome our new sheriff and his deputies to our town," he announced. He then went on to introduce each man.

Eloise was smiling as she eyed Jace and Grant with interest. They were both handsome with their dark good looks, but there was something about Jace Madison— a confidence and sense of power about him—that attracted her more. She had to admit to herself that Hank did look special wearing his deputy's badge. She'd been thinking of trying to catch him for a while, but Jace was, after all, the sheriff. She made up her mind right then and there that, by the end of the social, she and Jace were going to be on a first-name basis. She started making her plan.

"I see a few of you boys brought your instruments with you, so I'm sure we're going to get some dancing in tonight. Everyone have a good time, and make Sheriff Madison and Deputy Richards welcome in our town," Reverend Davidson concluded.

Jace and Grant shook hands with the preacher and then paused to speak with Hank and Walt for a moment before moving off to make the rounds. Hank and Walt didn't even bother to speak to each other. They just went their separate ways.

The food was ready to be served, and the musicians wasted no time in striking up a tune, adding even more gaiety to the already lively gathering.

Jace made small talk with those he met, but all the while he found himself glancing around for some sign of Sammie. He was looking forward to seeing her this night. In fact, he'd been thinking about her for most of the day, remembering the pure pleasure of holding her in his arms. He spotted Mary and her son sitting at a table with Jim Peters and several other women, but he didn't see Sammie anywhere. Walt had told him she planned to be there. He hoped she hadn't gotten too caught up working at the stable to get away in time.

Realizing the direction of his thoughts, Jace turned his focus back to his main reason for attending the social— meeting everyone. This wasn't a true social event for him. It was part of his job. He had to establish his authority in town and let everyone know that he could be counted on if anyone needed help in any way.

"I'm going to see how Mary's doing," Grant told him. "She and Jonathan are sitting over there at the table with Jim Peters."

"Have you seen Sammie anywhere?"

"No, not yet. Did Walt say when she would be getting here?"

"I didn't ask him."

"Well, let's check with Mary. If anyone knows what Sammie's doing, it should be her."

They made their way over to the table where Mary and her son were sitting with Jim Peters and three other women. One lady was older and appeared to be Jim's wife. The other two were young. One was a blonde and the other a brunette. They were sitting with their backs to the men, so they couldn't get a look at their faces. Jace and Grant suspected they might be Jim's daughters.

As the lawmen drew closer, the two young women looked their way, and Jace realized to his surprise that the shapely blonde was Sammie. He'd known she was lovely, but the transformation in her appearance tonight was amazing. Dressed in a demure gown with her hair worn down around her shoulders, she bore little resemblance to Sammie the stable hand, not that he hadn't enjoyed seeing her wearing pants.

Tonight, she was every bit a lady, and a beautiful one, at that.

He was utterly captivated.

Chapter Fourteen

"Good evening," Jace and Grant greeted those seated at the table.

Though the greeting was for everyone, at that moment, Jace only had eyes for Sammie.

"You know Mary and Sammie," Jim said, "and this is my wife, Dee, and my daughter, Eloise. Why don't you join us?"

"Yes, please do," Eloise invited, staring at the two men with open interest. They were every bit as handsome close up as they had been from a distance, and she was determined to find a way to get to dance with both of them before the night was over.

"Thanks," Jace and Grant said.

Jace took the chair between Sammie and Eloise, while Grant sat beside Mary.

Jace's full attention was on Sammie, and he said with a smile, "I take it you're not going back to work when you leave the social tonight?"

Sammie smiled back at him. "You could tell that, could you?"

"I think it's safe to say we all could," Grant put in. "You look real pretty tonight, Sammie."

"Why, thank you, Grant."

Everyone laughed except Eloise. She managed only a tight smile. She wasn't pleased that the men were paying more attention to Sammie than to her. She was prettier than Sammie. She knew it, and she was smarter than Sammie, too. After all, she'd gone back East to school, and her parents had money.

"What do you think of our town so far, Sheriff?" Dee asked, wanting to strike up a conversation. She was interested in learning more about this man who'd come to help the people of Lawless.

"I think most of the people here are good, honest, law-abiding citizens. They're friendly, and they care about their town. If they didn't, I wouldn't still be here," Jace answered.

"We appreciate what you're trying to do," Dee said earnestly. "And I know Jim has already told you that if there's ever anything you need us to do, you only have to ask."

"I thank you for that," Jace said. "The day may come when I have to take you up on that offer, but let's hope it doesn't."

"That's right," Jim put in. "And now—tonight is a night meant for us to enjoy ourselves. What do you say, Dee? Shall we dance?"

"Why, that's the best idea you've had in ages, Jim dear," his wife responded. She stood up to allow him to lead her out among the dancers.

With Mary holding Jonathan, Grant didn't know if

they'd get the chance to dance tonight or not, but he figured it couldn't hurt to ask. He was looking forward to taking her in his arms again. The memory of the kiss they'd shared the night before had stayed with him all day. He'd gone to the Tumbleweed for lunch and had ended up staying in the kitchen to eat so he could spend some time with her while she cooked.

"Would you like to dance, Mary?" he invited.

"I'd love to, but with Jonathan—" She was thrilled by Grant's invitation, but knew it wouldn't work well to try to dance and hold her son at the same time.

Sammie had been hoping something just like this would happen for Mary. She immediately spoke up. "You can't turn down a dance with the new deputy in town, Mary. He might arrest you or take you in and lock you up. You go on. I'll watch Jonathan for you."

"Are you sure?" Mary didn't want to impose on her friend.

"Absolutely. You know Jonathan's my favorite date."

Mary handed her son over into Sammie's keeping, and the little boy went without protest. Sammie had always doted on Jonathan and he loved her back. Mary knew she owed her friend dearly for this act of kindness and would tell her so later. Right now, though, all that mattered was being in Grant's arms. The thought of being close to him again left her breathless.

"Shall we?" He stood up and offered her his hand in a most gallant manner.

Mary took his hand and a delightful tingle of awareness shivered through her at the heat of that simple touch. She let him draw her out to the area that had been set off for dancing and went straight into his arms.

"I wanted to tell you, Mary, you look lovely tonight," Grant said as they began to dance.

For the first time in what seemed like a lifetime, Mary actually found herself blushing. "Why, thank you."

"There's no need to thank me. I'm just telling you the truth," he responded. Then he fell silent, just wanting to enjoy this moment of holding her near.

Eloise was watching the new deputy dancing with Mary, and she grew highly irritated. She had no idea why the good-looking deputy had decided to dance with the widow before he danced with her, but she was determined that she wasn't going to sit there alone all night long or suffer the unwanted attentions of some of the low-class men from town.

Eloise was sure, since Sammie was watching the baby, that the new sheriff was hers for the taking. With her parents away from the table, she knew they wouldn't hear her brazen ploy, so she decided to go for it. She certainly had nothing to lose.

"Jace?" She said his name sweetly, making sure she sounded totally innocent as she touched him on the arm to draw his gaze away from Sammie and the baby. She wanted his attention focused on her. "Would you care to dance?"

Jace was surprised by the other woman's request. He preferred to stay with Sammie. He wanted to use this time to talk with her and get to know her better, but there was no polite way to refuse the Peters girl. He accepted her invitation. "That would be nice, Eloise."

They stood up, and he led the way out to join the others.

Sammie watched them go and realized she should have expected as much from Eloise. The other woman had just proven again how aggressive, conniving and downright brazen she was. A twinge of jealousy went through her, though, as she watched Eloise being held in Jace's arms, gazing up at him as they began to dance. She frowned in surprise at her own reaction to the sight. She had no claim on him, and yet . . . after the kiss they'd shared, she'd believed there was something special between them. She glanced up again to see Eloise laughing at something Jace had said, and her frown deepened.

"Sammie?" Jonathan said, sounding a bit agitated.

His little voice drew her full attention back to him.

She looked down at the toddler to find him gazing up at her with open adoration, and her scowl vanished. The pure, unconditional love she saw in his innocent eyes touched her deeply.

"What do you want, little love?" she asked as she kissed him on the top of his head and hugged him close.

Jonathan just squealed and snuggled closer to her.

Mary was enjoying every moment of her dance with Grant, but when she caught sight of Sammie sitting all alone at the table with Jonathan, she felt truly guilty. She looked around and wasn't surprised to see Jace dancing with Eloise. If she'd been a gambling woman, she would have bet money that it had been Eloise who'd asked Jace to dance and not the other way around, but it didn't really matter. When this dance was over she would go back to taking care of her son. She didn't want Sammie to feel like a babysitter tonight, although the fantasy of escaping and spending the rest of the evening alone with Grant was a wonderful one.

"Is something wrong?" Grant asked, surprised by her troubled expression. He'd been enjoying their dance and wondered what he'd done to upset her.

"No, no, nothing's wrong," she hastened to reassure him. "In fact, if I had my choice, I'd keep dancing with you all night. It's just that I was feeling guilty for enjoying myself so much, while Sammie is watching Jonathan." Mary couldn't believe that she was being so open about her feelings with Grant when she'd known him such a short time, but there was just something about him that encouraged such confidences.

"If it will make you feel any better, remember, Sammie did volunteer," Grant told her.

"That's true." Her guilt eased a little.

"And I have to tell you, I'm glad you find dancing with me enjoyable. Years ago, my mother didn't hold much hope for me when it came to dancing."

"Why?"

"I've never been the graceful type," he said wryly.

"You're doing fine now," Mary complimented him, and then teased, "Have you been practicing a lot?"

"Hardly. I couldn't tell you the last time I danced with a pretty woman. I think you just got lucky tonight."

"I know I did." Mary looked up at Grant, seeing strength and intelligence in him. He was a rare man, indeed, and she knew she was blessed that he'd come into her life.

Her response surprised him, and he grinned down at her. "Why, thank you, ma'am. I'll try to make sure I don't disappoint you."

"You won't," she replied softly, and then fell quiet to enjoy what was left of this time in his arms.

* * *

Eloise was determined to take advantage of her dance with Jace to learn all she could about him. She bombarded him with question after question, trying to keep a conversation going. She was finding it a little difficult, though, for he was turning out to be a man of few words. He answered her questions mostly with a simple yes or no. She wasn't sure if she was intrigued by his vague answers or annoyed by them, so she kept trying.

"Do you think you're going to enjoy being here in Lawless?" Eloise asked, wanting to keep Jace's full attention focused on her. She'd noticed that he kept looking around.

Jace had been suffering through her inane attempts to make conversation, but the frivolity of her last question affirmed that she was just the kind of female he'd thought she was. He found himself wishing the dance would end soon. His expression turned serious, though, as he answered, "There's nothing enjoyable about what's going to happen once Harley King gets back."

"You can handle him," she went on, believing she was impressing Jace by complimenting him and dismissing any fears she had of the outlaws. "I've heard everyone talking about what a good job you did in Los Rios."

Jace knew it was naïve of her to think everything was going to work out perfectly. He knew from experience that that was seldom the case, but he didn't bother to try to explain it to her. There was no point.

When, at last, the music ended, Jace escorted her back to the table where Mary was once again cuddling her son. He looked down at Sammie as the musicians began to play again, this time a slower tune, and he thought their timing couldn't have been better.

"I think it's time we had a dance, don't you?" His gaze was intent upon Sammie as he held out his hand to her.

"I'd like that." She put her hand in his and let him draw her away from the table.

They made their way out to join the other couples.

Sammie went into Jace's arms without a word, and a jolt of sensual recognition at being held so close to him trembled through her. She followed Jace's lead, and they moved smoothly about the dance area together.

"Life in Lawless is already safer just because you're here," Sammie said, giving him a smile.

"What makes you say that?"

"Just take a look around tonight. It seems like forever since we were able to get together this way. The word's out about you and Grant, and there's a growing feeling that you really will be able to clean things up."

"I'm glad people believe in us, but with killers like the King Gang, it's still going to be dangerous—and deadly. I hope with Grant, Hank and your brother working with me, we'll get the outlaws behind bars pretty fast."

"Speaking of my brother, where is he?" She suddenly realized she hadn't seen Walt for a while.

"He and Hank are working. This is their first night on the job. I sent them out to make the rounds and keep an eye on things. We don't need any surprises. I want this to be a very quiet night in Lawless."

"You don't like surprises?" Sammie teased, wanting to lighten the mood between them and turn their conversation away from the outlaws and the danger that lay ahead. She wanted to enjoy the night, and the look Jace gave her then set her heart to racing.

"It depends on what kind of surprises you're talking

about," he answered in a low voice. "There was one surprise I've had since I showed up in Lawless that I've enjoyed."

"What was that?"

He grinned down at her with a devilish gleam in his eyes. "Finding out you were a girl—and a real pretty one, at that."

"Oh!" She was left breathless by his remark.

In that moment, if they hadn't been dancing in front of everybody, Jace would have kissed Sammie. He controlled the impulse, but it wasn't easy. He told himself sternly that he couldn't give in to the attraction he felt for her. He had a job to do, and she could end up in danger if he let himself be distracted in any way. Bringing peace to Lawless was a serious job, and it demanded his full attention.

He said nothing more as they continued to enjoy their dance together, moving as one to the music.

Ben and Catherine were looking around, checking out the smiling, happy crowd as they made their way to the table where Grant was sitting with Mary and the Peters family.

"How are things going?" Ben asked as he shook hands with Grant and Jim.

"Everyone seems to be having a good time," Catherine remarked.

"Yes, we are," Mary answered, "thanks to the new lawmen in town."

"Speaking of which, has anybody seen Hank? We've been trying to find him," Ben asked.

"Jace put Hank and Walt to work tonight. Our new deputies are making sure everything is peaceful," Grant told them.

"If that's the case, then it looks like they're doing a good job," Catherine said.

"So far," Ben added, sounding a bit uneasy.

"Have there been any signs of trouble?" Grant asked, suddenly worried that he might have missed something while he'd been enjoying himself with Mary.

"No, nothing that I know of," Ben said. "It's just a feeling I've got. With Harley and his gang of killers still out there somewhere on the loose, I'm not going to relax my guard too much."

"We're with you on that," Jim agreed. Their light-hearted mood became a little more sober. "Why don't you join us?"

Ben and Catherine did just that, joining those gathered at the table.

Eloise was frustrated. The new deputy hadn't given her a glance since he'd returned to the table with Mary. She'd hoped to dance with him next, but it didn't look as if that were going to happen. With her parents sitting right there with her, she couldn't very well ask him to dance as she had the sheriff, so she was trapped—and she was bored.

Eloise feared it was going to be a very long night, especially after she heard Grant say that Hank was off somewhere in town doing his job as a deputy and wouldn't be attending the social at all. Hank had been her last and final hope of salvaging the night.

Eloise's mood turned sullen as she envisioned herself sitting there through dance after dance. It was too humiliating even to consider. She turned her thoughts back to

Hank, and wondered just where in town he might be working. Hank was certainly nice-looking enough and his family did have money. Looks and money were two of her primary considerations for a suitor. True, he was a rancher, but the fact that he was now a deputy intrigued her a little. She began to wonder if she could sneak away from the social and find Hank. Certainly, a little adventure would beat sitting there looking pathetic.

"I just saw some friends I want to talk with," she told her mother. "I'll be back in a little while."

"All right, dear," Dee said. "Have fun."

Eloise escaped from the table and disappeared into the crowd of mingling townsfolk. Her determination to leave the social grew stronger.

Hank was out there somewhere.

She was going to find him.

When the dance ended, Jace and Sammie returned to the table to find Mary and Grant talking with an elderly little gray-haired lady who'd come to sit with them.

"Jace, I'd like you to meet Celia Miller," Mary said, making the introduction. "Celia runs one of the boarding-houses in town and she also babysits Jonathan for me while I'm working."

"It's nice to meet you, Mrs. Miller," Jace said.

"Please call me Celia, Sheriff Madison," she invited. "And if you ever get tired of staying down at the jail, I'll make space for you. Grant here is already thinking about taking a room at the house."

"I'll do that."

Jace turned his attention back to Sammie. He would

have liked nothing better than to spend the entire evening alone with her, but regretfully, he couldn't.

"Are you leaving?" Sammie asked, wanting him to stay with her. She wanted to dance with him again.

"I have to. Grant and I need to make the rounds and introduce ourselves to everybody, but I do want another dance with you before the night is over."

"I'll save you one," she promised.

Jace chatted with his aunt and uncle for a moment, and then duty called.

"Grant, are you ready?" Jace looked at his deputy, who was deep in conversation with Mary.

"If you are," he said, getting up.

"Hurry back," Mary said.

"We'll do our best," Grant promised her.

Sammie watched as Jace and Grant moved off to talk to the others in attendance.

"They are two special men," she told her friend.

"Very." Mary agreed, her gaze lingering on Grant.

"They certainly seem that way," Celia agreed, having overheard their conversation.

The festivities of the evening weren't over just because Jace and Grant had left them, but right then it seemed that way to Sammie and Mary.

Chapter Fifteen

Eloise knew she couldn't go too far in her search for Hank, but she had to try. She made her way around the church and down the street a short distance, hoping to catch a glimpse of him. The way her luck had been going so far that night, she held little hope that she would see him, so she was delighted when she spotted him down the block, close to the general store. Knowing she had the perfect excuse to go to him, Eloise hurried the rest of the way down the street.

"Why, Hank, it is you," Eloise said as she drew near.

"Eloise, what are you doing out here all by yourself?" Hank asked, sounding surprised to see her.

"I was running an errand at the social when I thought I saw someone down here by the store. I didn't know it was you, so I thought I'd better check to see who it was."

"You shouldn't have come down here alone," he cautioned. "What if it hadn't been me? It might have been dangerous for you."

"But it is you," she countered pertly with a smile, "and since you're a deputy now, I don't have anything to be afraid of, do I?"

"Only your father, if he finds out you were roaming the streets after dark."

"You won't tell him, will you?" She glanced coyly up at him.

"No, your secret is safe with me." He chuckled.

"Thank you." She smiled at him in the moonlight. "Why don't you walk me back to the social?"

Hank had planned to meet up with Jace there shortly, so he agreed. "All right. I'll see you safely to your father."

Glad to have Hank to herself for at least that much time, she went on, "Jace told us that you and Walt were working tonight, and I was sorry to hear that."

"Why?" He glanced down at her, frowning.

"Because I was looking forward to seeing you," she told him in a more sultry voice.

"Now that I've taken on this new job, I'm not going to have much free time anymore."

"So you're really serious about this? You're serious about being a lawman?"

"Yes," he answered solemnly. "I am."

Eloise looked up at Hank, impressed. She'd always just thought of him as a rancher—a well-to-do rancher, but a rancher just the same. Now she was seeing him in a whole different light, and the change in him intrigued her.

"Just be careful. You know what you're going to be facing when the gunmen return."

"I know."

"I wouldn't want anything to happen to you."

"You wouldn't?" Her admission surprised him a little.

He'd always thought of her as a flirt and a tease. He'd never thought she was serious about anything.

Eloise decided it was time to be daring. They were almost back to the church, but she saw a small alley off to one side, and decided to take advantage of it.

"No, I wouldn't," she answered, and in a completely bold move, she took his arm to draw him into the privacy of the little dark hiding place.

"We need to get you back." He wasn't sure what she was up to.

"This won't take long," she purred as she drew Hank down to her for a kiss.

Hank wasn't about to refuse. He knew Eloise could be a wild one, and he decided to take full advantage of the situation.

She'd issued the invitation.

He was accepting.

Hank crushed her against him and hungrily returned her kiss.

Eloise found his embrace heavenly. She would have stayed in his arms longer, but the distant sound of the musicians beginning another song forced her to draw away from him.

"I'd better get back."

"You sure?" Hank had been enjoying himself and wasn't eager to let her go just yet.

"Yes. I don't want my parents to come looking for me."

They moved out of the shadows, holding hands, and started on again, only to run into Jace and Grant.

Eloise saw the change in Jace's expression when he saw them, and she knew immediately that he wasn't pleased.

"You're supposed to be working with Walt tonight," Jace said sternly to Hank.

"We were for a while; then we split up. I found Eloise down by the general store, so I thought I should make sure she got back here safely."

Hank's concern for Eloise's safety would have been admirable under normal circumstances, but Jace knew he shouldn't have let it overrule his responsibilities as a deputy. He had wanted Hank to stay with Walt tonight to make sure the two of them could get along. They had a serious job to do, and he wanted to make sure both men were committed to it.

"She's here now," Jace pointed out, waiting to see what Hank would do.

"Thank you, Hank." Eloise could tell trouble was brewing.

Hank nodded to her, and she moved away quickly to find her parents.

The memory of Hank's passionate kiss stayed with Eloise and left her smiling. She was glad she'd been a little wild that night. Those few minutes with Hank had been worth it.

Now that Jace and Grant were alone with Hank, Jace looked his cousin in the eye.

"Do you want this deputy's job or not?" Jace demanded of Hank. He didn't have time to play games. The situation in Lawless was deadly. A part-time effort wouldn't work.

"You know I do," Hank answered seriously.

"Then act like it. I hired you to do a job, and I trusted you to do it. Don't make me regret my decision."

"All right."

Jace glared at him. "Go find Walt, and the two of you

stay together. You're got to watch out for each other. The gunmen we're dealing with are cold-blooded killers."

Jace was right, and Hank knew it.

"You know where I'll be." Hank's mood was dark as he headed off to find Walt. His cousin's angry rebuke had embarrassed him, even though he knew it was deserved. All the same, he had enjoyed Eloise's seductive kiss, and now that he was going to be in town on a regular basis, he planned to see a lot more of her.

Jace and Grant were on edge as they stood there a moment longer, away from the crowd.

"I expected more out of Hank," Jace said in a disappointed tone.

"Well, he couldn't have been holed up anywhere with her for too long. She only left the table a short while ago."

"You were watching her, were you?" Jace asked teasingly.

"It's my job. You told me to keep an eye on things around town, so I have been," Grant said with a grin. "Of course, there are some things I like keeping an eye on more than others."

"And I get the feeling that Mary might be right at the top of that list."

"You noticed that, did you? What about you and Sammie? You seemed to be making sure she stays out of trouble."

"It's a hard job, but somebody's got to do it," Jace chuckled. "We'd better get back. She promised me another dance."

They returned to the social to find Reverend Davidson looking for them.

"I noticed you were gone for a while. Was there some kind of trouble?" he asked, worried.

"No, everything is quiet tonight."

The preacher smiled. "Good. You are such a blessing to our community. It's so wonderful to have a peaceful night like this."

"I appreciate the thought, Reverend," Jace said, "but this is probably the calm before the storm."

"I'll pray that you're wrong, Sheriff," the minister said.

"You do that. I'd like to be wrong about the King Gang coming back."

They returned to the festivities, mingling for a while before making their way back to the table.

A slow song had just started up, so Jace didn't waste any time. He went straight to Sammie.

"You owe me another dance."

"And you're here to collect?" she countered, looking up at him.

"That's right."

Without another word, they went out to join the other couples.

"Your timing couldn't have been better," Sammie said.

"Why is that?"

"The dancing stops when they start serving the food, and they're setting up for that now."

"I'm glad Grant and I made it back in time."

"Because you wanted to dance with me again or because you're hungry?" she teased.

"Both."

They laughed.

"It's good to know you're an honest man, Jace Madison, but it would have been much more romantic if you'd said it was because you wanted to dance with me," Sammie said coyly.

Jace gazed down at her, thinking how lovely she looked tonight and how she truly did deserve the truth from him. He was completely serious as he admitted to her, "I did."

Sammie was surprised by the intensity she heard in his voice, and she looked up to find his dark-eyed gaze warm upon her. She was spellbound, and for a moment, time seemed to stand still. It was as if they were alone in the world, as if all the activity around them didn't exist.

"I'm so glad you came to Lawless," she said softly.

"So am I," Jace responded.

"All right, folks! It's time to eat!"

The announcement came as the music ended, and they were both jarred back to reality.

Reverend Davidson came to stand before the food tables to say grace, and as soon as he finished, the rush began.

"Are you ready to eat?" Sammie asked Jace.

"Since we can't dance any more, I guess we'll be forced to."

"I know it's a sacrifice for you, but if we hurry we can get near the start of the line."

"Let's go."

Sammie led the way and Jace followed, helping himself to generous portions of Mary's chicken, along with cornbread and vegetables.

"It's a shame Mary didn't make one of her apple pies," he said, looking over the desserts.

"Try the lemon cake. It's delicious."

"Are you sure?"

"I'm positive, and if you don't like it, I'll finish your piece for you."

"I don't think we'll have to worry about that."

After they'd piled their plates high, they returned to the table. Before long, everyone else was back at the table with them, enjoying the delicious meal.

"How long do these socials usually last?" Grant asked.

"Just until nine o'clock," Mary answered, "and that's good, because as soon as we're done eating, I have to take Jonathan home and put him to bed."

It was obvious the toddler was getting a bit fussy, but between Mary and Sammie and the food, they were able to keep him pretty well occupied so he didn't bother anyone else while they were dining.

As everyone finished eating and nine o'clock drew near, the preacher once again stood before everyone.

"I want to take this moment to thank all of you for coming out tonight," Reverend Davidson announced. "It has been a long time since we've had a social event like this, and I hope this can become the start of a regular church activity for us again. Please bow your heads and let us close this wonderful evening with a prayer." He led them in a heartfelt prayer of thanksgiving for the blessings that had been bestowed upon them, and asked for God's protection for their town and the people in it. "Good night," he bid them. "I'll see you all at church on Sunday."

Jace went to say good night to his aunt and uncle, while Grant stayed with Mary, Jonathan and Sammie.

"Did you come with anyone else?" Grant asked Mary. He was concerned about her getting safely home. Although there had been no sign of Ned around town, he still didn't trust the mean drunk not to sneak back and try to cause more trouble.

"Sammie and I came over together," Mary told him.

"Then Jace and I will walk you both home."

"Good." Mary was looking forward to spending more time with Grant. She gathered up her son and, after bidding good night to those still lingering at the table, got ready to leave.

Sammie regretted that the evening was already coming to an end, but she was delighted at the prospect of being with Jace. She knew he had serious duties to tend to, and she was glad they would have at least a little more time together. After tonight, she didn't know when they might get the opportunity again, and she wanted to take full advantage of it. The feelings Jace roused within her surprised and excited her. She'd been attracted to other men in the past, but there was something about this lawman that touched her. She wanted to get to know him better—much better.

"Ready?" Jace asked when he returned from saying good night to his relatives.

"It's that time," Grant agreed.

Mary was carrying a very sleepy Jonathan as they left the church grounds on their way to her house.

Chapter Sixteen

"Thank you for the dance tonight," Mary told Grant. "It's been a long time since I've done any dancing."

"Well, you haven't forgotten how," he complimented her.

"You mean I didn't step on you or hurt you?" she teased.

"No, ma'am. Not at all."

They were all laughing as they reached Mary's home.

"I'll see you in the morning," Jace told Grant.

"I'll be there," Grant answered as Jace and Sammie left.

Mary looked up at Grant in the moonlight. "Would you like to come in for a while? I've got a surprise for you."

"You do?" He was intrigued.

"Yes, come on in," she invited as she started indoors. "The lamp's right here by the door."

As they went inside, Grant smelled something delicious, and he hoped that his guess would be right about the surprise she had for him.

Grant quickly took care of lighting the lamp while Mary tended to her sleepy son. While she disappeared to the back of the house to see about putting Jonathan to bed, he took the time to look around the small sitting room. It was a warm, inviting room, and he realized it felt like a home. The feeling was a rare occurrence for him. For years now, home for him had simply been a rented room somewhere. The room he'd taken at the boarding-house was better than the hotel had been, but it was still just a rented room.

"With any luck, Jonathan will fall asleep in no time," Mary said as she rejoined him. "Now, come on out to the kitchen."

"Is that where my surprise is?" he asked.

"Yes, it is." She lit the lamp on the kitchen table.

There in the middle of the table was an apple pie.

"I was hoping that was what smelled so good when we came in."

"I made it just for you. Have a seat."

Grant sat down at the table while Mary got a knife and forks and two dishes.

"How big a piece would you like?" she asked as she cut a good-sized slice and put it on a plate.

"That'll do," Grant said. Then he directed her, "You take the piece you just cut, and I'll finish the rest."

She laughed in delight at his quip. "Didn't your mother teach you any table manners?"

"Should I have said please?" There was a glint of mischief in his eyes as he challenged her.

Mary pushed the rest of the pie toward him, just to see what he would do.

"Don't think I'm not tempted," he said. "But I'll behave myself and take whatever you give me."

She quickly cut him an even larger slice and served it, then sat down across from him to enjoy her own piece of pie. There was something very intimate about having Grant at home with her, and she quietly watched him as he hungrily devoured the pie.

"I've said it before and I'll say it again: You are one talented cook," he complimented her as he finished off the treat.

"I'm glad you enjoyed it. I hoped you would."

"What if I hadn't walked you home tonight? What were you going to do with the pie then?"

"I would have served it to you at lunch tomorrow."

"Well, I'm glad I didn't have to wait."

"So am I."

They sat talking, just enjoying each other's company.

"I'd better go," he told her regretfully as it grew late. "But I'll see you tomorrow for lunch."

"I'll be watching for you," she said.

Grant got up and Mary followed him to the front door. Grant stopped and turned to her. "I had a real good time tonight."

"So did I."

"You're a very special woman, Mary Smith," he said softly.

He moved to embrace her, and she went willingly into his arms. As he held her close, she linked her arms around his neck and drew him down to her for a kiss.

Their kiss started out sweetly, but a flame of desire ignited between them, and Grant responded eagerly to that fiery need. He crushed her to his chest as he deepened the kiss.

Mary found being held so close to his hard strength intoxicating, and she gloried in the heat of his nearness.

"You really don't have to go just yet, do you?" she asked breathlessly when they ended the kiss.

Grant had a one-word answer for her, and it was the answer she was waiting to hear.

"No."

Mary didn't hesitate. She took his hand and drew him down with her to sit on the sofa.

They said no more.

Words weren't necessary.

They came together again, sharing kiss after passionate kiss.

Grant pressed her down upon the welcoming softness of the sofa, and she wrapped her arms around him, holding him even closer. She loved the feel of his hard, lean body against her. When he began to caress her, she thrilled to his touch. They were caught up in the excitement of their need for one another and were surrendering to the delight of exploring their passion—

When the pitiful sound of a cry jarred them apart.

"It's Jonathan," Mary whispered miserably. She was torn between closing her eyes again and pretending she hadn't heard him, and forcing herself to leave the haven of Grant's arms to see to her son.

Grant gazed down at her, at her flushed cheeks and the invitation in her eyes. He wanted to keep kissing her. He told himself he was a gambling man and the odds were good that Jonathan would fall back to sleep. With that thought, he bent down to kiss her again.

Mary returned his kiss with abandon.

This was Grant . . .

And they were alone . . .

For a moment, they were totally consumed by the power of their desire, and then Jonathan began to cry even harder, his sobs turning into tortured wails that no mother could ignore.

Mary knew when he cried like that, something truly was wrong. Her motherly instinct drove her from Grant's arms.

"I have to go check on him."

Grant understood, and he realized, too, that things had been getting a little too hot between them. "I'd better leave."

Mary was shocked that he would have even suggested it. "No, you don't have to leave. Just wait here. I'll be right back."

She gave Grant another sweet, quick kiss before hurrying off to see to Jonathan.

Grant watched Mary go, all the while wishing he could just take her back into his arms and keep her there. He understood her need to see to her baby, though, so he got up to pace the room, wanting to ease the hot ache deep within his body.

Grant realized then that it was probably a good thing Jonathan had kept crying and hadn't fallen asleep. There was something very special about Mary, and his passion for her had started to run away with him. Grant knew he needed to keep his desire for Mary under control, for he didn't want to take advantage of her. He didn't want her to think that he was no better than one of the drunks from the saloon.

The sound of Jonathan's cries were coming closer, and

he was just turning to look in the direction she'd gone when Mary appeared with her son in her arms.

"Grant, I'm sorry. He's not usually this fussy at bedtime," Mary said as she held Jonathan close, trying to calm him.

"It's all right, Mary. I understand. Let me see if I can help." He could tell she was upset, so he went to her and took the miserable toddler in his arms.

"You want to hold him—now? When he's like this?" She was shocked. Most of the men she knew ran in the opposite direction when there was a screaming child around.

"I'll rock him and see if it helps," he offered, gazing down at Jonathan with tenderness.

Mary said nothing as Grant carried Jonathan over to the rocking chair in the corner and sat down with him.

"Well, big guy, what's bothering you tonight? Did you want to stay at the social and dance with some of the ladies?" Grant asked in a deep, gentle tone.

Mary was amazed when, at the sound of Grant's voice, Jonathan quieted and after a moment or two, curled up and relaxed against his chest. It was almost as if her son had found a haven in Grant's arms, too. She moved off quietly to sit down nearby and watch as Grant continued to talk to the little boy in a low, mesmerizing tone. They remained that way, intimately quiet together as Jonathan drifted off to sleep. When Grant felt the last of the tension drain out of the child's small body, he looked up at Mary and smiled.

"Do you want me to take him?" Mary asked in a whisper.

"No, not yet. Let's make sure he's really out."

They waited a while longer until they were certain Jonathan was deeply asleep, and then Mary led the way to the back bedroom. Grant carefully laid the sleeping child down on his bed and covered him with his blanket. They stood together in the darkened room, watching Jonathan for a moment longer; then Grant took Mary's hand and drew her silently from the room. Grant closed the door behind them and then looked down at her in the shadows of the hallway. He didn't speak, but lifted one hand to cup her cheek before bending down to give her a gentle kiss.

And it was in that loving, tender moment that Mary realized Grant made her feel like a real woman again.

Since her husband's death, she'd been numb inside, but now, because of Grant, all that had changed. She felt alive. He had only been in her life for a short time, but she had come to truly care for him. And after watching him with Jonathan tonight, she realized just how special he was.

When they ended the kiss, they made their way quietly back to the parlor.

"It's getting late. I'd better go," he told her regretfully.

"But I want you to stay," she said softly.

"Believe me, I want to stay. You are a very tempting woman, but if I don't go now, I might not go at all."

At his words, Mary blushed, knowing he was right. "Will I see you tomorrow?"

"You know it," he promised her, gathering her in his embrace for one last passionate kiss before putting her from him.

"Good night." Mary watched Grant leave, and in that

moment, she realized she was falling in love with him. After the kisses they'd shared, the thought did not surprise her. It thrilled her.

When Grant had disappeared into the night, Mary closed up the house. She went to check on Jonathan once more before seeking the comfort of her own solitary bed. As she lay alone in the darkness, she wondered if Grant was thinking of her. She hoped that he was.

Grant headed straight to the rooming house, wondering all the while if he was going to get any sleep that night. The way he felt at that moment, he seriously doubted it. And the thought made him smile. If he had to lose a good night's sleep, he couldn't think of a better reason for it than thinking about Mary.

When Sammie and Jace reached her house, after making a detour to be sure all was well at the stable, she was in no hurry to be parted from him.

"Would you like to sit here on the porch for a while?" Sammie invited.

"Yes, I would," Jace accepted, wanting their time together to last as long as possible.

They sat down on the porch swing, enjoying the peace of the evening.

"How long have you lived here in Lawless?" Jace asked, wanting to know more about her and her family. He'd heard the Madison side of the feud, and now he wanted to know more about the Preston side of it.

"We've been in the area for years. I'm sure your uncle told you how we used to own the ranch next to his."

"Yes, he told me how bad things got when the drought hit."

"Things were bad, all right." The bitterness was evident in her tone, and her expression grew dark as she told him, "It's especially hard to cope with a drought when your neighbors won't give you access to the only water around. Did your uncle tell you how his ranch hands drove our cattle off and shot at our ranch hands when they were trying to get to the water?"

Jace just nodded.

"We weren't the only ones who lost everything. Most of the others just packed up and left, but my father was still alive then, and he didn't want to go. That's when we started the stable here in town. He died a while back, and Walt and I have kept it going. It's all we've got."

"You've done a good job with it."

"It's hard work, and—" she paused, wanting to lighten the mood, "it's just a real shame that I don't get to dress up much when I'm there."

"I think we've discussed that already."

They both smiled, remembering their earlier conversation.

"What about you?" Sammie challenged. "Why did you decide to become a sheriff?"

She was surprised when Jace paused and was quiet for a long moment.

Jace rarely talked about Sarah, but he knew Sammie deserved to know the truth.

He began slowly, "Some years back, I was ranching up near San Gabriel. I was engaged to be married, and my fiancée and her mother were killed when an outlaw gang robbed the stage they were on."

"Oh, Jace—I'm so sorry—" The unexpected news horrified Sammie, and she could tell it wasn't easy for him to talk about the pain of his loss. She gently reached out to touch his arm.

He didn't respond to her show of sympathy as he went on, "I joined up with the sheriff's posse to track her killers down. It wasn't easy, but we finally caught up with them." He looked at Sammie, the memory of that day still burning deep within him. "It felt good bringing Sarah's killers in. Real good. So I've stayed at it ever since."

Sammie gazed up at him in admiration. "You're a fine man, Jace Madison."

"I'm just a man who believes in seeing justice done."

"And you're good at it, Jace, very good. Lawless is blessed to have you."

"The job's not done yet," he cautioned her.

"It will be."

"You've got that much confidence in me, do you?"

"Yes, I do," she answered. "In fact, Mary told me she thought you and Grant might be our guardian angels, and I'm beginning to think she was right."

"I've been called a lot of things in my life, but never a guardian angel." He chuckled.

"Well, now you have," she added. "You rescued Mary from Ned, and you're going to save the town—"

"I hope you're right, but Grant and I won't be doing it alone. Your brother's helping us, and Hank, and, with luck, the rest of the town."

"You know you have my help," Sammie promised softly.

Jace looked down at her as she sat beside him, and his gaze went over her lovely features in a gentle caress. Sammie was such a spirited, beautiful woman; he felt an over-whelming need to be close to her. He turned and, without a word, slipped an arm around her.

Just that simple touch thrilled Sammie, and her breath caught in her throat as he gathered her near. She didn't resist, but went eagerly to him. He kissed her then, softly, tenderly at first, and when she responded without reserve, he deepened the exchange.

Sammie needed no further encouragement. She wrapped her arms around Jace, clinging to him. The power of his kiss sent ecstasy through her. When his lips left hers to trace a path of fire down the side of her neck, feelings she'd never experienced before flamed to life within her. Instinctively, she pressed herself more tightly against him, wanting to be closer to him, needing to be closer to him.

Jace obliged, holding her tightly as his lips sought hers again in a devouring exchange that set their senses reeling. They shared kiss after passionate kiss as the heat of their desire for one another grew.

Jace found Sammie's kisses intoxicating. He wouldn't have stopped kissing her, except the sound of a wagon and team passing through the streets of town intruded and brought him back to the reality of just where they were and what they were doing. Even so, he still didn't want to let her go, and he was reluctant to move completely away from her.

"Jace?" Sammie whispered his name as she drew back to look at him in confusion, wondering why he'd broken off the kiss. "Why did you stop?"

The innocence of her question touched him, and he couldn't help smiling gently down at her.

"Someone might come by."

"Oh." At his words, she realized just how caught up she had been in the thrill of the moment. She'd never known such excitement. No other man's kisses had ever affected her this way, leaving her mindless in her need to know more of him.

Jace leaned over to her and lifted one hand to caress her cheek as he kissed her one last time. It was a sweet, gentle kiss.

"Good night," he said in a seductive voice just barely above a whisper. He stood up to leave.

Sammie got up from the swing, too, and went to where he was standing at the porch steps.

Jace looked down at her. "You need to go on inside now, so I know you're home safe."

"In a minute," she said in a throaty, seductive voice as she pulled him down to her for one more kiss.

He wasn't about to resist her daring ploy, and he enjoyed every minute of it. When they finally moved apart, he went down the steps, deliberately distancing himself from the temptation of her.

"Go on inside now," he directed.

"Your word's the law, so I guess I'd better do it," she said, remembering her conversation with Walt the night before.

"That's right." Jace grinned.

"I'll try to remember that," Sammie said softly. She turned to go, then looked back at Jace one last time. "Good night."

"Good night." He waited there, keeping watch as she went in and closed the door behind her.

Jace didn't start to move away until he saw lamplight

coming through the window; only then did he start back down to the sheriff's office. He was alert for any kind of trouble on the way and was glad that there was none. When he reached the jail, he let himself in and got ready to call it a night.

As he bedded down, his thoughts were completely on Sammie—how she'd been dressed like a boy that first night they'd met and how beautiful and feminine she'd looked tonight. Her transformation had been amazing. He would never have guessed that she could have changed so completely, but she had. She'd been the prettiest woman at the social tonight, and there was no denying that he'd wanted her when they'd been alone there on her porch.

The memory of Sammie's kisses haunted Jace, and he realized he hadn't felt this way about a woman since Sarah. The thought brought him up short. He tried to be logical about what he was feeling for Sammie. He told himself he was in Lawless to bring down the King Gang, and he had to concentrate on doing his job. But even as he cautioned himself, Jace knew it was too late.

He was already involved with Sammie.

The passion she aroused in him in could not be denied.

She was an incredibly exciting woman.

Jace knew, though, that Sammie's safety and the safety of the whole town depended on him. He couldn't let himself relax in his vigil to bring peace to Lawless. He was going to do his job and do it right.

Jace courted sleep, but it was long in coming.

Chapter Seventeen

It was getting late, and Dennis wasn't happy with the way things had been going in the Tumbleweed that night. The boys had been drinking heavily and were rowdier than usual. He could tell some of them were just plain looking for a fight. He'd managed to keep things under control so far, but it had been his experience when dealing with drunks that violence could break out at the drop of a hat.

Dennis had been hoping Jace and Grant would come by after the social. Their presence might have helped calm the place down a little, but the church event had ended some hours before and neither lawman had shown up. Resigned, he kept his hidden shotgun close at hand while he kept serving up drinks.

"You're not smiling," Lilly said as she came to stand at the bar with him.

"There ain't a lot to smile about tonight," he grumbled.

"You noticed that, too, did you?" She grimaced. It had

already been a long night, and they still had a few hours to go before closing time.

"I keep expecting trouble," Dennis answered, keeping his voice low.

"I hope you're wrong."

"So do I." He turned away to wait on two of the men who'd come to the bar for refills.

At that moment the violence Dennis had been expecting broke out. Two men who'd been involved in a poker game at the back of the saloon charged to their feet. They knocked the table aside as they went at each other, fists flying.

"Get out of here, Lilly," Dennis ordered, not wanting her to be in harm's way if the fight escalated.

She wasted no time taking refuge in the kitchen.

Dennis was determined not to let the violence get out of control. He left the bar and went over to where the two men were battling it out. He was bigger and meaner than either one of the drunks, so he stalked right up to them and grabbed one by the back of his shirt just as he started to lunge at the other.

"Stan Collins! You know I don't like fighting in my saloon!" he shouted as he dragged Stan to the swinging doors and tossed him bodily outside. That done, he turned back to the other drunk, Zeke Miller, who was coming after him in a rage. In one deft move, Dennis snared him, too, and gave him a hard shove out the doors.

Hank had sought out Walt after his run-in with Jace earlier that evening, and the two of them had stayed together ever since, making the rounds and keeping an eye on things. They understood that they had to get used to working together, so they concentrated on doing their jobs and tried to put their personal feelings aside. It wasn't easy for either one of them, but they were both determined to prove to Jace and Grant that they were strong enough to do it.

They had just been coming up the street as they finished their last rounds for the night when they saw the two men being thrown out of the Tumbleweed. They watched the drunks land heavily in the street and then get up again and charge back inside when some of the other men standing in the bar's doorway yelled at them, taunting them.

Hank looked over at Walt. "For a while there, I thought we were going to get off easy tonight."

"I guess this isn't our lucky night, after all." Walt had been looking forward to stopping in at the Tumbleweed for a drink. He hadn't anticipated going in to break up a fight. "Let's check it out."

They quickened their pace. As they drew near they could hear the sounds of chaos erupting inside. They paused just outside the swinging doors to take a quick look into the saloon, and they could see the battle raging while Dennis was shouting at the crowd of drunks to stop.

Hank and Walt knew they had to break the fight up fast before it got completely out of control.

"We'd better get in there before somebody decides to go for a gun and Dennis pulls his shotgun," Walt said, leading the way.

Walt slammed the doors wide and stalked in just as a chair went flying through the air and crashed into the far wall.

Stan Collins was drunk, and when he got drunk he got mean.

Zeke Miller had been so drunk himself that he'd forgotten how ornery Stan could get. He was learning his lesson now, though, as they continued to attack each other with savage, vicious blows, and a bigger fight erupted around them. They were both so caught up in the riot going on that they didn't even notice the two lawmen joining in the fray.

Hank followed Walt as he stormed right into the mix, and the battle was on. They made their presence known quickly. With sober determination, they took on the drunken rowdies. They were going to bring peace to Lawless, even if they had to fight to do it.

And fight they did.

It was a brutal, chaotic brawl.

Hank and Walt even turned on each other once, but were quick to realize their mistake and go after the others.

Any of Dennis's customers who'd dared join in the fight were left bruised and battered on the saloon floor as the two deputies continued their mission.

Hank had finally cornered Zeke and was pummeling him heavily when he caught sight of Stan sneaking up behind Walt as the other deputy engaged in a serious fight with one of the rougher cowboys. Stan was carrying a chair and Hank realized Walt was in big trouble. He didn't hesitate to help Walt.

"Walt! Look out!" he shouted as he turned and quickly threw himself at Stan.

The chair went flying from Stan's grip as Hank tackled him to the floor and knocked him unconscious with one savage blow to the jaw.

Walt was completely shocked when he realized what had just happened. He hurried to finish off the man he was fighting before going over to where Hank was slowly getting to his feet.

The two deputies stood there, looking at each other in silence for a moment as the commotion in the saloon came to an abrupt end. Both men were bloodied and worse for the wear, but they'd won the fight and they'd won it by working together.

Walt wiped blood from the corner of his mouth as he looked Hank in the eye. It was hard for him to do it, but he said, "Thanks."

"You were a little busy," Hank quipped, looking around at the overturned tables and chairs and feeling much better now that the ruckus was over, "so I thought I'd give you a hand."

"I appreciate it," Walt said and he put his hand out to Hank.

The two deputies shook hands.

"Good job, boys," Dennis said, coming to join them. "How about a drink? On me."

"That sounds real good, Dennis," Hank told him.

Walt and Hank followed him to the bar.

"All you boys! Get this place picked up! *Now!*" Dennis ordered, glaring at the troublemakers who were slowly getting moving again. He went to pour the deputies their drinks.

"Bad night?" Hank asked as he came to stand before the bartender.

Dennis slanted him a sidelong grin. "There've been worse nights, believe me, but now that we've got you helping out, things are going to be getting better—a lot better. That was one smooth move you put on Stan. Maybe this time, after dealing with you, he'll learn to keep that temper of his under control a little better. Are you planning to lock him up for the night?"

Hank looked over to where the drunken Stan was just barely moving on the floor where he'd left him. "No. I think I'll just have a few words with him and set things straight before we go. We need to let the boys know that Lawless is a peaceful town now, and we want to keep it that way."

One of the men drinking at the far end of the bar who hadn't been involved in the fight gave them a derisive look. "You'll be changing your tune once Harley and his gang get back."

Walt and Hank both turned deadly glares on the man as Walt answered, "No, Harley's the one who's going to be changing his tune. Jace Madison is putting the law back in Lawless, and we're here to help him."

"I'll drink to that," Dennis proclaimed loudly, lifting his own glass of whiskey. "Come on, boys. Show the deputies some respect. These two are fine lawmen, and they're going to help keep things quiet around here."

Most of the men in the bar joined him in lifting their glasses to Walt and Hank.

It was some time later when Walt and Hank left the Tumbleweed for the sheriff's office. Hank's talk with Stan had gone well, and the deputies had a feeling it would be a while before Stan and Zeke got drunk again and started any more trouble. When they returned to the sheriff's office, they found Jace was already there, bedded down in the back room. They tried to be quiet.

Jace had been asleep, but when he heard Walt and Hank return, he roused himself and got dressed to come out and talk to them. He stopped in the doorway, surprised by the condition they were in. There was no doubt they'd been in some kind of a fight. He just hoped they'd won.

"What happened to you?" he asked sharply.

Hank and Walt exchanged glances and then just grinned at him.

"Oh, we ran into a little trouble down at the Tumbleweed, but it wasn't anything we couldn't handle."

"You sure about that?" Jace asked warily as he looked between them.

"We're sure," Walt told him.

"No shots were fired," Hank said.

"So I can rest easier now, knowing my deputies can take care of trouble in town without firing a shot?"

"That's right. Hank watches my back real good for me." Walt glanced over at Hank.

Jace noticed the change in his attitude. "What are you talking about?"

"One of the drunks came after me with a chair, and Hank got to him just in time."

Jace had to admit he was pleased by the news. He looked at his cousin with renewed respect. "Good job, Hank. If we're going to make this work, we've got to watch out for each other."

"We will," Walt assured him.

"I'm counting on it. You two go on now and get some rest, but be back here by noon tomorrow."

The two deputies left the office. They had started to head in their separate directions when Walt told Hank, "Thanks again. I owe you one."

"Let's just hope I never have to collect," Hank said, smiling slightly as they parted for the night.

Chapter Eighteen

Harley and his men had been riding hard all day, and they were more than glad to stop for the night. Tired and out of sorts, they were real sorry they'd run out of liquor. They were still days away from reaching Lawless, and there were no other towns around where they could find a saloon. As darkness claimed the land, they ate what lean fare they had and sat around the campfire.

"I've got a hankering for the girls at the Tumbleweed and the liquor, but you know what I want even more?" Pete said as he finished his sparse meal.

"What?" Harley asked from across the campfire.

"Those hot meals that Mary the cook serves up."

"I'm with you on that. She serves up some fine grub," Harley agreed, and so did the others. "If things keep going this smooth, it won't be too much longer 'til we're back," Harley went on. "We covered a lot of ground today."

"How soon do you want to ride out again, once we get

back? You got any ideas on what our next job is going to be?" Al asked Harley.

"I've been thinking about a few," he answered.

The rest of the gang was interested in hearing what Harley had on his mind.

"Like what?" Pete asked, joining the conversation. He'd worked with Harley for a long time and knew how smart he was. It was no secret the gang leader was always planning ahead.

"I don't know about you boys, but I'm tired of just robbing stages. We can make a much bigger haul if we go to the source," he began intriguingly.

"'The source'?" Ken asked. "You thinking about robbing banks?"

Harley looked over at Ken. "That's right. There's a lot more money to be made that way."

"Now I know why I like riding with you so much, Harley," Ed said, smiling greedily at the prospect.

Harley went on, "It'll take more planning, and it'll be more dangerous, but it'll be worth it in the long run."

"Yes, it will," Al agreed.

They were a greedy, amoral bunch of men, who trusted Harley completely. If Harley told them to do something, they did it. They never questioned his judgment, for he'd proven time and again that he could outsmart everybody.

They talked long into the night, anticipating the money they would steal, after they rested up and enjoyed themselves in Lawless for a time.

Pete was the lookout that night, and it was as they were bedding down that he noticed the faint glow of a campfire in the distance. He quickly alerted Harley and the others. Harley got up and went with him to take a look.

"What do you think?" Pete asked.

"I think we'd better put out our campfire," the gang leader ordered sternly.

"Do you think it might be a posse?"

"It's hard to say, but I'm not going to take any chances."

"What are we going to do?" It didn't matter to Pete that it was nighttime. He was ready to saddle up and go after whoever was camped out all those miles away.

"We're not going to do anything right now. They'd hear us coming this time of night. We'll go after them just before dawn."

"What are we going to do if it is a posse?"

Harley smiled coldly at him. "We'll kill them before they have a chance to draw on us."

"And if it's not a posse?"

Harley shrugged, still smiling. "If it's not the law, we still might get something worthwhile out of it. You never know."

The other men knew what Harley was thinking and found themselves looking forward to the raid. They bedded down, waiting for the long, dark night to pass.

Harley stayed awake for quite a while, keeping an eye on the other campfire. He didn't like surprises, and he wasn't about to let himself be caught off guard. If the time ever did come when the law tracked him down and tried to bring him in, he was going to fight to the end and take as many lawmen down with him as he could. He wasn't about to be arrested and put on trial, and then hanged for all to see. That wasn't his way. When his time to die came, he was going to choose the way he was going out. It wouldn't be up to any jury.

Harley never fell into a deep sleep. He was up before dawn and ready to ride. He roused his men, and within minutes they headed out in the direction where they'd seen the distant campfire.

Ned was in no hurry to move on that morning. He knew he still had a few days of travel before he would reach any town worth stopping in, so he took his time getting up as the eastern sky brightened.

He found out real fast that had been a mistake.

Ned was still lying there taking it easy when he heard his horse stirring restlessly. He kept his gun belt next to him when he bedded down in case of trouble, so he drew his sidearm and started to get up to see if there was some wild critter nearby that was scaring his horse. Getting to his feet, he managed to take only one step before he heard someone shout at him.

"Hold it right there!" The commanding, deadly voice cut through the silence of the early-morning hour.

Stunned, Ned froze.

"Good, good. Now, don't try anything. Just throw your gun down and raise both your hands up where I can see them!"

Again, Ned did as he was told. He wasn't the bravest of men, and judging from the sound of the voice, he figured he would have been dead before he could have reached cover. But even if he had managed to escape and make it to the rocks nearby, he still would have been unarmed and would have ended up dead anyway, so there was no point in offering any resistance.

"What do you want?" Ned called back.

No one answered.

GET UP TO 4 FREE BOOKS!

You can have the best romance delivered to your door for less than what you'd pay in a bookstore or online. Sign up for one of our book clubs today, and we'll send you **FREE* BOOKS** just for trying it out...**with no obligation to buy, ever!**

HISTORICAL ROMANCE BOOK CLUB

Travel from the Scottish Highlands to the American West, the decadent ballrooms of Regency England to Viking ships. Your shipments will include authors such as CONNIE MASON, CASSIE EDWARDS, LYNSAY SANDS, LEIGH GREENWOOD, and many, many more.

LOVE SPELL BOOK CLUB

Bring a little magic into your life with the romances of Love Spell—fun contemporaries, paranormals, time-travels, futuristics, and more. Your shipments will include authors such as KATIE MACALISTER, SUSAN GRANT, NINA BANGS, SANDRA HILL, and more.

As a book club member you also receive the following special benefits:

- **30% OFF all orders through our website & telecenter!**
  (Plus, you still get 1 book FREE for every 5 books you buy!)
- **Exclusive access to special discounts!**
- **Convenient home delivery and 10 days to return any books you don't want to keep.**

There is no minimum number of books to buy, and you may cancel membership at any time. See back to sign up!

*Please include $2.00 for shipping and handling.

YES! ☐

Sign me up for the **Historical Romance Book Club** and send my TWO FREE BOOKS! If I choose to stay in the club, I will pay only $8.50* each month, a savings of $5.48!

YES! ☐

Sign me up for the **Love Spell Book Club** and send my TWO FREE BOOKS! If I choose to stay in the club, I will pay only $8.50* each month, a savings of $5.48!

NAME: _____

ADDRESS: _____

_____

TELEPHONE: _____

E-MAIL: _____

☐ **I WANT TO PAY BY CREDIT CARD.**

☐ VISA   ☐ MasterCard   ☐ DISCOVER

ACCOUNT #: _____

EXPIRATION DATE: _____

SIGNATURE: _____

Send this card along with $2.00 shipping & handling for each club you wish to join, to:

Romance Book Clubs
1 Mechanic Street
Norwalk, CT 06850-3431

Or fax (must include credit card information!) to: 610.995.9274. You can also sign up online at www.dorchesterpub.com.

*Plus $2.00 for shipping. Offer open to residents of the U.S. and Canada only. Canadian residents please call 1.800.481.9191 for pricing information. If under 18, a parent or guardian must sign. Terms, prices and conditions subject to change. Subscription subject to acceptance. Dorchester Publishing reserves the right to reject any order or cancel any subscription.

JOIN NOW!

Silence reigned.

Ned's terror grew, and, coward that he was, he began to shake.

Harley looked over at Pete and Al and directed, "Go down there and find out who we're dealing with here."

The two outlaws did just that. Guns drawn, they left their hiding places among the rocks and made their way down to where the lone man was standing in obvious fear. Pete positioned himself in front of the man and kept his gun trained on him while Al quickly went through his saddlebags.

"Is he the law?" Harley shouted down to them.

"He ain't got no badge," Al yelled back.

"No, no, I ain't no lawman!" Ned cried out.

"What's in his saddlebags?" Harley called down.

"A little money."

"Good."

With their guns still aimed at the stranger, Harley and Ed stood up from where they'd been hiding and started down to the campsite. Ken stayed back to keep watch for any trouble that might come their way.

Never before had Ned had so many guns pointed at him at once. He believed he was looking death in the face as the other outlaws closed in around him. He began to tremble even more violently as he waited for what would happen next. Only when the man who seemed to be the leader came to stand in front of him did Ned know a moment of hope.

"You're Harley King!" Ned gasped, staring at the outlaw. He'd only seen Harley once before, and that had been on his first day in Lawless, before Harley and his gang had ridden out. Even so, there was no forgetting him. Ned didn't know if this was a lucky moment for him or if he was going to be dead before he could even use the information he had to try to save himself.

"That's right," Harley snarled, getting in Ned's face. "I am Harley King." He glanced over at his men. "How much money does our friend have, boys?"

Pete shouted out the amount, which was less than fifty dollars.

"Is that all you got?" Harley looked at him in disgust. "What do you think? Is your life worth more than that? You got any more cash on you?"

Ned was stuttering and stammering as he cowered before King. In a desperate bid to save his own life, he looked up at the outlaw and said, "No, I don't have any more! That's all the money I've got, but I got something else I know you'll want more than money."

"I don't like spineless weasels who try to play games with me." Harley's eyes narrowed and his threatening expression turned even more intimidating as he glared at Ned.

"I'm not playing any games!" Ned all but shrieked. "It's true! It's true! I do have something you need!"

"And just what is that?" Harley demanded.

"Information!" Ned squeaked out. "I got information you need!"

"You think you know something I don't?" Harley challenged sarcastically.

Ned knew this was his one and only chance to save himself, so he tried to be calm as he faced his tormentor.

"I know I do," he managed in a more steady tone as he looked the outlaw straight in the eye.

Harley glowered at him. "And just what is it you know that's so important?"

Gathering all the gumption he had, Ned told him, "I just came from Lawless. There's a new sheriff and deputy there. They've taken over, and they're waiting for you to come back!"

"Oh, really?" Harley was skeptical.

Ned went on to explain how he'd had a little run-in with the lawmen and had left town. He didn't give Harley the details. That humiliation didn't need to be known. "The sheriff's name is Jace Madison and the deputy is Grant Richards—"

Al was in his face in an instant, demanding, "Did you say Jace Madison is in Lawless?"

"That's right! Him and his deputy! They've taken over the place. They're the same lawmen who tamed Los Rios."

"I know who they are," Al said tersely. He looked at Harley and smiled coldly. "If he's telling the truth, this is going to be fun—real fun."

"Madison is the one who tracked down the gang you used to run with, isn't he?" Harley asked.

"That's right. Right after the stage robbery near San Gabriel, I split from them. They went their way and I went mine."

"And you're still alive to tell about it."

"That's right, but Buck and Vic aren't. For some reason, I got lucky. Nobody ever came after me, but I tell you, it's gonna feel real good to get revenge on Madison for what he did to Buck and Vic." Al gave an evil grin. He couldn't wait to confront Jace Madison. He was going to enjoy killing the lawman.

"You're going to have to be careful when you go back to Lawless," Ned put in, trying to sound like he was smart enough to advise them on how to handle the new men in town. "They're gonna be setting a trap for you."

Harley gave a harsh laugh. "They can try, but Lawless is our town. They're the ones who are going to be caught in a trap—the trap we're going to set for them."

"But these two know what they're doing. They're the ones who tamed Los Rios," Ned warned.

"They weren't dealing with us in Los Rios," Harley said as he looked closely at the weasely man, trying to read him. "Your tale is a good one, but why should I believe you?"

"Because I know I'm a dead man if you think I'm lying." He waited in silence to see what was to come.

"What do you think, Harley?" Ed spoke up.

"Do you trust him?" Pete asked.

"I think our 'friend'—" Harley eyed the stranger cowering before him. "What's your name?"

"Ned Ballantine."

"I think we can trust our friend Ned Ballantine."

"Why?" Pete wondered. He thought the stranger looked like a fool.

"Because Ned's going to ride right back into Lawless with us and show us just what's going on there."

Ned's eyes widened in shock. He'd been relieved that Harley was believing him, but he'd never expected this turn of events. "You want me to ride with you?"

Harley pinned him with a deadly glare. "That's right. You're going to be right there with us when we ride down Main Street."

"Why? I told you everything I know! Why don't you just take what money I have and let me go?"

"Because you're the only one who knows what this new sheriff and deputy look like. We're going to need your help when we get back there. Are you ready to saddle up and ride with us?"

Ned knew what he had to say. "Yes."

"Then pick up your things and get ready to head out. We've got a lot of miles to cover today."

"You're really gonna trust me?"

Harley fixed him with a look that sent fear through Ned. "That's right. I'm really going to trust you . . . until you give me a reason not to."

Ned said nothing more. He knew he was lucky to be alive. He scrambled to do as he was told.

As he got ready to ride out, Ned remembered the fantasy he'd had the other night about returning to Lawless as a member of the King Gang, and he realized his fantasy had just come true. That was exactly what was going to happen. He started smiling, even as he was still shaking in his boots. Jace, Grant and Mary were going to be real sorry they'd given him trouble.

Harley went over to talk with Al. "I know you want revenge on these two we're going after."

"You're right. I do. Vic and Buck were my friends."

"You'll get your revenge, but just don't go losing your head and making any mistakes. Sheriff Madison and Deputy Richards are going to find out real quick that they came to the wrong town and took on the wrong gang."

"Are you really sure you want this Ned to go with us?" Al asked, looking over at the stranger. Something about the fellow just didn't seem right to him.

"He'll serve his purpose when the time comes," Harley stated coldly.

His men had learned over the years not to question him, so Al shut up.

"How are we going to handle these new lawmen when we get back to town?" Pete wondered.

"If they really are the same two who cleaned up Los Rios, it's not going to be easy, but we'll do it. Let's ride," Harley ordered. They had many miles left to cover, and he had to start planning their strategy.

Al seldom got excited about things anymore, but he was eager to return to Lawless. As they mounted up he was smiling at the thought of getting even with Jace Madison for what he'd done.

Chapter Nineteen

More days passed, and it seemed a sense of normalcy almost settled over Lawless. The church was almost full on Sunday and people were freely moving about on the streets again. Most of the townsfolk realized this peace wouldn't last, but they were enjoying it while they could.

Jace and Grant worked with Hank and Walt each day, teaching them the basics of law enforcement. They were both pleased that the tension between the two men had eased. They were working well together, and that was exactly what was needed to form a successful team.

Their goal was to keep the town safe at all times, and so far they'd been successful. Not that Lawless had turned into the peaceful town Los Rios had been when they'd left it, where the biggest problem some days was a troublesome dog, but at least no one had been gunned down or robbed in the past few days.

* * *

For Mary, her daily routine became a welcome one. Every afternoon, Grant showed up for lunch at the Tumbleweed and ate his meal in the kitchen with her. They even occasionally managed to steal a quick kiss before he left her, and she would then spend the rest of the day smiling. She longed to spend more time with him, and she believed he felt the same way about her, but she knew that until the King Gang had been dealt with, he would remain focused on his job of keeping the town safe from the murderous outlaws. Understanding the situation as she did, she treasured what time they had together and prayed that the confrontation to come would be over soon and that everyone would be safe.

Sammie relived the night of the social over and over again in her fantasies—the excitement of dancing with Jace and then being alone with him at home on the porch swing. Just the wonderful memory of his kiss still had the power to thrill her. She desperately wanted to be alone with him again, but there had been no opportunity. She was tempted to seek him out, but with Walt now working as a deputy, she had no time. She was spending so many hours working at the stable that she was beginning to feel as if she should just move in and live there with the horses.

For his part, Jace was discovering that Sammie was a real test of his self-control. She was a constant temptation. He found himself thinking about her and watching for her around town, and he knew he couldn't afford any distraction right then. With the looming danger of the King Gang's return, he couldn't risk losing sight of the real reason he was in Lawless.

Now, sitting in the sheriff's office with Hank, Jace realized it was getting late and he needed to go out and take a look around town. They had established this routine over the past few days, and they were both growing accustomed to it. One of them would make the rounds while the other stayed behind at the office in case of an emergency.

Tonight, it was his turn.

"I'm going to go check on things," Jace said.

"I'll be right here if you need me," Hank assured him.

"Don't go falling asleep on me, now," Jace said, pleased that there had been no trouble so far that evening.

"You don't like things being nice and peaceful in Lawless?"

"I do like things being nice and peaceful, but I'll be jealous if you get a nap and I don't."

They were both chuckling as he walked out.

Jace made his way through the darkened streets of Lawless. The Tumbleweed was noisy. It was obvious that some of the men inside were rowdy, but it didn't seem as though anything out of the ordinary was going on, so Jace didn't bother to go in. He couldn't afford the luxury of relaxing and having a drink at the bar with Dennis, even though he would have enjoyed it. He had the rest of the town to patrol and protect.

Jace continued, finding the streets were quiet. He was satisfied that all was well that night until he came within view of the stable. He was surprised to see that the side door was open and light spilled out from inside.

Cautiously, Jace went to investigate. It wasn't normal for Sammie or Walt to be working this late, so he drew his gun, just in case. He wanted to be ready for trouble. Jace reached the doorway and cautiously looked inside, but he saw no sign of anyone moving about.

Stepping back into the shadows, he called out, "Sammie? Walt? Are you in here?"

"Jace?" Sammie was working with an injured horse in the back, and she hurried out of the stall at the sound of his call. Her heartbeat quickened when she saw him appear in the doorway.

"You're here," Jace said when he saw her coming his way. He holstered his gun and went inside, relieved that nothing was wrong.

"Yes, and it's good to see you," she said, smiling brightly at him. She'd been working since early that morning and knew she looked a mess, but she also knew there was nothing she could do about it. She was with Jace, and that was all that mattered!

"Are you all right? I was concerned when I saw the door was still open." His gaze went over her, enjoying the sight of her in her work clothes. She'd been gorgeous in her dress the other night, and he still saw her as that same beautiful woman, even dressed as she was now.

"I'm fine," she answered, wiping her hands on a clean cloth as she joined him. "Doc Malloy brought his horse over a little while ago. It had pulled up lame on him, and he thought I'd better take a look at it tonight. So it's just business as usual around here."

"I'm glad there's nothing else wrong."

"Now that you're here, everything is right," she said as she looked up at him. "Walt's been telling me how you've been working with him. Is he doing a good job for you?"

"He's doing fine, learning fast, and he and Hank are working well together."

"That's good news. Walt told me how Hank stepped up and helped him that night at the Tumbleweed. I knew it was going to be hard for the two of them to get along, so I'm glad things are better between them."

"So am I. I need to be able to count on my deputies to do the right thing, no matter what kind of situation they're in."

"Walt is a good man. He's an honorable man," she said.

"I know that. I wouldn't have hired him if I hadn't believed it." He noticed her whip hanging on a hook nearby and added, "I'm just thinking, though, that I may have made a real big mistake by not hiring you and Mary as deputies instead. Between your whip and her frying pan, we would have had quite a few secret weapons going for us."

"Has anyone ever hired any female deputies before?" she asked, truly curious and trying to imagine herself facing the dangers that Jace faced every day. It was an intimidating thought.

"Not that I've heard of, but I'm always ready to try something new if it will make things better."

"You're willing to take risks, are you?" Sammie's tone was daring as she gazed up at him. She wanted to go into his arms and kiss him, but she knew she couldn't. They were standing right there in the stable where anyone could walk in on them. He was treating her almost as if the other night hadn't happened, and his behavior left her emotions in turmoil.

Jace heard the change in her tone of voice and found himself staring down at her, remembering how good it had felt to hold her close and kiss her. He tried to concentrate on their conversation, but she was proving to be too much of a temptation. "I have to take risks. That's what I get paid for. It's a part of my job."

Sammie wanted to kiss him so badly, she decided it was worth the risk to be brazen. She didn't know when they'd ever be alone together again and she wanted to take full advantage of the moment. "What about right now, Jace? Do you want to risk kissing me while we're here alone in the stable?"

Jace was intrigued by her daring offer.

"You're right," he admitted slowly. "It would be risky."

"And why is that?" she challenged.

"Because," he began as he closed the distance between them, unwilling to deny himself this chance to hold her, "I don't know if I'll be able to stop kissing you once I start."

"Oh—" Her heartbeat quickened and her breath caught in her throat at his seductive words.

Jace said no more. He reached out and drew her to him. Sammie went willingly, and when he bent to kiss her, she met him in that exchange. His mouth moved hungrily over hers, and she responded passionately. She was thrilled at being back in his embrace. His kiss was as heavenly as she remembered.

"I'm glad I had to work late tonight," she said huskily when they broke off the kiss and were just standing there wrapped in each other's arms.

"So am I," Jace said, kissing her again. "I'm going to make stopping by here a regular part of my nightly rounds."

"I'd like that," Sammie told him in a soft whisper as she lifted her lips to his. "I can always find some reason to be working late."

Jace needed no more of an invitation. Any and all risks were forgotten. He kissed her deeply once more. When the kiss finally ended, Jace didn't say a word. He just walked away from her, heading for the door.

"Jace?" Sammie was confused and devastated. She feared he was leaving her, but her fears were soon laid to rest.

Jace closed the door and returned to sweep her up into his arms.

"There are some risks I'm willing to take, but right now, I don't want to risk being interrupted," he said, kissing her.

Sammie was breathless as he carried her to a secluded, shadowed corner of the stable and laid her down on a bed of fresh hay. Jace grabbed a saddle blanket from nearby and spread it out next to her. She quickly shifted to lie on it and then lifted her arms to him in silent invitation.

Jace went to her and stretched out beside her, drawing her full length against him. He knew she might be dressed like a man, but there was nothing manly about the softness of the ample curves pressed so intimately against him. Sammie was all woman, and he wanted her.

Moving over her, he kissed her deeply, wanting to tell her without words what she meant to him.

Sensations Sammie had never before experienced began to pulse deep within her as Jace held her.

Instinctively she moved against him.

She wanted to get even closer to him.

She never wanted to be apart from him again.

She was home, and with the overwhelming feeling of rightness came the realization that she had fallen in love with Jace.

The revelation startled her.

It hadn't taken long. They'd only known each other for a short period of time, but from the first moment she'd seen him riding into town, she'd sensed that he was special, and now she knew it for a fact. Jace was everything she'd ever wanted in a man, and his every kiss just left her wanting him more.

Jace had tried to ignore the feelings Sammie stirred within him. He had tried to concentrate only on the task of bringing peace to Lawless, and he had—until now. Holding her in his arms and kissing her again had pushed everything else from his mind. In this moment, there was only the two of them, alone there in the stable, sharing kiss after devouring kiss as their desire grew by leaps and bounds.

The logical part of Jace was warning him that he was supposed to be out making his rounds, not kissing Sammie, but, right then, logic had no part in what was driving him. Right then, being with Sammie was all that mattered.

Sammie had never been so intimate with a man before. Just being this close to Jace thrilled her. When he began to caress her, excitement trembled through her. She returned his caresses, eagerly sculpting his hard-muscled back and shoulders.

Jace was caught up in his need for Sammie.

He wanted her.

He wanted to strip away their clothing and bury himself deep within her. Jace knew by her heated, passionate response to his touch that if he tried to make her his own, she would not resist him.

And it was that very thought—knowing her pure innocence was his for the taking—that jarred him back to the reality of just where he was and what he was doing.

Jace had always considered himself a strong-willed man, but at that moment he had his doubts. He knew he should put some distance between him and Sammie. He knew he should do what was right, but the fiery heat of the desire she aroused in him was almost too strong for him to overcome. His willpower was being tested to the extreme, and he wondered if he could hold out.

With all the self-control he could muster, he managed to rein in his passion. It wasn't easy, but he did it, ending their kiss and stopping his caresses. He shifted away from the temptation of her soft, enticing curves and sat up, deliberately not looking at her.

"Jace? What is it? Is something wrong?" Sammie was a bit disoriented by his sudden withdrawal from her. She hadn't wanted him to stop kissing and caressing her. The thrill of his touch had created an excitement within her she'd never experienced before. She'd been in heaven there in his arms.

"Yeah. Something's wrong," Jace managed to answer in a gruff, frustrated voice.

Sammie was shocked and confused by the harshness of his response. She immediately feared she'd done something wrong. A sense of abandonment filled her, and she sat up, feeling embarrassed and completely unsure of herself.

"What did I do?"

Jace cast a sidelong glance her way, all the while struggling to keep from giving in to the need to reach out and take her back in his arms. He could see she was confused by his actions, and he wanted to ease her torment.

"You didn't do anything wrong," he hastened to reassure her. "The problem isn't with you."

"But—"

"The problem is with me." He looked over at her.

"I don't understand."

"You're an innocent," Jace said, "and I want to make sure you stay that way."

Unable to sit there beside her any longer, he stood up. His body was on fire with his desire for her, and he knew he needed to physically distance himself from her before his resolve weakened and he made love to her.

"I have to go now."

Sammie didn't say anything as he made his way to the door to let himself out. When he started to leave, she called to him in a soft, inviting voice.

"Jace—"

He stopped to look back at her questioningly.

"Want to take one more risk?" Sammie deliberately said this in a daring tone. Though she was feeling a bit insecure, she wasn't about to let him just walk away from her like this. Getting up, she crossed the stable to stand before him. "I want you to kiss me good night."

She didn't have to ask twice.

Jace reached out and took Sammie in his arms. He wanted to hold her close. He wanted to lie down with her on the blanket again, but he didn't. With utmost care, he gave her a soft, cherishing kiss that left her even more breathless, and then he released her and moved away.

"You are a real temptation, you know," he said in a husky voice.

"And you are a real strong man," she returned, smiling up at him.

"Good night," Jace said gently, his dark-eyed gaze warm upon her.

"Good night."

Sammie stepped back to watch him as he headed outside. At that moment she heard the faint, distant ringing of the fire bell.

"Jace! Listen!"

He turned back to look at her, confused by her sudden frantic reaction. "Listen to what?"

"That bell—it means there's a fire somewhere in town!" She rushed outside to try to figure out where the fire was.

Jace was already looking up at the night sky, and he spotted the eerie glow in the distance.

"There!" He pointed out the glow to her.

"Oh, no!"

"What is it?"

"That's the direction of Mary's house!"

Chapter Twenty

Sammie ran back into the stable and grabbed as many buckets as she could carry, then put out the lamp and hurried back outside to where Jace was waiting.

"Let's go! And say a prayer that it's not Mary's house!"

Jace took several of the buckets from Sammie as they raced off in the direction of the fire.

Other people in town had also heard the fire bell, and were running from their homes carrying buckets to help out, too.

Sammie's heart was all but broken when they turned the corner and she actually saw which building was burning.

"It is Mary's house!" she cried in agony. "But where is Mary? Where's Jonathan?"

They ran even faster to join up with those who were already throwing buckets of water on the raging blaze.

"Where are Mary Smith and Jonathan?" Sammie shouted.

"I don't know!" the men answered.

"She may be trapped inside, Jace!" Sammie turned to Jace, horrified.

"Stay here!" he ordered.

Sammie watched in disbelief as Jace threw down his buckets and ran toward the burning building, trying to find a way inside to search for Mary.

Jace couldn't get near the front of the house, so he circled around back. Staying low to avoid the heat and smoke, he moved in closer to the back porch. He tried to look in a window, but the smoke was too heavy to see anything. Just as he was about to try to enter the building, he heard someone yelling his name.

"Jace! Don't go in there! We're safe!"

He backed up and looked over to see Mary running toward him, carrying a screaming Jonathan. Sammie was by her side. He heaved a sigh of relief as he backed away from the inferno.

"Thank heaven I found her, and I got to you in time!" Sammie said, looking up at him with pure adoration. The thought that this man would run into a burning building to save a woman and her child made her love him all the more.

Jace looked down at Mary, who was in shock over the turn of events. "Are you and Jonathan all right? Do we need to get you to a doctor? Were you burned or injured?"

Mary looked up at him with tears streaming down her face. "No, thank God. I managed to get us out in time."

Jace went to Mary and put an arm around her to support her. He drew her even farther away from the blazing building, wanting her out of harm's way.

Sammie remained right beside her. She tried to take Jonathan from Mary to hold him, but he was clinging so tightly to his mother, and screaming and crying so loudly in terror, that she finally gave up.

When they were safely away from the heat and smoke, Jace ordered, "Stay right here so I know where the three of you are."

"But all our things—" Mary was frowning, trying to understand what was happening.

"Don't even try to go near that house." His tone was stern and brooked no argument. He looked at Sammie. "Make sure she stays right here."

"I will," Sammie promised.

"I'll be back," he told them, leaving the two women so he could join up with the men battling the blaze.

Mary was standing there as if in a trance, watching her home burn to the ground. Fortunately, Jonathan had quieted some. Sammie gently patted the little boy's back, wondering what she could do to help the little boy and his mother.

Across town, Jim Peters came running into the sheriff's office. "Where's Sheriff Madison?"

"He's not here. What can I do for you?" Grant asked.

"There's a fire across town! We need all the help we can get to keep it from spreading!"

Grant was on his feet following Jim out the door. "Let's go!"

As soon as they were outside, Grant realized where the fire was. He knew a moment of horror at the thought that it was close to Mary's home.

"Jim, does anybody know what's burning?" Grant asked as they raced across town.

"I don't know for sure. It looks like it's close to Mary Smith's house, though."

"That's what I'm afraid of," Grant said grimly, fearing for Mary's and Jonathan's safety and also worrying that Ned Ballantine might have had something to do with the blaze. "Whoever's place it is, let's just hope they got out safely."

Neither man said any more as they raced to the scene. When they reached the site and saw that it was Mary's place, Grant was furious. He left Jim and ran to where he saw her standing with Sammie.

"Mary, you weren't hurt?" he asked, rushing up to her.

"Oh, Grant." Mary went straight into the heavenly shelter of his arms, clinging to his strength. "Thank God you're here."

He held her close, wanting to shield her from the horrors that surrounded her. "Thank God you got out of there in time. If something had happened to you or Jonathan . . ."

Grant looked down at her, cherishing the fact that she was not hurt. He knew he should be helping the others fight the fire, but first he needed to reassure himself that she truly was safe and protected.

"How did the fire start?" he finally asked. If she told him anything suspicious had happened, he was ready to immediately start searching for Ned.

Mary looked up at him, ashamed. "It was an accident. I should have realized it could happen, but I never dreamed—" She looked down at Jonathan nestled against her. "I was cooking in the kitchen, and I let him have the run of the house. I heard a crash in the sitting room and knew he'd broken something. I was on my way there to check on him when I heard him scream, and I knew something was wrong. It all happened so fast." Mary shuddered visibly as she mentally relived that terrifying moment. "By the time I reached the front of the house, I found the lamp shattered and the sitting room in flames, but Jonathan was all right. I tried to put out the fire using the quilt I keep there on the sofa, but it was no use. The fire was out of control and the smoke was so heavy that I just grabbed up Jonathan and ran out of there as fast as I could. Luckily, one of the neighbors saw the flames and everybody started showing up to help."

Grant was relieved that neither she nor her son had been injured, and he was relieved to know that the fire had truly been an accident. He'd known Ned was a lowlife, but he hadn't thought he would stoop so low as to deliberately trap Mary and her child in a burning house to claim his revenge against her.

As he kept his arms protectively around her, he watched the house burning. The efforts of the townsfolk were keeping the fire from spreading to other houses, but there was no way to save any of Mary's belongings. It angered Grant that in her young life she'd already suffered so much. First, she'd lost her husband and had to raise her son alone, and now she and Jonathan were going to be homeless. Her circumstances left him wondering why some people were lucky and others always seemed to fall on the hard times. He didn't know the reason, but he knew he would do whatever he could to try to make things right for her.

"Sammie," Grant called. "Stay with Mary while I go see if I can help."

Sammie stayed supportively by her friend's side while Grant joined the others who were fighting the fire.

It was nearly an hour later when they gave up, realizing there was nothing more they could do. All that was left of Mary's home was a pile of smoldering ruins, and the stench was nauseating.

It was past midnight when Jace and Grant stood together with Hank and Walt, watching as the other volunteers left to return to their own homes.

"I'm proud of them," Jace said. "They put up a good fight."

"Let's hope they can do the same thing when Harley King comes back," Grant remarked.

"That'd be real good," Hank and Walt agreed.

"I'm just glad it wasn't Ned who started the fire, but I still don't know what Mary's going to do now that she's lost everything," Grant said, worried about her. He knew she was a strong woman. She'd proven it by what she'd accomplished since her husband's death, but it was one thing to be a young widowed mother who had a home and could support herself and her son by cooking at the Tumbleweed. It was another to face the future completely devastated, without a home or any possessions to your name.

Jace glanced over at Grant and saw his dark expression. In all the years they'd worked together, he'd never known Grant to care so deeply about anyone before. He knew Grant had lunch with Mary every day at the saloon, and he'd noticed how much attention he'd paid to her at the social the other night. "Why don't we go see what we can do to help them."

"All right."

"I'll go to the office and stay there until you get back," Hank offered.

"Thanks," Jace told him. "I shouldn't be too long."

They started over to where Mary was standing with Sammie and a few of her other friends from town.

"Grant and Hank are staying at the boardinghouse, but I've got another room you can use," Celia Miller was telling Mary. "You can move right on in tonight. That way, Jonathan will feel at home when he wakes up in the morning, and he won't be too scared. I know it won't be the same as waking up in his own bed, but it'll be as close as we can get for right now."

"Thank you, Celia," Mary replied, her voice emotionless. She was numb through and through. The shock of losing everything had left her frozen inside.

"Thank you, Celia," Sammie echoed her friend. She didn't have an extra bedroom in the small house that she and Walt shared, but she'd been ready to offer Mary her own bedroom. Sammie realized Celia was right about Jonathan; since he spent most of his days at her home while Mary worked, he would feel safe there.

"Why don't we start on over?" Sammie suggested, wanting to get Mary away from the terrible sight of the blackened ruins of what had once been her home. It looked bad now in the darkness, and she could well imagine what they were going to face in the morning light.

They had no more than turned away when Jace, Grant and Walt reached them.

"Where are you heading?" Walt asked. He expected to hear that Mary would be staying at their home and he was surprised when Sammie told them of Celia's suggestion.

"We'll be in touch in the morning, then, to see what more we can do to help you," Jace told Mary.

She merely nodded. As she started to turn away, she looked up to find Grant watching her, his dark-eyed gaze intent. She'd seen him working hard beside the other men, fighting the fire, trying to save her home for her, and knew he meant the world to her. She said his name in a shuddering breath as she lifted her tear-filled gaze to his, "Grant—"

"I'll get back over to the office later," Grant told Jace, going to Mary's side and putting a supportive arm around her shoulders.

Jace nodded. "Show up whenever you can."

They shared a look of understanding and parted ways.

Walt looked at Jace. "Do you need me any more tonight?"

"I think we'll be all right. You can call it a night. I'll see you tomorrow."

Jace looked back over to where Sammie was accompanying Mary to the boardinghouse. He'd known the kisses they'd shared in the stable earlier that night had been fiery, but he'd never dreamed the night would end up with this kind of a blaze. He definitely liked the heat of Sammie's kisses better. He shook his head at the thought and started back to the office.

Jace knew it was sad that Mary had lost her home, but there was some good news with the tragedy—no one had died or suffered any injuries. Houses could always be rebuilt. When loved ones were lost, they were lost forever.

He'd learned that lesson the hard way.

Jace pushed the thought away as he went back to work.

* * *

Sammie stayed at the boardinghouse with Mary, helping her get settled in with Jonathan. They were all surprised when Doc Malloy, after hearing about the tragedy, stopped by to check on them.

"How are you doing?" he asked Mary as he spoke with her privately in the parlor.

"I don't know," she answered him honestly. "I feel . . ."

"Lost?" he offered.

She nodded. "What am I going to do?"

"At times like these, you just have to live life one day at a time."

"Just like when my husband died."

"That's right. It's the only way to cope with these tragic, life-changing events," he said sympathetically. "I brought some laudanum for you." He handed her the small bottle of opium tincture. "If you find you can't sleep at night and need something to help calm you, a few drops of this in a glass of water or with food will help you fall asleep."

"Thank you." She was touched by his thoughtfulness.

"If you need anything else, come see me in the morning."

"I will."

He let himself out and was at the front door when he saw Sammie coming down the hall from the kitchen.

"I gave Mary some laudanum to help her sleep. If you think she needs anything else, just send word over."

"Thanks, Doc."

"By the way"—Doc Malloy was smiling as he asked—"with all the excitement, did you get a chance to take a look at Shadow?"

Sammie couldn't believe all that had happened since

he'd brought the horse by the stable earlier. "I started to, but got interrupted."

"I understand."

She knew he thought she was talking about the fire, and she let him go right on thinking that. She wasn't about to mention the fact that Jace's unexpected and very exciting visit to the stable had been the cause of the interruption.

"I'll take care of Shadow first thing in the morning, and I'll let you know how he is."

"I appreciate it, Sammie. I'll see you tomorrow."

She saw the doctor out and closed the front door behind him before going to check on Mary, who hadn't come out of the parlor yet.

"Want to come out to the kitchen with us?" Sammie invited when she found her friend standing with her back to the room, staring out the window into the dark, dark night. She went to Mary and put a gentle hand on her shoulder. "Come on. I think you could use a big piece of the cake Celia baked earlier this afternoon."

Mary didn't say anything. She just nodded and went along with Sammie to the kitchen.

Fear was eating at her. She wanted to go get Jonathan and hold him again. She'd come so close to losing him tonight. If anything had happened to him—

Mary shuddered at the thought and then made up her mind that she wanted to carry her son in her arms with her for the rest of her life. She smiled at the thought. Active, independent little boy that he was, Jonathan would not tolerate that treatment for long.

"You smiled for a minute," Sammie said, stopping in the hallway.

"I was thinking of Jonathan. I don't want to let him

out of my sight ever again. What if I hadn't been able to get to him in the fire?" The panicky thought returned.

"But you did," Sammie hastened to reassure her friend, wanting to calm her fears.

"I know, and I smiled because I was trying to imagine keeping him on my lap for the rest of his life. I want to just hold on to him forever and keep him safe."

Sammie couldn't help it. She chuckled at the image of Jonathan sitting on his mother's lap when he reached his teenage years.

"That might work until he's about four or five, but I think you'd have a problem when he gets to be older— and especially when he gets to marrying age." She was happy when Mary actually smiled again.

"Thanks, Sammie. I love you."

"I love you, too, Mary, and I am so glad that you and Jonathan are safe."

Sammie hugged her.

"Now, come on. Let's get some of Celia's cake. Jonathan's enjoying it."

They went to the kitchen to join the others.

Chapter Twenty-one

Al Denton was sitting by the campfire, smiling and feeling satisfied with himself. "If we can pull this off—"

"We're going to pull this off," Harley stated emphatically.

"You're right. We are. Things are going to work out just fine."

"But how can you be so sure those two lawmen will believe any of this?" Pete asked Al.

"Judging by the way Jace Madison went after Vic Lawrence and Buck Carson after that stage robbery in San Gabriel, he's never going to forget why he became a lawman. I'm just damned lucky that I split up with Vic and Buck when I did, and I'm damned lucky they never talked. If they'd told Madison about me, he would have come after me once he finished with them, but he didn't. That's what makes this so good. He doesn't know anything about me, but I know all about him. I know how to get to him—and this is the way."

"You think so?" Pete still had his doubts.

"I know so. You lure him out with that stagecoach, and you'll see."

"I want to believe you're right, Al," Harley told him, "but Jace Madison didn't earn the reputation he's got by being stupid. Don't you think he'll suspect something if we use a stage robbery to set him up?"

"Not if we play it the way I'm thinking."

"Let's hear it."

Harley and the others listened as Al told them his plan to draw the new sheriff into a deadly trap.

"Ned told us there's just him and his deputy. Once we get them out here, it'll be a simple matter to ambush them, and then you've got your town back, Harley," Al finished.

"I do like the way you think, Al."

"Thanks. Now let's do it. Jace Madison is going to be sorry he ever went after Vic and Buck. He's going to pay for seeing my friends hang, and I'm going to be the one who sees that he does pay."

Ned sat beside the campfire with the outlaws, listening as they made their plans. They were intimidating men, and he was glad he was on their side and not against them. Cold-blooded killers that they were, they were the kind of men who shot first and asked questions later. When it came to taking down Sheriff Madison and Deputy Richards, he was looking forward to being a part of it. If the lawmen stayed alive long enough and he got the chance, Ned was going to make them pay for humiliating him. He smiled at the thought. He kept smiling as he imagined what he would soon be able to do to Mary, too. Paying her back for hitting him with that frying pan was going to be real enjoyable.

The gang bedded down for the night, looking forward to reclaiming their town. In just a few more days, they would be back in Lawless, relaxing and enjoying the liquor, the food and the women at the Tumbleweed.

"What do you think?" Jace asked Grant two days later as they sat together in the sheriff's office early in the afternoon. Walt and Hank weren't due in for a little while, so they had some time to themselves.

"I think these quiet days have been nice—real nice," Grant said.

"I agree with you there. It's just a shame they can't last."

"I haven't heard any new talk around town, have you?"

"Not a word, and I think that's what's bothering me. Harley believes he can outsmart everybody, so we can't relax our vigil for even a minute. I wouldn't put anything past him."

"You know, we could have stayed in Los Rios," Grant pointed out, joking.

"We could have," Jace agreed, "but then we wouldn't have met Mary and Sammie."

Grant didn't need to ponder the benefits of those meetings for long.

"Good point. The women of Lawless are definitely more intriguing than the girls back in Los Rios," Grant said. "Just look at your first run-in with Sammie at the stable."

"You know, I've been trying to forget about that."

"I don't know why," Grant joked. "You have to admit, she is handy with that whip of hers."

"That she is, and Mary is good with her frying pan, too. You just got lucky. She didn't have to use it on you."

"I'm glad I'm a gentleman. I think the frying pan would have hurt a lot worse than Sammie's whip."

They both laughed.

"Those two do know how to protect themselves. That's for sure," Jace said, impressed.

"And I'm glad. Can you imagine what would happen if we turned them loose on Harley?"

"He'd deserve everything they gave him and then some."

The door to the office opened just then and Hank came in.

"Lou Johnson, down at the stage office, stopped me when I was passing by and told me that he needs to see you right away," Hank told Jace.

"Did he say what it's about?"

"The stage was due in early this morning, and there's been no sign of it."

Jace frowned at the news. "I don't like the sound of that. Was it carrying anything of value? A payroll or any gold shipments?"

"Lou didn't say."

Jace stood up, a sense of unease gripping him. He didn't like missing stagecoaches. "I'd better go talk to him."

"I'll come with you," Grant said, getting up, too. "Thanks, Hank."

They left the sheriff's office and headed across town to speak with Lou, the elderly stage office manager. They found him awaiting them anxiously.

"Sheriff Madison, Deputy Richards, I appreciate your coming over so fast."

"Hank told us you think there might be some trouble with this morning's stage," Jace began.

"That's right. I'm getting real worried." Lou was frowning as he explained, "The stage should have been here no later than eight this morning, but there hasn't been any sign of it."

"How often does it run this late?" Grant asked.

"Good ole Murray is the regular driver on this run, and that's why I'm worried. This ain't like Murray. This ain't like him at all. He's always right on time."

"Is the stage carrying anything worth stealing? Any gold or payrolls?" Jace asked.

"No, nothing like that," Lou answered, and then seeing what the lawman was thinking, he added, "If you're thinking the King Gang might be behind this, I doubt it. In all the time Harley's been coming to town, he and his men have never bothered any of the stages going through."

"Were there many passengers due in this trip?"

"I'm not sure how many. We never know. It changes all the time."

"All right, we'll go check it out for you," Jace said, prepared for anything now. He couldn't believe Lou thought his stage line was safe from the likes of Harley and his men.

"I appreciate it, Sheriff."

Jace was on edge as they left to return to the sheriff's office.

He remembered the last time he'd gotten word about a stagecoach running late.

He remembered, too, the reality of what had come later when they'd found the wreckage of that stage.

Learning that Sarah had been killed in the robbery had devastated him and changed his whole life.

"What do you think?" Grant asked.

"I'm hoping the stage just broke down somewhere, but . . ."

"But what?"

"If it did break down, why didn't the driver just unhitch one of the horses and ride into town for help?" The fact that he hadn't left Jace expecting real trouble.

"I guess we're going to find out. Do you want both Hank and Walt to come with us?"

"There is no 'us.'" Jace glanced over at Grant. "I want you to stay here. Hank can ride with me."

"Are you sure? We can leave Hank and Walt here, and I can go."

"No. If anything should happen here in town while we were gone, neither of them has the experience to handle it."

Grant backed off, knowing Jace was right, but not liking the situation just the same. He didn't like it at all.

Hank was still at the office when they returned.

"The stage is running real late, so we're going to take a ride out and see if we can find it," Jace told Hank. "I want you to ride with me."

"All right. I'll meet you down at the stage office." Hank left to saddle his horse.

"How long do you think you'll be gone?" Grant asked Jace.

"I hope the stage isn't too far out of town. With any

luck, we'll make it back before dark." He got his rifle, saddlebags and extra ammunition.

"That would be good."

"Yes. It would."

"Be careful."

"We will be."

They shared a knowing look as Jace walked out.

Jace was hoping to see Sammie at the stable when he went to get his horse, and he wasn't disappointed. He stopped just inside the main doors to watch her as she walked toward him. His gaze raked over her, and he couldn't help smiling. He made no attempt to disguise the fact that he was watching her, and he wondered again how he'd ever thought she was a boy.

Sammie was smiling, too, as she went to speak with Jace. Just the sight of him standing there looking so handsome quickened her heartbeat. She'd been thinking about him that morning and regretting that they hadn't had any time alone together since the night of the fire. She'd been spending all of her free time with Mary, helping her try to put her life back together.

"This is a nice surprise," she said as she stopped before him.

"Yes, it is," he said, realizing then just how much he'd been missing her.

"To what do I owe this visit?"

"Hank and I are going to be riding out soon."

It was then she noticed he was carrying his rifle and other gear, and she grew uneasy. "Where are you going? What's wrong?"

"We're not sure anything is wrong yet," he began. "Lou

let us know that the morning stage is running real late, so we're going to try to find it."

"Harley and his men could be the ones behind this, couldn't they?"

"That thought crossed my mind."

"Well, watch out and hurry back." She took a step closer to him, knowing that they were alone in the stable for at least a moment. "I'll miss you."

"Don't worry. I'll be back." He responded to her unspoken invitation and leaned down to give her a quick kiss. It was broad daylight and he didn't want to do anything that could damage her reputation.

"You'd better be. I'll be waiting right here for you."

"I'll keep that in mind."

Jace went on to saddle his horse and mount up.

"Be careful, Jace," Sammie called out to him.

He nodded to her, letting his gaze linger on her for one last moment before starting down to the stage office to meet up with Hank.

Sammie watched him ride off, eagerly anticipating his return. Somehow, she was going to find a way to get him in the back of the stable again. Smiling at the thought, she picked up her pitchfork and returned to work.

A short time later Jace and Hank were riding out of Lawless.

"It'd be real nice if they didn't break down too far out," Hank said, not at all eager to spend long hours in the saddle looking for the missing stagecoach.

"My hope is that we'll run into the stage on its way into town," Jace replied.

"That would be good," his cousin agreed, "but I doubt we'll get that lucky."

And they didn't.

Mile after endless mile passed with no sign of the long-overdue stagecoach.

"It gets rougher from here on," Hank warned Jace as the landscape turned rockier. "And there's a canyon up ahead. My guess is, if there was going to be some kind of an accident, it probably would have happened there."

Jace considered the possible dangers of riding into a canyon. "How many ways are there through here?"

"There's only the main road," Hank offered.

"So there's no real way for us to split up?" Jace asked thoughtfully.

"No. We'll have to ride in together."

Jace realized he could be overreacting, but he wanted to be prepared for every possibility. If the King Gang was trying to set him up for an ambush, the canyon would be the place to do it.

"All right, we've got no time to waste. Let's do this, but if you see anything unusual, let me know. This could be something Harley's set up for us."

Hank tensed as he considered what they'd face if the outlaws tried to ambush them. "I'll keep an eye out."

They continued on, keeping a close watch on their surroundings as they searched for the missing stagecoach.

At the far end of the canyon, Harley and his men were ready and waiting. It had been a simple thing to go after the stagecoach. There had been no one riding shotgun and only one passenger, so they'd had little trouble. Now the stage was their bait as they waited for the sheriff and his deputy to show up.

Harley was counting on the two lawmen letting their

guard down when they made it almost completely through the canyon without any trouble. When they finally spotted the broken-down stagecoach, they would be unprepared for an ambush.

Now it was just a matter of biding their time. Ned knew what the new sheriff and his deputy looked like, so Harley was counting on him to identify them when they showed up.

Ned was scared as he crouched, hidden among the rocks with the gang. He'd been in a few gunfights over the years, but he'd never shot anyone down in cold blood before. The way Harley and his men had killed the stagecoach driver and the passenger had scared him bad. A part of him wanted to turn tail and run, but he knew if he tried it, he would be shot dead by Harley or one of the other outlaws. So he was staying put, gun in hand, waiting to see what was going to happen once Sheriff Madison and Deputy Richards showed up.

Al was particularly proud of himself as he watched for some sign that the sheriff was coming. He was certain the lawman would show any time now, and, when he did ride up, Al was going to wreak his vengeance upon him, for what he'd done to Buck and Vic. It was going to feel good to pay him back, and he hoped he got the chance to let Sheriff Madison know just who he was before it was all over.

Al smiled thinly as he waited.

Chapter Twenty-two

It was late in the afternoon when Harley spotted two riders in the distance and alerted Ned.

"Does that look like Madison and his deputy coming?" Harley asked Ned.

Ned scrambled to get a look and recognized Jace Madison immediately. "Yeah, that's the bastard who locked me up."

"Good, good." Harley was smiling. His plan had worked out perfectly. Nobody was smarter than he was—nobody. "All right, get ready." He signaled the men who were already in position some distance away.

They cocked their rifles in preparation for what was to come.

Al was close enough to hear Ned positively identify Jace Madison. He settled down in his hiding place and lifted his rifle to take aim at the lawman. As soon as the two riders were within range, he was going to see that Buck and Vic were finally avenged.

* * *

Jace and Hank said little as they covered the rugged miles with no sign of the missing stage. They focused solely on their search, not allowing themselves to be distracted.

"There, up ahead," Jace alerted Hank when he first caught sight of the stagecoach.

It was still a ways off, but even so, they could tell one of the front wheels had been badly damaged.

"No wonder Murray didn't make it to town," Hank remarked.

"Let's just hope nobody got hurt." Jace was grim. The wreck that had killed Sarah and her mother and another passenger had been much worse than this, but, even so, he knew whatever impact had caused such damage to the wheel had been serious.

They hadn't ridden too much farther when they spotted the team safely tied up nearby.

"The team's there, so I think Murray and whatever passengers he has with him are probably sitting in the shade somewhere, waiting for us to show up and rescue them," Hank said.

"Think we've made them wait long enough?"

"Yeah. We'd better go see what we can do to help."

"It'll be a trick figuring out a way to get them back to town, but we'll manage." Jace glanced over at Hank. "I don't see anything unusual, but be ready, just in case." Jace drew his sidearm.

Hank, too, drew his weapon.

They slowed their pace and rode cautiously toward the damaged stage, keeping an eye out for some sign of the driver and passengers.

Jace caught sight of it first—the glint of sun on steel up in the rocks ahead.

"It's an ambush!" Jace shouted at Hank. He leaned low and put his heels to his horse's sides just as the first shots rang out. In that instant, he was hit and thrown from his horse.

"Jace!" Hank yelled in horror as he rode to escape the hail of gunfire. He reached the rocks on the steep hillside and threw himself from his horse's back to scramble for cover. He desperately worked his way among the rocks, trying to get as high up as he could to return the gunmen's fire. The way things looked, he figured he was a dead man, but he planned to take a few of the outlaws with him.

"Nice bit of shooting there, Al," Harley said as he kept an eye on the other lawman.

Al just nodded, satisfied that he'd claimed his revenge. "Looks like Lawless doesn't have a sheriff anymore."

"That's good. That's real good. Now, let's see if the boys can take care of the deputy, too," Harley said, signaling Ken and Ed to close in on him.

Hank knew he was in trouble. He stayed low, dodging among the rough boulders as he fought his way up the hillside. He was just making a break toward what he thought looked like better protection when a bullet slammed into his back. Hank collapsed and fell, rolling down the steep incline and into a deep ravine.

Harley shouted, "Did you get him?"

"It looks like it!"

"You see anybody else coming?"

"No," they called, looking back the way the two lawmen had ridden in.

"All right, Ken! Ed! Go check on him! We got the sheriff!" he ordered. Then he looked at Al and Ned. "Let's see if he's dead."

Gun in hand, Harley stood up and started down to where Jace Madison lay facedown on the ground. Pete climbed down from his hiding place to join them there.

"Looks like Lawless is your town again," Ned said, wanting more than ever to ingratiate himself with the killers.

"Yes, it does," Harley agreed arrogantly. "Madison and his deputy may have managed to take over Los Rios, but they weren't up against us there."

Harley reached Jace, who lay unmoving, on the ground. He saw blood on the ground by his head and reached down to turn him over to get a look at him. He was startled when Jace let out a low groan, and Harley didn't like to be startled.

"Damn!" Harley swore as he stared down at the unconscious lawman. "Looks like you ain't as good a shot as you thought, Al!"

Al was standing nearby, and he was instantly angry and humiliated that he'd missed. "You mean he's alive?"

"Yep. You only grazed him," Harley taunted. The men who rode with him were good shots, but this just proved what he'd always believed—none of them were as good as he was.

Al was furious—furious that he hadn't hit Madison clean and furious that Harley was taunting him about it.

"Let me take care of it right now," Al snarled, coming to Harley's side. "I'll finish what I started." He drew his sidearm and took aim, ready to shoot the sheriff at point-blank range.

"Don't." Harley's order was harsh as he shoved Al's gun aside.

"What the hell do you mean, 'don't'?" Al challenged the outlaw leader.

"I got an idea," Harley said, smiling coldly as he knelt down to get a look at the sheriff's head wound. He stood up and turned to Pete, ordering, "Doctor him up as best you can and get him ready to ride. As soon as Ed and Ken get back, we're heading for Lawless."

"Wait! We set up this ambush to kill Madison and his deputy, and now you want to take him back into town alive?" Al demanded.

"That's right. I do." Harley didn't like being questioned or having to explain himself to anybody.

"He's right, Al," Pete put in. "Madison's worth a lot more to us alive than dead. We can take him back in and show the good folks in Lawless why they shouldn't go hiring any sheriffs when we ain't around."

"So shooting the other sheriff wasn't good enough to show them?" Al raged.

"We're going to make an example out of good old Sheriff Madison here," Harley said, looking coldly at Al as he began to wonder how smart the other man really was.

"How are you going to do that?"

"We're going to put him on trial and hang him—just like he did your partners."

At his words, Al immediately calmed down. He actually managed to smile. "A trial and a hanging? Let's get him back to Lawless."

Ken and Ed were making their way through the maze of rocks, searching for the fallen lawman.

"How far up did he get?"

"Not too much farther," Ed said, keeping a close lookout just in case their aim hadn't been true.

As they reached the site where they believed the lawman had been hiding, they made a gruesome discovery.

"That's why we couldn't see him after he went down," Ken said at the sight of the man's lifeless body, sprawled on the rocks at the bottom of a steep, narrow, rocky ravine.

"We'd better climb down there and check on him."

"Why? He's dead, and even if he ain't, he will be soon enough." Ken holstered his gun.

"You sure?"

"Yeah, let's go tell Harley."

The two gunslingers made their way back to join the others, and were shocked to find the bloodied sheriff still alive. Madison's head was bandaged and his wrists tied in front of him as Al and Pete kept him on his feet.

"What are you going to do with him?" Ken asked.

"I got a plan for him. Don't you worry about that," Harley said. Then he demanded, "Is the deputy dead?"

"We shot him in the back, and he fell into a ravine." Ken went on to reassure him that the deputy had had no chance of surviving the fall.

Jace had been only vaguely aware of his surroundings as the gunmen supported him between them. The violent, agonizing pain in his head proved he was still alive, but he didn't know for how long. He was caught up in a disoriented, pain-filled daze, barely able to stay on his feet, but when he heard the gunman tell Harley that Hank was dead, the shock of it jarred him.

Hank is dead?

The words echoed through his soul, and in that moment, a fierce, cold-blooded rage surged to life, empowering him. Jace reacted violently, jerking himself free of the outlaws' hold to launch himself bodily at Harley.

Harley was caught off guard by Jace's attack, but dodged his charge. He hit Jace on the back of the neck with his pistol and then savagely punched him in the stomach, leaving him doubled up on the ground.

"Come on, lawman. Want to try to take me again?" Harley challenged as he stood over him, gun still in hand.

Jace looked up at the murderer, and when Harley saw the look in his eyes, he realized just what a dangerous man Jace Madison was. Harley understood how he had been able to tame Los Rios, and he was going to be real glad to see him hang.

"How come you're keeping him alive?" Ken asked.

"Because we're going to use him to help us teach all the folks in Lawless a lesson they'll never forget," Harley said. "Put him up on his horse. I want to reach Lawless before dark. We're going to let everybody know that we're back in town when we ride in."

"What do you want to do about the stage team?" Ed asked.

"Turn the horses loose."

There was no discussion about the dead driver and passenger. They'd just been in the way of Harley's plan and had paid the price.

Jace was barely conscious as the outlaws dragged him to his feet again and shoved him over to his horse and up into the saddle. Wracked with pain, he struggled to clear his thoughts as he fought to stay in the saddle.

Hank is dead—

Trapped as he was, Jace wasn't sure how he was going to do it, but somehow, some way, this gang was going down. Knowing that Grant and Walt were ready and waiting in town gave him the strength to stay in the saddle as they covered the long miles back.

Al and Ned were enjoying the long ride back to Lawless. Though they had both wanted Jace Madison dead, they were glad now that he hadn't been killed with the first shot. They rode up next to him to taunt him.

"You know, it's good to finally meet you face to face," Al said, looking Jace over and smiling.

Jace didn't say a word. He kept his gaze downcast as they continued to ride along, trying to deal with the pain from his head wound. He wondered how Ned had come to be riding with the outlaws, for he certainly was nothing like the other gunmen in Harley's gang.

"Yep, it sure is," Al went on, chuckling evilly.

"So you and Jace here are good buddies?" Ned asked.

"Oh, yeah. Jace and me, we go way back. We go all the way back to San Gabriel."

Jace had wanted to ignore his tormentor, but at the mention of San Gabriel, he tensed and glanced quickly over at him.

"Ah, so you remember those good old days in San Gabriel. Me and my friends Buck Carson and Vic Lawrence used to hang out there a lot." Al deliberately paused, waiting to see Jace's reaction, and he wasn't disappointed.

Jace clenched his fists.

"You remember Buck and Vic, don't you? We were riding together then. Why, we even pulled off a stage robbery near San Gabriel. We took in a big haul that day. You remember that robbery, don't you, Madison?"

"I remember," Jace said harshly.

"The posse out of San Gabriel thought they were good, but they weren't," Al mocked. "I know they finally managed to track down Buck and Vic, but they never caught up with me." Al could tell he was really getting to the sheriff, and he was enjoying every minute of it. "You rode with that posse, didn't you, lawman?"

"That's right. I did."

"And you never knew you didn't bring in the whole gang—until now."

"Who are you?" Jace ground out.

"My name's Al Denton. Remember that name, lawman."

"Don't worry, Denton. I won't forget." Jace fell silent.

Al laughed at Madison's frustration. Reining in, he and Ned fell back to ride among the other gunmen.

The gang continued on until they were just on the outskirts of town. Only then did Harley rein in.

"What are we stopping here for?" Pete asked, voicing the question in the minds of the other gunmen.

"Remember how I told you I wanted to teach this town a lesson? Well, now's the time." He freed his rope and ordered Pete, "Get our good friend the sheriff there off his horse."

Pete didn't ask Harley what he was about to do. He just did what he was told. He dismounted, pulled Jace down off his horse's back and dragged him over to stand before Harley.

"You boys ready to have some real fun?" Harley asked.

"Yeah, boss. What have you got in mind?" Ed returned.

Harley didn't bother to answer. He just gave a loud yell that startled the horses as he lassoed Jace.

Now Jace knew what was coming. He fought to free

himself, but he had no chance as Harley took off at a gallop down the main street of town. Jace tried to stay on his feet and keep up by running behind him, but it was hopeless. He lost his balance and fell, and was dragged down the street behind Harley's horse.

Chapter Twenty-three

Grant was growing more and more worried as each hour passed and they heard nothing from Jace or Hank. Getting up from the sheriff's desk, he began to pace restlessly around the office. He looked over at Walt, who was sitting nearby watching him.

"It's getting late. It's almost sundown. They should have been back here by now."

"I know." Walt was feeling the same tension. "We can get a posse together and ride out after them if you want."

"It's so late, it wouldn't do us much good. By the time we got everybody saddled up and ready to go, it'd be dark." Grant went to stand at the window and stare out. He was gripped by an overpowering sense of unease, and he wasn't sure why. "Where the hell are they? What could be taking this long?"

"It could be the stage was damaged in some way, and they're helping bring it back into town."

"I hope that's all it is." He decided to get out of the office for a while to ease his restlessness. "Walt, I can't just sit here. I'm going to go take a look around town."

Grant had just reached for the doorknob to start outside when he heard the sounds of screams and wild shooting coming from across town.

"That sounds like trouble. Bad trouble." Grant stopped to listen.

"It might be the King Gang returning." Walt remembered other times when the outlaws had ridden back into town this way. They were always out of control, so he and Sammie had made it a point to stay in the stable, out of harm's way.

Grant went to the gun case to grab his rifle and some extra ammunition. "Let's go out the back. There's only the two of us right now, and if it is the gang, we need to take them by surprise."

Walt got his rifle, too, and followed Grant out the back door.

The sounds of gunfire continued as they ran silently through the alleyways of town. When they worked their way in close enough to get a look at what was happening, they spotted Harley and his men riding triumphantly down the street. The outlaws were shouting at folks and firing their guns wildly into the air. It was only as the riders finally passed by that Grant and Walt saw why they were celebrating.

"It's Jace!" Grant exclaimed, horrified by the spectacle playing out before them. Jace was bloodied and looked beaten as they led him past their hiding place. Harley King had lassoed him and was half leading, half dragging him behind his horse as he rode through town.

Grant swore vilely at the sight. He would have loved to ambush the gang right then and there, but he knew Jace would be caught in the middle of the gunfire. He was forced to bide his time.

Grant was grim as he looked over at Walt. "It looks like we got some work to do."

Walt, too, was shocked by the sight of Jace being dragged into town this way. "Where's Hank? Did you see him? Was he with them, too?"

"No. He's not with them." Grant's expression darkened. "And if they didn't bring him in, I'd say he's dead."

They shared a look of understanding, realizing the deadliness of the situation they were facing. Walt was furious that Hank had been in trouble and he hadn't been there to help him.

"Look! Ned's riding in with Harley King." Walt was surprised to see the mean drunk riding past them with the outlaws. "He was never a part of the gang."

Grant was surprised to see Ned, too. "I don't know. Maybe he went looking for Harley to tell him we were here, so he could get even with us."

"I wouldn't put it past him."

"We've got to get Jace away from them as fast as we can. Right now, I'd say he's lucky to still be alive."

"I wonder where they're taking him? That house where they usually stay is down the street from the sheriff's office, but I doubt they'd take him there."

"We'll have to watch and see. Once we figure out what they're doing, we can start making our plan." Grant realized the gang was reining in. "Looks like they're stopping at the Tumbleweed." He didn't like that at all. Mary was there working and with Ned back . . .

"What do you want to do?"

"We've got to get the word out that they're back."

"Sammie will do that for us. Let's go down to the stable and tell her what's going on. She'll want to know about Jace." He could only imagine how his sister would react to the news.

"All right. You ready?"

"I'm ready," Walt replied.

"We're going to do whatever it takes to save Jace and this town, and we're going to need all the help we can get from the townsfolk to do it."

They made sure to stay out of sight as they crossed town.

Harley dismounted and went to where Jace was standing unsteadily in the street behind his horse. He took the rope off the lawman and shoved him into the saloon, slamming the swinging doors wide as he walked in. His men followed, keeping an eye out just in case anyone in town was thinking about trying something.

"We're back," Harley announced harshly, staring around at all the wide-eyed, obviously uneasy patrons in the Tumbleweed.

Dennis was horrified at the sight of Jace, but he kept his expression controlled and tried to act as if there was nothing untoward going on. "I can see that."

"And Lawless is our town again."

"I can see that, too," Dennis said, hoping to mollify the gang leader. "What'll it be, Harley? The usual?"

"That'll be just fine," Harley said.

He shoved several tables out of the way, then grabbed a single chair and pushed Jace down to sit in it, isolated and alone in the middle of the room.

A low murmur went through the saloon as everyone stared at the bloodied, wounded lawman and wondered what the killers were going to do next. Dennis wanted to grab his shotgun, but knew he didn't stand a chance alone against the whole gang. He quickly poured Harley's drink and set the glass on the bar.

Leaving Jace there, Harley went to the bar to pick up his drink and took a deep swallow.

"Good stuff."

"I aim to please."

"You're a smart man, Dennis. I like that about you." Harley eyed him for a moment, then looked at the other men drinking in the saloon. "I want you all to know that the deputy who rode out with your sheriff is dead, and Sheriff Madison here is under arrest."

"Arrest?" Dennis couldn't stop himself from asking.

"That's right," Harley answered. "Me and the boys arrested him for trying to take over our town, and now he's going to stand trial for that crime. We want to do things like real law-abiding citizens. Ain't that right, boys?"

Pete, Ned, Al and the others all agreed.

Harley's smile was feral as he let his gaze sweep around the room. "We're gonna lock him up in the jail tonight, just like he did Ned, and then we're going to hold the trial right here tomorrow night, so be ready. I expect all of you to be here. You understand me?"

The men in the saloon muttered the response Harley wanted to hear, so he turned his back on them to finish his drink.

Hiding just inside the door to the kitchen, Mary had seen and heard everything that had just transpired. She was standing there physically shaking from the outrage that filled her. She could tell Jace was hurt, but she couldn't tell how badly, and the thought that Hank had been ambushed and killed horrified her.

Mary knew she had to do something and fast. Her first impulse was to charge out into the saloon with her cast-iron skillet, but she controlled herself. She had to find Grant and Walt. She'd seen them earlier that afternoon, but had no idea where they were now. She knew she had to get word to Sammie, too, but she had to be careful. She didn't want the gang getting suspicious of her. The situation was going to be tough enough as it was.

Sammie had been hard at work when she'd heard the gunshots and the shouts and realized the gang was back in town. The thought frightened her, for she knew there could be no avoiding the ultimate showdown with the outlaws now. With Jace and Hank gone, her brother and Grant were the only deputies left to protect Lawless. She knew she had to help them in whatever way she could. Grabbing up her whip and her gun, Sammie was just starting toward the back door of the stable to sneak out when Grant and Walt showed up.

She saw the look on her brother's face and realized immediately that something terrible had happened.

"What is it? What's wrong?" she demanded as they worked to secure the door behind them.

Walt hesitated, unsure how to tell her about Jace.

His hesitation convinced her he was keeping something back, and it deepened her fears. She grabbed his arm and glared up at him.

"Walt! Tell me!"

Walt had dealt with Sammie long enough to know he couldn't hide anything from her. He met her gaze straight on. "The stage trouble was a setup. Harley and his men are back in town and they've brought Jace with them."

The horrifying thought that Jace had been killed tore through her. "Is he . . . ?"

"No, no, he's not dead," Grant hastened to reassure her. He told her what they'd seen and how they'd watched the gang go into the saloon with Jace.

"Oh, thank God, he's alive," she breathed, trembling from the power of the emotions that assaulted her. "What are we going to do? How are we going to help him?"

"I don't know yet, but we will," Grant said firmly. "Nothing's going to happen to Jace."

"Did they bring Hank in with them, too?" Sammie asked.

"No. We don't know what's happened to Hank. He may have gotten away or—"

"All right." She cut him off, not wanting to think about the alternative.

"We have to get the word out to everybody in town we trust and let folks know what's going on," Grant directed.

"We need to let Ben know, too," Walt added.

They were silent for a moment, thinking of how the rancher was going to react to the news that his son was missing.

"I'll take care of it," Sammie declared.

"How?" Walt recognized her determined tone of voice and knew whatever she'd decided to do, there would be no stopping her.

"I'm going down to the Tumbleweed to try to talk to Mary. I'm sure she's heard everything that's happened.

She can help us, and I'll tell as many other folks as I can on the way back."

"One of us should go with you," Grant said.

"No. I'll be less conspicuous by myself. It's getting dark enough now that I don't think anybody will see me. You just wait here."

"Tell Mary to be careful. Ned rode back in with Harley and his men," Grant told her.

"Ned wasn't part of the gang." She was shocked by the news.

"I don't know how they happened to meet up, but he must have been the one who let the gang know Jace and I had come to Lawless," Grant said.

"All right, you two stay here in back where nobody can see you, just in case someone tells Harley that you're both here in town. This won't take long," Sammie promised, hurrying off.

Grant and Walt immediately started trying to figure out the best plan to free Jace, find Hank and reclaim the town from the killers.

"Mary!" Lilly called out as she hurried into the kitchen. "Dennis wants you to stay in the kitchen. Ned rode in with Harley and he was wondering why you weren't out there serving food. Dennis told him you weren't working the tables anymore."

Mary knew she would be forever grateful to Dennis for his help. "What's going on out there? How is Jace?"

"It's hard to tell. It looks like he might have been grazed by a head shot. He's conscious and sitting up, so I don't think the wound is too bad. Did you hear what Harley's planning to do?"

"I heard everything, and we've got to do something fast."

"But what?"

Just as Lilly was speaking, Sammie appeared at the back door.

"Mary," she called quietly, staying outside. She didn't want to risk being seen by anyone who might come to the kitchen doorway, which opened into the saloon.

Mary hurried over with Lilly to talk to Sammie and quickly told her everything she knew. She saw the pain in her friend's eyes as she learned what was happening to Jace.

"We're going to get Jace away from them," Sammie swore. "We just have to figure out how to do it."

"We will," Mary vowed, knowing she could count on Lilly's help, too. Lilly had no love for the cruel and deadly gunmen.

"If you hear anything else that might help us, send word right away," Sammie told Mary.

"Don't worry. I will."

Sammie left the Tumbleweed then, slipping through the back alleys so she would not be seen. She stopped to warn the undertaker and then went to the Peters's home to let Jim know. Both men promised to notify all their friends about what was going on. When Eloise heard the news that Hank might have been killed, she was devastated, and made her father promise to round up the men responsible. Jim did, and he told Sammie he'd be ready whenever she needed him. She promised to send word the following day when they were prepared to act.

Sammie returned to the stable, where Walt and Grant would be making their plan. As she headed back, though, she knew she had to try to see Jace, just to reassure herself that he really was alive. The street in front of the saloon was deserted, giving her the opportunity she needed to sneak up close to one of the windows and get a quick look inside. She spotted Jace right away, seated in the isolated chair, his shirt bloodied and his hands tied in front of him. Sammie could tell he'd been through hell, but his stoic expression revealed nothing of what he was thinking or feeling. Hurrying off into the night, she was ready to do whatever she had to in order to free him.

Chapter Twenty-four

It was almost dark when Hank stirred and regained consciousness. Agony tore through him with every movement, so he stayed still, trying to remember what had happened. Opening his eyes took an effort, but he finally did it. He stared blankly up the steep walls of the ravine, and slowly the memory of taking a bullet in the back and falling forward returned.

He shifted his position, and a groan escaped him.

From the fierceness of the pain searing through him, it was obvious to Hank that he wasn't dead. He was wondering, though, if death might not have been a better option than the agony he was experiencing.

Using all the strength he could muster, Hank managed to lever himself up into a sitting position and brace himself against a rock for support. He took a moment to assess his physical condition and discovered that the bullet that had hit him in the back had passed cleanly through, coming out near his left shoulder. He knew he was lucky to be alive, for if the bullet had hit him an inch or so the other way, he wouldn't have been sitting there struggling to figure out how he was going to save himself. Hank knew only two things for certain—he was weak from loss of blood and the hard fall he'd taken, and he was all alone. Jace was dead.

Hank's prospects were dim as he faced the reality of his situation. There was the slim hope that someone would eventually come looking for him, but even so, there was no way anyone would ever find him at the bottom of the ravine. If he wanted to stay alive, he had to climb out of there on his own.

Hank lifted his gaze to the top and, seeing that the sky was growing dark, he knew he had to try to make his move now. Lying in the ravine overnight was not going to help. He would only get weaker.

Hank had always thought of himself as a strong, determined man. But the climb he was facing would be a true test of not only his physical strength but his fortitude as well. Hank had never been particularly religious, but at that moment he understood more fully the challenges some folks faced in life and why they did need God's help to get through the hard times.

As Hank struggled to his knees so he could begin to haul himself up the steep slope, he offered up a prayer for God's help. He locked his jaw against the pain that tore violently through him. Reaching out with his good arm, he grabbed hold of a big rock to slowly lever himself upward.

Meanwhile, back in Lawless, Dennis was serving up a lot of drinks to the gunmen. He wanted to get them as drunk as he could as soon as possible. He grew more and more furious as he watched Ned acting like a big shot with the gang. He had to keep an eye on the man to make sure he didn't try to get back to the kitchen where Mary was working. He didn't trust Ned at all.

Dennis wondered if Harley realized what Ned was really like. He knew it might cause some trouble within the gang if he brought the subject up, so he decided it was worth a try. The more the outlaws fought with each other, the better chance the town had to find a way to get rid of them.

When Ned came back to the bar for a refill a short time later, Dennis was ready to make his move.

"Give me another drink," Ned ordered arrogantly. He was riding with the Harley King Gang now. No one was going to mess with him. In fact, he'd been thinking about paying Mary a visit back in the kitchen. He'd been keeping an eye out, watching for her to come wait tables, but the bartender and the two working girls had been the ones who'd served the food tonight.

"Aren't you supposed to be drinking sarsaparilla?" Dennis deliberately spoke loud enough so everyone heard him.

"Why, you—" Ned was instantly furious, not to mention uneasy about how Harley would react if he overheard what the bartender had said. "Those days are over, and you damn well know it!"

Harley and Pete were standing down the bar a ways, and they looked over to see what all the shouting was about.

"What's the problem, Ned?" Harley asked.

Ned was glaring at the bartender, but didn't answer, knowing how an explanation would make him look to Harley.

When Ned didn't answer him, Harley looked at the bartender. He wanted an answer. "What are you two talking about?"

Dennis smiled and picked up his rag to start wiping down the bar as he told Harley the whole story of what had happened between Mary and Ned. He explained how the new deputy had brought Ned to the saloon and made him drink sarsaparilla and apologize to her in front of all the customers. When he finished telling the story, everyone in the saloon was howling with laughter and taunting Ned.

Harley had listened to Dennis's story with growing anger. His tale about Ned abusing Mary the cook left Harley enraged. He stalked down the bar to confront Ned.

Ned saw Harley coming and wondered what the problem was. As he drew near, he saw the look in Harley's eyes and started to shake.

Harley stopped in front of him and leaned down into his face. He loomed over Ned threateningly.

"I'm gonna tell you this once, Ned," Harley said slowly. "You stay away from Mary or I'll break both your arms."

"But that Mary's a bitch," he yelped back, trying to defend his own actions.

"She may be that, but she's the best cook within a hundred miles. You leave her alone or you'll answer to me."

Ned was terse as he quickly responded, "All right."

Harley could tell Ned was too weak-willed and spineless to defy him, and he liked that. "Did she really hit you with her frying pan?"

Ned glanced over at Dennis, knowing there was no point in trying to lie his way out of that one. He told Harley in disgust, "Yeah."

Harley started laughing then.

Ned got his whiskey from Dennis, gave the bartender a dirty look and started back to his table.

"Ned, when you get done with that drink, we're going to lock up our outlaw in the jail. You want to help guard him overnight?"

Ned looked back at Harley. His anger was easing at the thought that he'd at least get to torture the lawman for a while, even if he couldn't get to Mary. "Yeah, I can do that. In fact, I just might enjoy it."

"I figured you would," Harley said, knowing he'd read the other man right. Truth was, having Ned around bothered him. He wanted to party all night long; getting Ned out of the way would work just fine.

Jace was still sitting in the chair, bound and bloodied and aching all over, wondering how long the outlaws were going to keep him there on display. He had no chance of making a break for it, so he had to bide his time and take whatever abuse they threw at him.

Al had taken a seat at a table close by and had been taunting him about what a bad bunch of trackers the posse out of San Gabriel had been to have missed his trail when he'd split up with Vic and Buck. Jace was careful to keep his expression blank, for he did not want the gunman to know that the taunts were getting to him.

The truth was, though, that Al's words stirred emotions in Jace that he kept under tight control deep within him. Thoughts of Sarah and the life they'd planned together returned, and though he had come to accept the reality that she was gone, the pain of losing her was still there, even after all these years.

Jace drew a ragged breath and fought for control. He

had no time for emotion right now. He had to concentrate on finding a way to free himself and save this town.

When the outlaws had first brought him in, he'd feared the men from town who were in the Tumbleweed drinking, or maybe even Dennis or the saloon girls, would tell Harley about Grant and Walt. He had been listening to the conversations around him and had not heard anyone mention his deputies to Harley or his men. That knowledge gave him the strength he needed to keep fighting. Grant and Walt were out there somewhere, and he was sure they were working on a plan to bring the outlaws down.

Jace was surprised when Harley called his men up to the bar to talk to them. He'd expected them to keep partying all night, and he wondered what they were up to.

"All right, boys, it's time to take the sheriff over to the jail and lock him up for the night. Ned, you ready?"

"Oh, yeah. I'm ready to lock him up, just like he did me." Ned was smiling at the thought.

"You be my guest," Harley told him. Then he looked at Pete, ordering, "Pete, you go along with Ned. I want to make sure nothing goes wrong before the trial tomorrow night."

Pete was not happy. He wanted to stay in the saloon and enjoy some time with Lilly, but he said nothing.

Harley looked around at the men from town who were still sitting there drinking, and said, "Like I told you before, this town is ours. Remember that, and come on back tomorrow night for the trial. It's gonna be a good one." He was chuckling as he finished, "Get him out of here. I'm tired of looking at him."

Pete and Ned went over to Jace and hauled him up to his feet. They pushed him ahead of them out of the saloon.

Harley turned back to Dennis, who was watching Jace leave.

"You got a problem?" Harley demanded.

"No. No problem at all. You want another whiskey?"

"Damned right, I do! Let's get this party going!"

Pete went ahead of Ned and Jace to make sure there was no one around the sheriff's office who might give them trouble. As he'd expected, the place was deserted. Since they'd killed the deputy and had the sheriff with them, he believed it was going to be a real quiet night. Not that quiet appealed to him. He'd been looking forward to a rowdy night at the Tumbleweed, but he understood why Harley wanted him with Ned. Even wounded as he was, this lawman could easily give Ned trouble if he got the opportunity.

Pete threw the door open and got the lamp lit just as Ned brought Jace inside.

"Where's the keys?" Ned asked.

Pete found them on the desk and tossed them to Ned. "Enjoy yourself."

"Oh, I am enjoying myself."

Jace moved back to the cell area and waited as Ned unlocked the cell door.

"Get in there, Sheriff," Ned ordered. "I want to see you behind bars."

Jace walked into the cell and sat down on the narrow cot.

"You look real good in there, lawman, but I got a feeling, come tomorrow night, you won't be sitting in a cell anymore. You're gonna be swinging from a tree somewhere."

Jace didn't say a word, but he lifted his gaze to stare straight at Ned.

Ned saw the power of the hate in Jace's eyes and quickly locked the cell door before going back out to sit with Pete.

"He's all locked up, good and safe, back there. Now, all we got to do is wait for tomorrow. That trial is going to be fun."

"Not as much fun as spending tonight with Lilly and Candy would be."

"That's true enough," Ned agreed. "You want to go on back over now that we got him locked up?"

Pete would have liked nothing more, but he knew what would happen if he showed up back at the saloon after Harley had told him to guard the sheriff.

"Damn right I want to, but I ain't going to. Harley told me to do this, and I'm going to follow orders."

"Maybe he'll send one of the other boys over to relieve you later, so you can party some more."

"No. He won't. We're stuck here for the night, so we might as well try to get comfortable." Pete knew he was in charge, so he locked the office door and sat down at the desk. He didn't want to risk letting his guard down at all tonight.

Ned went into the small room Jace used for his own and lay down on the bed. He was smiling as he stared up at the ceiling. Who would ever have thought that he'd end up in Sheriff Madison's office, running things? Life was good some days, real good. He'd ridden back into town with the King Gang, and nobody was laughing at him now.

Jace stretched out on the cot and closed his eyes. He didn't know if he'd get any rest that night, but he had to try. He had to get some of his strength back. If he had some fight left in him, he'd have a better chance of making a break for it tomorrow—if the opportunity arose. With Grant and Walt still out there, he had hope.

As he lay on the hard cot, his thoughts turned to Sammie, and he wondered how she was. He hoped Walt would keep her out of harm's way. He didn't want her getting caught up in any of the dangerous situations that might arise with the King Gang back in Lawless. He wanted her safe.

Try as he might to put thoughts of Sammie from him, Jace couldn't. An image of her as she'd looked at the social the other night played in his mind. She had been all beauty and grace that night—a vision of loveliness—and her kisses had left him hungry for more.

Jace had believed after losing Sarah that he would never love again, but he realized now Sammie had changed all that. Just in the short time they'd known each other, she had found a way into his heart. Jace hoped he would get the chance to tell her so.

When Sammie made it back to the stable, she told Walt and Grant what she'd learned from Mary—that Jace was going to be locked up in the jail tonight and then put on trial tomorrow night at the Tumbleweed. She also told them how she'd stopped to warn some of the folks in town about what was going on.

"Now we've got to get the word out to the Circle M and let Ben know that Hank is missing," Grant said, knowing how devastated the Madison family would be by the news. "We also need to tell the other ranchers what's happened here in town, so they can send some men to help us."

"Do you want me to go tell Reverend Davidson? He could ride out of town without any of the King Gang knowing it," Sammie offered.

"That's a good idea," Walt agreed, "but we're still in deep trouble. We've got to figure out how we're going to get Jace out of that jail before Harley puts him on trial. We can't just try to shoot our way in. They'd kill Jace before we even got through the door."

Sammie and Grant both knew he was right.

"Whatever we do, it's going to take some serious planning. We need to find out who's going to help us, and then we have to figure out how to break Jace out of there without alerting all the other outlaws."

"Judging from the way they've acted in the past, when Harley and his men drink all night, they usually don't start moving until mid-afternoon the following day," Sammie said. "So, we'll have that much time to get ready."

"All right," Grant said. "I'll go tell Reverend Davidson what's happened."

"No, you won't," Sammie ordered. "You two stay right here, out of sight. We don't need any more trouble tonight."

"But Sammie—" Walt started to protest.

The look she gave him shut him up. He knew his sister well enough to know when not to push her.

"You be careful," Walt cautioned, worried about her being on the streets at night alone.

"Don't worry. I'll be right back," she said as she picked up her whip and started from the stable.

Reverend Davidson was quick to answer the door when she knocked. "Sammie, is something wrong? Please, come in."

He held the door wide and she slipped inside. He closed the door tightly behind her.

"Do you want to sit in the parlor and talk?"

"No. There's no time. The King Gang is back."

"I thought as much when I heard the gunshots. What are Jace and Grant doing? Do they need help?"

"Yes, we need help, but Jace is in trouble," she began. She quickly went on to tell the minister everything that had happened. "We need you to ride out to the Circle M and let the Madisons know what's happened to Hank and ask them to send whatever men they can to town to help us."

The reverend was tortured by the terrible news that Hank was missing and presumed to be dead. "I'll leave at sunup."

"Thank you. We figure Jace should be safe enough until Harley starts this 'trial' of his tomorrow night, but we've got less than twenty-four hours to rescue him and get rid of the gang once and for all."

"Anything more you need me to do, you just let me know."

"We will, Reverend. Thank you." Then she added, "Maybe you could say some prayers for Jace."

"You care for our new sheriff, don't you, Sammie?" he asked perceptively.

Sammie drew a ragged breath and fought back tears as she answered him, "Yes, I do. I love him, Reverend."

"Then you pray for him, too, Sammie."

She nodded, unable to say any more. She left the reverend to return to the stable. As she made her way through the dark streets, she knew this night was going to be the longest of her life.

Chapter Twenty-five

Walt and Grant were holed up in the stable, working on their plan.

Walt told him, "In the past, Harley and his gunmen have always ended up sleeping it off back at the old sheriff's house they took over."

"All of them?" Grant questioned.

"Usually, yes. Of course, things could be different this time, who knows? We'll just have to try to keep track of every one of them as the night goes on."

"If you're right and they do end up there at the house, we'll have to think of a way to flush them out tomorrow. It could prove deadly if we try to go in after them."

They were still discussing all possible courses of action when they heard someone come into the stable. They immediately fell silent and drew their guns.

"Sammie?" Mary called her friend's name in a voice just above a whisper as she stopped inside the door. She'd gotten off work and wanted to check in with Sammie before she went home to Jonathan at the boardinghouse. When she didn't get a response to her call, she moved farther into the stable. "Sammie? Are you in here?"

When Grant and Walt realized it was Mary, they left their hiding place to talk to her. Neither man holstered his gun, though, until they made sure she was alone.

"Mary," Grant said, stepping forward out of the darkness.

"Oh, Grant, Walt. You frightened me for a minute," Mary said, breathing a sigh of relief at the sight of the two men. "Where's Sammie?"

"She's gone to talk to the reverend," Walt told her. "Have you found out anything new?"

"They took Jace over to the jail and locked him up a while ago. Harley sent Ned and another outlaw named Pete to guard him all night."

At the news, they knew their earlier assumption had been correct. There was no safe way to break Jace out of the jail.

As they were talking, Sammie returned.

"Oh, Mary, I'm so glad you're here." She went to hug her friend, relieved to know she was safely away from the Tumbleweed.

"So am I."

Sammie looked at the men. "I talked to Reverend Davidson and he's going out to the Circle M first thing in the morning."

"Good." They knew what a hard trip that was going to be for him to make.

"Have you come up with a plan yet? What are we going to do to get Jace out of jail?" She looked at Grant.

"We're not going to do anything until morning," Grant answered.

"Morning?" Sammie was shocked. She'd been hoping to take action right away. "Why do we have to leave Jace locked up there overnight? I know we're worried about what might happen in a shootout, but what if he needs to see the doc? We should be heading over to the jail right now!"

"Sammie," Walt said sternly, even as he realized how much Jace meant to her. He'd had a feeling she was coming to care for the man, but he knew now it was much more than that. "Jace was wounded. We know that, but we don't want to get him killed trying to save him."

"What if we got one of the saloon girls to help us?" Sammie suggested. "She could go over pretending to want to pay a visit to Ned and Pete, and then we could follow her inside the jail and break Jace out."

"I like the idea of distracting them, and I know for sure Lilly is on our side," Mary began, "but there's no way she can help us tonight. Those fools are all over her and Candy. If she suddenly disappeared, Harley and his boys would miss her right away and start asking questions."

Sammie fell silent, desperately trying to think of a way to rescue Jace. "Then what can we do in the morning? How can we get the upper hand?"

Mary was thoughtful and then glanced over at her friend. "Well, Ned and Pete will probably be wanting something to eat, so I'd have an excuse to go over to the jail, and I know they'd let me in if they saw I was carrying a food basket."

Sammie suddenly lit up. "Mary—"

"What?"

"How have you been sleeping lately?"

"Fine, why? What are you talking about?" She was completely lost by Sammie's question.

Sammie was smiling slyly as she looked at her friend. "Remember what Doc gave you the night of the fire?"

Mary's eyes widened as she realized what Sammie was thinking. "Sammie, you are a genius! An evil one, but a genius!"

Grant looked at Walt, totally confused by the conversation. "What's going on?"

Mary was quick to explain, "Doc gave me some laudanum to help me sleep the night of the fire. He said that I could just put it in a drink or mix it with my food."

"All Mary has to do is mix it into the food she's going to make for them in the morning. If it works as well as the doc said, they'll be sound asleep in no time and we can get Jace out without firing a shot!" Sammie said excitedly.

It would work. She was certain of it.

She looked at Mary. "How much do you have left?"

"Almost all of it. I was afraid to take too much in case Jonathan woke up during the night and needed me."

"Good. Bring it all with you tomorrow. And Mary, can you borrow a dress from Lilly for me?"

"What are you thinking of doing?" her brother demanded.

"I'm not going to let Mary go over to the jail, not with Ned there," Sammie insisted. "Ned won't recognize me, and Pete's only seen me here at the stable. I doubt that he'll know who I am. If Mary can borrow a dress from Lilly, I'll get all dressed up like a dance hall girl and go carry the food to the jail. I'll flirt with them while they're eating so we can be sure the plan works."

"But what if they try something?" Walt demanded.

"I'll have my whip."

"And I can always be waiting somewhere close by with my frying pan," Mary put in, ready to back Sammie up.

"No, you're not going anywhere near that jail," Grant ordered. "Walt and I will back Sammie up. If there's trouble, we'll be there."

"But—"

"Don't even think about it. These men are deadly," Walt said harshly, thinking of Hank. "It'll be hard enough worrying about keeping Sammie safe. We don't need you putting yourself in danger, too."

Mary didn't like being left behind, but she knew she was helping to save Jace by using her expertise in cooking. "All right, but I wish I could be there, just to see them pass out."

"I'll tell you all about it," Sammie promised.

Grant and Walt were still uneasy, but knew it was the best plan anyone had thought of yet.

"I'm proud of you," Grant told Mary and Sammie. Then he looked at Walt and said, "We'd better watch out, though. These two are a lot smarter than we are."

"I know." Walt had to smile. Sammie and Mary were something when they got together.

"Once Jace is out of jail and we have Ned and Pete in custody, we'll only have Harley, Al, Ken and Ed to worry about, and we can get the folks from town to help with them," Grant said thoughtfully. "But tomorrow morning, Walt and I are going to stay real close so nothing happens to you, Sammie. Nothing."

Mary smiled at Grant, knowing as long as he was there, her friend would not be in danger. "Right now, I've got to get back to the boardinghouse. Jonathan's probably still up waiting for me."

"Bring the laudanum with you in the morning, and I'll meet you at the Tumbleweed," Sammie repeated to make sure everything went right. "We've got to save Jace."

"We will. I'll show up even earlier than usual so I can get the dress from Lilly without anyone else finding out what's going on. There's a nook off the kitchen where you can change. What time do you want to meet? I usually show up about ten or ten-thirty, and we don't even open until after eleven."

"Earlier is better. Let's make it ten. We know Harley and the others will still be asleep then, and that gives us our best chance."

Sammie gave Mary a quick hug as she started to leave.

"Kiss Jonathan for me tonight," Sammie told her.

"I will."

They were both excited and scared.

Walt and Sammie went to the back of the stable to give Grant and Mary a moment alone together.

"Are you coming to the boardinghouse tonight?" Mary asked.

"No. It's better if I don't. I don't want to put anyone else at risk. If someone out there has told Harley about me and Walt still being here in town, things could get ugly real fast."

Mary wrapped her arms around him and rested her head on his chest. "I'm so glad you're here to protect us."

Grant held her close, cherishing the moment. "Our plan tomorrow could turn deadly. I want you to be very careful. Don't take any unnecessary chances. I want to know that when this is all over, you'll be right here with me."

Mary lifted her head to look up at him, admiring the determination she saw in his expression. "I will be. There's nowhere else I'd ever want to be." Then, knowing she had to say it now, that this was the moment she'd been waiting for, she whispered, "Grant, I've fallen in love with you."

Her words touched him to the depths of his soul as he gazed down at her. "I knew I was taking a big risk being with you, but it's been the best risk I've ever taken, Mary. I love you, too."

Her heartbeat quickened at his tender words. "You do?"

"Oh, yeah," he said softly, claiming her lips in a hungry exchange that told her all she needed to know about the depth of his love.

Grant did not want to let her go, but he knew Jonathan was waiting for her. He finally ended the kiss and took a deep breath.

"You'd better go now, before I decide to keep you with me all night," he said, regretting that they had to part.

"I wish I could stay."

"So do I."

He kissed her one more time and then she moved out of his embrace.

"I'll see you tomorrow," Grant promised.

She nodded and started for the door.

"Mary—"

She looked back at the tall, powerful man who meant the world to her.

"I love you," Grant repeated tenderly.

Tears of joy filled her eyes and she told him in an emotion-choked voice, "You are my guardian angel."

Before he could say any more, she slipped out into the

darkness of the night to make her way back to the boardinghouse—and her son.

Grant just stood there for a few minutes, coming to grips with what had just happened.

She loved him . . .

Mary loved him. . . .

Mary meant the world to him, and as soon as Jace was free and the gang had been dealt with, he intended to spend the rest of his life with her, returning that love.

"Mary's gone?"

The sound of Walt's question brought Grant back to the real world.

"Yes." He turned serious again.

"Then we'd better get some rest, too. Dawn's going to be showing up real early tomorrow. Let's bed down back here. That way, if anybody tries to look for us at the hotel or my house, we won't be found."

"I'm going to go on home for now," Sammie told her brother. "But I'll be back early to start getting ready."

She didn't think anyone connected to the gang was watching as she left, but wanting to be cautious, Sammie locked up the stable as if it were any other night. She desperately wanted to sneak past the jail to try to see how Jace was doing, but she feared she might be discovered, and that would ruin everything.

Their plan was going to work. She was sure of it. She just had to wait a few more hours to start putting everything in motion.

Knowing she had to be ready to move quickly in the morning, Sammie went home and got cleaned up. She took her bath and washed her hair that night. If she was going to fool Ned and the other gunman into believing she was a new dance hall girl in town, she had to look and act the part.

It was late when she finally went to bed, and though she was exhausted, sleep would not come. Thoughts of Jace haunted her. She prayed fervently that his injuries weren't severe and that he was doing all right in the jail cell. Remembering the way he'd looked sitting in the chair in the saloon left her crying silently into the night.

Sammie wanted Jace with her.

She loved him, and she deeply regretted now that she'd never told him the truth of her feelings for him.

Sammie calmed her runaway emotions by telling herself Jace would be free again tomorrow, and she would tell him she loved him then.

Hank was thankful for the pale moonlight as he edged ever closer to the top of the ravine. If the night sky had been cloudy or moonless, he would never have made it this far. The moon had shed just enough light to allow him to continue his climb out of the hellhole he'd found himself in.

He was exhausted, but giving up meant certain death, so he couldn't quit. He fought on, inch by inch, making his way ever higher. Dizziness assailed him, so he had to be careful not to lose his balance and fall back into the seemingly bottomless pit. Several times he'd almost lost his grip. He was certain it was only by the grace of God that he'd survived this long.

Hank had no idea how many hours it had taken him when he finally managed to reach the top and shift his weight up and onto solid land. He lifted his head to look around for any sign of a campfire, but the countryside was deserted, with no sign of life as far as he could see. Collapsing back on the hard, unforgiving ground, Hank lost consciousness and lay unmoving under the cover of the night.

Pete was bored and angry at being trapped in the sheriff's office with Ned, while Harley and all the other boys were having a good time at the saloon. Ned had fallen asleep in the back room, and that was fine with him. He considered Ned an idiot and would be glad when he parted ways with the gang. Needing some excitement in his life to make up for what he was missing over at the Tumbleweed, he got up and went back to where Jace was locked up.

"Well, Sheriff, how you liking your jail here?" Pete asked, standing close to the cell so he could see Jace lying on the cot.

Jace got up and walked over to face the murderer who was taunting him. "It's a fine jail. You're going to find that out for yourself real soon."

"You really shouldn't go talking that way to me. You're not the law around here anymore. We're back, and we've brought our own brand of justice with us. You're going to find out all about that tomorrow at your trial."

Jace reacted instantly, reaching through the bars to grab Pete and slam him forward against the metal bars. Jace held the stunned outlaw pinned there as he told him, "Don't talk to me about justice. You and your friends enjoy what you do. You enjoy killing innocent people in cold blood."

Pete regained his senses quickly and jerked violently away from Jace's hold.

He told himself he wasn't intimidated.

Jace was no threat to him.

The man was locked up behind bars.

Pete had all the power—he had the keys and a gun.

Pete backed away, saying, "If people get in our way, they pay the price."

"One day you're going to pay for what you've done."

Pete laughed and started to walk away. "No, I'm not. You're going to be the one paying up—tomorrow, big time."

Pete went back out to the office and shut the door behind him. He'd half expected Jace to start shouting at him, but instead, silence reigned. He went to look out the office window in the direction of the Tumbleweed and scowled as he thought of all the fun Harley and the others were having with Lilly and Candy.

Sitting back down at the desk, he tried to get comfortable so he could sleep. He hoped that tomorrow he'd get the chance to enjoy the company of those ladies, too.

Chapter Twenty-six

Hank stirred and opened his eyes. He had no idea how long he'd been lying there. Though it was still dark out, he could see that the sky was slowly starting to lighten in the east. He shifted his position and immediately paid the price as agony ripped through him. He uttered a pain-filled groan and was shocked when suddenly a large dark shape loomed over him.

Panic threatened.

He had no gun to defend himself—

He had no strength to run—

And then Thunder whickered.

"Thunder?" Hank was stunned to find it was his horse standing over him. Never before had he known such a sense of relief. He'd always believed Thunder was the best horse he'd ever owned, and the stallion had just proven it. Most horses would have run off, and possibly eventually made their way back home, but Thunder had remained where his master had fallen.

Thunder nudged Hank's shoulder with his nose, as if wondering why he was still lying there and urging him to move.

"Good boy," Hank said, reaching up to pet him as he slowly levered himself up to a sitting position.

Hank knew this was his one and only chance to save himself. Somehow, he had to mount up and get back to his family's ranch. It took every ounce of strength left in him to get to his knees and then slowly to his feet. He balanced himself against the horse as he fought to get his foot in the stirrup. It wasn't easy, but finally he managed to pull himself up onto Thunder's back.

Slumped over, barely holding on, Hank urged Thunder, "Home, boy. Let's go home."

He was weaving unsteadily in the saddle as Thunder began the trek back to the Circle M.

Reverend Davidson had gotten little sleep that night. He'd spent the long, restless hours praying fervently for Hank Madison and his family, for Jace to be rescued and for the safety of everyone in town. At dawn's first light, he was already saddled up and on his way. The miles seemed endless as he rode for the Circle M. It was going to be an agonizing time for the family. He only wished there was some way he could ease their pain.

It seemed an eternity before the Circle M ranch house came into view, and he could see Ben Madison and some of his ranch hands had come out of the stable to watch him ride in.

"Morning, Reverend," Ben said cautiously, going out to greet him. He was frowning, for he knew this visit was unusual.

"Morning, Ben," Reverend Davidson replied as he reined in and dismounted. "I need to speak with you and Catherine."

Just the tone of the minister's voice set Ben to worrying even more. He grabbed his arm and asked urgently, "What's wrong? Has something happened in town?"

"Ben . . . I . . ."

"What is it?" Ben demanded, a deep, abiding sense of dread overwhelming him.

The reverend looked him in the eye as he answered, "The King Gang is back. They robbed the stage yesterday and set a trap for Jace. Jace and Hank rode out to look for the stage when it didn't show up, and they were ambushed."

"Dear God. No, not—" Ben stared at the reverend, tortured by the horrible news he feared was coming.

"There was a shootout. They wounded Jace and—"

"Hank! What about Hank?"

"He's missing, Ben. The outlaws didn't bring him back into town with them, so he may have been—"

"Don't say it!" Ben ordered harshly as a torrent of emotions tore through him.

Some of the ranch hands had come out to see what was going on, and they could tell by the look on Ben's face that something terrible had happened.

"What is it, Boss?" Gil, the ranch foreman, asked.

Ben didn't answer him. He just looked at the reverend and asked, "Where was the ambush?"

Reverend Davidson shook his head. "We don't know, but it must have been somewhere along the stage route into town."

"What about Jace? You said he was wounded. What have they done to him?"

"Harley and his men brought him back into town. They were telling everybody last night that they were going to put him on trial today and hang him."

Ben hadn't believed things could get any worse, but they just had. He was the one who'd asked Jace to come to Lawless to help the townspeople, and now . . .

Ben was grim as he looked to his foreman. "Hank's missing. He may have been killed yesterday in a shootout with the King Gang. Get everybody saddled up."

"Right away!"

Ben looked toward the house, dreading what he had to do next.

"Will you come up to the house with me, Reverend?"

"Yes, Ben."

Ben had done some hard things in his life, but nothing measured up to this—to telling his wife that their son might be dead.

The moment was as awful as he'd imagined it would be.

"What are you going to do, Ben?" Catherine was in shock.

"We're riding out right now. We're going to find Hank, and we're going to bring him home."

She went into his arms and clung to him, needing to feel his strength, needing to know there was some hope that her son was still alive.

Ben held her close for a moment, then put her from him and went to get his rifle. He was ready for trouble.

"I'm riding with you," Reverend Davidson said.

"Good. We're going to need all the help we can get."

They went back out to find all the ranch hands mounted up and ready to ride. They even had Ben's horse saddled for him.

"Gil, you and Frank ride out and tell the other ranchers what's going on in town. Tell them to get there as fast as they can. Harley's looking to hang Jace sometime today, and Grant and Walt will need help to stop them."

"We'll do it."

"The rest of you men, we're going to find Hank. He and Jace were ambushed by the King Gang yesterday, and no one's seen Hank since. We're heading out now to follow the stage route, and we're not coming back until we find him."

"Let's ride, Boss," they told him, their determination fierce.

Catherine was crying as she watched them leave, and she prayed fervently that her son would be found alive.

As she'd planned, Mary showed up at the Tumbleweed earlier than usual and went up to knock on Lilly's door. She wasn't surprised that Lilly was slow to answer after the night just past.

"Who is it?" Lilly called out wearily.

"It's me, Mary," she answered. "I need to talk to you."

Lilly was exhausted, but when she heard it was Mary, she jumped up, threw on her wrap and hurried to open the door. "What is it?"

"May I come in? I need to talk to you."

Lilly pushed the door wide for her and then closed it behind them.

"Are any of the gunmen still here?" Mary asked.

"No, they all went over to the old sheriff's house right around sunup."

"Were they good and drunk?"

"Oh, yeah. They're going to be sleeping for quite a while. Why? What's going on?"

"We're going to break Jace out of jail this morning, and I need to borrow one of your dresses."

Lilly had been drinking all night, too, and she was a bit confused. "What are you talking about? Why do you need a dress?"

Mary moved closer and quietly explained their plan.

"That's brilliant! Ned and Pete will never know what hit them!"

"That's right, and that's why we've got to get this done early, before the others wake up."

"Here." Lilly went to the small wardrobe in the back corner of the room. "I've got three. There's the black one, the blue one and the red one." She showed Mary all the dresses. "It's the red one that they all seem to like the best. Which one do you want for Sammie?"

Mary could tell why the men liked the red dress. It was low-cut and short, showing a lot of cleavage and leg. "The red one. We don't want them to take their eyes off of her."

Lilly quickly handed Mary the gown and the accessories she wore with it. "Do you want me to help Sammie get dressed?"

"You wouldn't mind?"

"Not at all. Let me get some clothes on, and I'll be right down."

Mary started to slip out of the room, then turned back. "Lilly—"

Lilly looked up.

"Thank you."

"No, Mary. Thank you, and Sammie. You're two strong, brave women, and I admire you both."

They shared a look of understanding, and then Mary quietly left, so Lilly could get dressed.

Sammie had hardly slept. She wanted nothing more than to get over to that jail and break Jace out. She got up early and went over to the stable to see how Walt and Grant were doing. She could tell when she first saw them that something was wrong.

"Sammie, I need to talk to you," Walt told her right away. "It's important."

"What?" She knew something was really bothering him.

"I'm having second thoughts about this plan of yours. I got a real bad feeling about it."

"It's going to be scary, but, Walt—" She looked her brother straight in the eye. "I love Jace. He means the world to me."

"I understand that, but there's got to be some other way. I don't want you putting yourself in danger like this. I want to keep you safe."

"I love you, Walt. You know that." Sammie looked up at her brother, deeply touched by his protectiveness. "But this is a matter of life and death. We've got to rescue Jace, and you know as well as I do that our plan is the best chance of doing that."

"I know," he conceded.

"And you also know that I'm the only one who can do this, and do it right. I mean, we could let you or Grant take over, but neither one of you could fit into one of Lilly's dresses, let alone distract Ned and Pete enough to get the job done."

Grant had been listening to their exchange, and he

couldn't help himself. He gave a short laugh at her outrageous comment. "There's nothing funny about this, but Sammie's right, Walt. There's no way Ned and Pete would believe either one of us was a new dance hall girl. She's the only one who can do this."

"Thanks, Grant," Sammie said, smiling.

"All right," Walt conceded, "but we're going to be close by, just in case anything does go wrong."

"I'm counting on it," she told him.

"Are you ready to go to the saloon?" Walt said.

"I'm ready. I want to get Jace out of that cell as fast as we can. We can't risk Harley showing up early and ruining everything."

"Get your whip," Walt ordered.

Sammie grabbed it and they started off to meet up with Mary at the Tumbleweed.

Mary and Lilly were waiting for her when they arrived and quickly ushered them into the kitchen. Mary was thrilled to see Grant. She wanted to go to him and kiss him, but controlled the need.

She had a job to do.

"We should be safe here. The saloon won't open for business for another hour, but you two stay out of sight, just in case somebody does walk in," Mary ordered the men.

There were a couple of chairs in a corner of the kitchen, so they went to sit there to await the results of the transformation. Sammie handed Walt her whip, then followed Lilly and Mary into the small room off the kitchen where Lilly had put the dress and accessories.

"Oh, my," Sammie said, a bit wide-eyed as she got her first look at the red dress.

"The boys really like this one," Lilly assured her.

"I bet they do."

Sammie ignored the sudden nervousness she was feeling and concentrated on the upcoming jailbreak.

She looked at Lilly and Mary. "Where do I start?"

"Get undressed," Mary ordered, and the transformation began. "I'm going to go start cooking."

Sammie enjoyed the times when she got to dress up for church socials, but this was a totally different feeling as she found herself corseted and stuffed into the low-cut, starkly revealing gown and wearing the flashy shoes that matched it.

Lilly stepped back to take a critical look at her when she'd finished fastening the back of the dress. She frowned.

"What's wrong?" Mary asked, sneaking into the room to see how things were going. She eyed Sammie from head to toe and thought Sammie looked gorgeous in the revealing gown. Of course, the red dress was something her friend would never have normally worn, but it certainly did emphasize her cleavage and her slim waist, not to mention her shapely legs. Walt wasn't going to like it one bit, but she had no doubt that Pete and Ned were going to be drooling over Sammie.

"She still looks too sweet," Lilly said objectively. "If they're going to believe you're the new saloon girl, then we've got to make you look like you know what you're doing wearing that dress."

"What do you mean?" Sammie asked.

Lilly grabbed a chair and pointed to it. "Sit down. I've got some more work to do on you."

Sammie did as she was told. She was willing to do whatever it took to make their plan work.

"How much longer do you think you'll be?" Mary asked.

"Not too much longer."

"I'll finish fixing the food and get it packed up."

Mary left Lilly alone again so she could complete Sammie's transformation.

Sammie sat perfectly still while Lilly worked on her hair, piling it up and pinning it on top of her head.

"That's better," Lilly said as she stepped back to study the hairstyle. Next, she took out the cosmetics she used every night and went back to work on Sammie. "This is almost the final touch."

Lilly put color on her cheeks and painted her lips a bright red to match the dress. She took out a red ribbon and artfully tied it around Sammie's neck, wanting to draw the men's attention to her throat and her cleavage, and then she gave her two dangling earrings to wear.

Stepping back one last time, Lilly studied Sammie with a critical eye.

"I think you're ready. Pete and Ned aren't going to be thinking about anything other than how good you look," she pronounced, pleased with how well the transformation had gone.

"Is there a mirror around?" Sammie was a little unsettled, wondering what she looked like.

"Not back here, but we should be able to get you into the saloon so you can see your reflection in the one behind the bar. Are you ready to go face the others?"

Sammie nodded and followed Lilly out of the room.

"Here she is, boys," Lilly said to Grant and Walt.

Sammie was watching her brother's expression carefully as she stepped out into the kitchen, and she would never forget the look on his face at the first sight of her.

"Sammie?" Walt couldn't believe the gorgeous, sexy woman in the red dress was his sister.

"What do you think?" Sammie asked.

Walt didn't say a word.

Grant was nodding in approval as he told her, "It's going to work. Ned and Pete aren't going to be thinking about anything except getting their hands on you."

"Here's your whip," Walt finally put in.

She took it from him.

"Good work, Lilly. Thank you," Mary said, completely impressed by the change in Sammie. Except for the look in Sammie's eyes, she saw no trace of her friend in the very sexy, heavily made-up woman standing in front of her.

"Glad to help. If you need anything else, just let me know." Lilly looked at Sammie. "Do you want to see yourself?"

Sammie nodded and Lilly led her into the closed-up saloon so she could get a look at herself in the mirror behind the bar. Sammie was shocked as she stared at her mirror image. She'd never dreamed the transformation would be so complete.

"I don't think Ned and Pete would recognize me, even if they knew me real well," Sammie told Lilly as she studied herself.

"Just remember to flaunt yourself when you're around them. They'll be expecting that. It's part of the job."

"I'll do it."

"And Sammie—" Lilly reached out and took her hand, proud of her daring. "Be careful. Don't trust those two for a minute. Don't turn your back on them. They are mean men—real mean."

"Thanks, Lilly."

She gave the dance hall girl a hug and started back to the kitchen where Mary, Walt and Grant were waiting for her. She paused only long enough to wind her whip up tightly so she could keep it hidden in the folds of her skirt on the way over to the sheriff's office. She planned to leave it just outside the door when she went in.

"Here's the food," Mary said, handing her the basket.

Sammie had the food and her whip. She was armed and ready. She looked over at Walt and Grant.

"Let's go get Jace out of there," Sammie told them.

Chapter Twenty-seven

Never before in her life could Sammie remember sashaying, but she was definitely doing it as she made her way down the street to the sheriff's office. She needed to be ready to face the outlaws as a saloon girl. She needed to act the part. Jace's very life depended on her convincing them she was from the Tumbleweed. She went up to the doorway and slipped her whip down on the ground before knocking loudly on the door.

"Hey, boys! You awake in there?" Sammie called out in a boisterous voice. "I got a present for you! It's from Harley! You'd better come and get it!" She said the last in an openly suggestive way.

Sammie heard someone moving around inside and drew a deep breath, thrusting her bosom forward just as the door was thrown open.

"What the hell do you—" Pete hadn't slept well at the desk and he had just dozed off again when she'd pounded on the door. What he'd planned to say flew from his thoughts as he stared at the gorgeous display in front of him. He'd seen some good-looking women in his time, but this one outdid the rest. "Well, well, well, what can I do for you, young lady?"

Sammie was ready.

"It's what I can do for you," Sammie said, smiling seductively up at him. She deliberately brushed against him as she walked past him into the office.

Pete was mesmerized and immediately on fire with desire for her. He couldn't take his eyes off her and merely pushed the door shut before following her over to the desk.

"What's going on?" Ned asked as he came out of the back room. Ned's eyes widened at the sight of the gorgeous, buxom blonde standing in the middle of the office. He'd never seen her before, but he sure was glad he was seeing her now. "Who are you?"

"My name's Sugar," she said in a breathless tone.

"Sugar suits you," Pete said, all but drooling as he stared at her cleavage. "You look real sweet."

"Why, thank you," Sammie said, giving him a come-on smile. "I've only been working at the Tumbleweed for a little while, but I'm liking it a lot."

"I'm real glad you're here." Pete hadn't seen her when he'd been at the saloon last night, but she had probably been upstairs taking care of business at the time. Having her here with him now was all that mattered.

"Last night, Harley told us to bring some food over to you this morning. He said you boys would be hungry after being locked up here by yourselves all night long. So I got up real early to take care of you."

"We're glad you did," Ned said.

"I'm hungry, all right," Pete agreed, "but not necessarily for food."

He reached out and ran a hand down her arm.

Sammie had feared they would try to paw at her and maybe try something even worse, so she artfully moved behind the desk and began to unpack the delicious-smelling foods from the basket, along with the dishes Mary had provided.

"Well, food should come first, don't you think? You do need to keep up your strength, you know." She couldn't believe she was saying these things, but she was going to do whatever was necessary to get Jace out of that jail cell. The door to the cell area was closed, so she hadn't gotten a look at him yet, but it wouldn't be long before she did if she could get these two started eating. Mary had used a lot of laudanum in her cooking that morning, and Sammie couldn't wait to see the results. "You should eat the food while it's hot."

"I do like hot things," Pete agreed, but he wasn't really thinking about the meal.

"What did you bring us?" Ned asked.

"Well, let's see . . . We've got some scrambled eggs and sausage and hot biscuits—"

The delicious aroma of the hot foods convinced the men that the meal should come first; they could play with Sugar after they'd eaten.

"You're going to stay here with us and keep us company, aren't you?" Pete asked.

"Of course. Harley wanted to make it up to both of you for all the fun you missed last night over at the saloon—and you did miss a lot of fun."

"No, we didn't," Pete said, still staring openly down her bodice. "The fun is here now."

"I'm glad you think so. Eat up," she encouraged them, "and then we'll see what other kind of excitement we can get going."

The two men wasted no time in helping themselves to the generous fare. They piled eggs and sausages on their plates, along with a few buttered biscuits, and sat down to eat.

Sammie moved about the office, casually looking around. "I've never been in a real sheriff's office before. Is that where the jail cell is?" She pointed toward the closed door.

"Yep," Ned answered, still chowing down. "And that's where we got the town's sheriff locked up right now."

"I heard all about that last night. That must have been frightening, getting in a gunfight with him and his deputy."

"Nah," Ned bragged. "It was easy. Harley knew how to set him up and he did it. They rode right into our ambush, didn't they, Pete?"

"They sure did. We thought the sheriff was dead at first, but Al's shot just grazed him. That was when Harley got the idea to bring him back to Lawless and put him on trial for everybody to see."

"I bet you're going to have a big crowd at the Tumbleweed tonight," Sammie told him. "Everybody was talking about it last night."

"I bet they were," Ned agreed.

"Harley's determined to teach this town a lesson. While we were gone, these folks went and hired the new lawmen, after we'd done killed the last sheriff. This time, Harley figured if he put Madison on trial and then hanged him for all to see, the citizens of Lawless would come to understand that this is his town and nobody is taking it away from him."

"Harley sounds like a very powerful man," she cooed, hiding her revulsion to the cold-blooded killer.

"He is. Nobody messes with him and gets away with it. Harley just shoots them."

"So you got the new sheriff all locked up back there." She moseyed over to the doorway to take a peek through the small opening at the top. She saw Jace standing in the cell looking her way, his expression hard, the look in his eyes unreadable. "He looks like a real mean man."

"Go ahead and open the door. We'll let him see how Harley takes care of his own."

"What do you mean?" she asked innocently as she opened the door to find herself staring straight at Jace. Her heart leapt at the sight of him.

"Why, Harley sent us a hot meal and he sent us you. It doesn't get much better than that first thing in the morning," Pete was saying as he took a second helping of the eggs.

"I'm glad you think so," Sammie purred.

A short time before, Jace had heard someone knocking on the office door and hadn't been too concerned until he'd recognized the woman's voice as Sammie's. He hadn't been sure whether to be furious with her for putting herself in danger by coming to the jail or thrilled that she cared enough to take such a risk. When she opened the door and stepped into the cell area, Jace couldn't believe what he was seeing.

"Why, hello there, Sheriff Madison," she purred, flaunting herself in front of him. "My name's Sugar. I'm the new girl over at the Tumbleweed. Harley had me bring some food over to Pete and Ned, so I thought I'd entertain all you boys for a while."

"Yeah," Ned called from the outer office, laughing derisively as he kept eating. "She's here to take care of me and Pete. We wanted you to see what you're going to be missing."

"I bet you're real sorry you're locked up in that jail cell now, aren't you, Sheriff?" Sammie asked, moving nearer. She wanted to reach out to him, but she couldn't. She had to force herself to keep smiling and keep up her act as she tried to control the powerful emotions flooding through her. It wasn't easy. Seeing firsthand how close Jace had come to being killed left her shaken. Even as beaten and bloodied as he was, though, she knew he was stronger than any man she'd ever met before.

"You're right. I am sorry I'm locked up," Jace told her, dealing with his own tumultuous emotions as he watched her strut before him.

Jace couldn't take his eyes off her. He'd always thought she was beautiful, whether she'd been wearing her working pants or the demure gown at the church social, but seeing her dressed in this saloon girl outfit was a whole different story. It was obvious that Sammie was up to something. He knew he had to be ready to act when the opportunity came. It was not easy, but he forced himself to concentrate on what was really going on.

Jace looked past her to see that Pete and Ned were

completely caught up in their eating right then, so he whispered to her, "Did you bring me a gun?"

Sammie faced him, still smiling broadly and leaned slightly forward to answer in a hushed voice, "No, there's no place to hide it in this dress, but Grant and Walt are right outside. Give me a minute. In just a few minutes, you'll be out of here." Then speaking in a normal tone, she asked seductively, "Do you like the view I'm offering you, Sheriff?"

Jace looked down the low-cut bodice of her dress again, but before he could say anything, she turned and strutted back into the outer office. She didn't want to risk arousing the outlaws' suspicions if she stayed with Jace too long.

She was thrilled to see that almost all the food Mary had prepared was gone.

It wouldn't be long now.

"It looks like you enjoyed your meal," she purred, watching them carefully to see if the drug was taking effect yet.

"That was some good food," Pete said. "Was there anything else you were supposed to deliver?"

"Yeah, Sugar," Ned added. "I do love your name. Do we get any kind of sweet dessert with this meal?"

"That's right, Sugar," Pete said, smiling big at her. "Harley did take good care of us this morning, sending you over our way. The food was delicious, and now we get to have some sweet fun with you."

Sammie had been afraid this might happen, but she kept smiling. "What kind of fun did you have in mind?"

"Hey, baby, you know what I want," Ned said, openly ogling her.

Pete was watching her, too, smiling broadly. "I want

the same thing. There ain't a better way to start the day than a good, hot breakfast and a good, hot woman—and you look real hot."

Sammie gave them both a flirtatious look. "This isn't exactly the best place to—heat things up, is it now?"

"We got the back room, Sugar," Ned suggested quickly. "Come on."

Ned went to her and snared her by the wrist, ready to draw her with him.

Sammie told herself again and again that the drug would start to work, that all she had to do was play along with them a little while longer.

"You don't want to wait and do it right, later tonight, on the big soft bed in my room at the Tumbleweed?"

"Any time I do this with you, I'm going to be doing it right," Ned said, just about drooling on her.

Sammie's reaction to Ned was pure revulsion. When Jace touched her, it was ecstasy, but just having Ned's hand on her arm made her flesh crawl. She could well imagine how horrible it would be to have to suffer through anything more intimate with him.

She was thrilled when she noticed Pete start to yawn.

"Looks like you didn't sleep too good last night," she said, trying to delay going anywhere alone with the sleazy Ned.

"You're right. I didn't. I had to sit here at the desk. Ned took the bed."

"Well, why don't we change that right now?" Sammie gently tugged her arm free of Ned's possessive hold on her. She looked up at Ned, batting her lashes at him as she told him, "If you got the bed all night, then Pete should have the bed all day."

"That ain't right," Ned argued.

Sammie heard a slight lazy drawl coming into Ned's words and prayed it was the laudanum taking effect on him, too.

"Yes, it is," Pete insisted. He got up from the desk and started back to the sleeping room. "Let's go, Sugar. It's been a real long time since I had a good-looking woman tuck me in."

She moved seductively over to him and looked up into his eyes, purring, "I can't wait to tuck you in."

The look in Pete's eyes told Sammie he wasn't too sharp right at that moment. If she could just kill a little more time, perhaps he'd pass out along with Ned, and then she could let Jace out of the cell. Her hopes were soaring as she took Pete's hand to lead him into the back room. She closed the door behind them, leaving Ned outside, fuming with frustration.

Back in his jail cell, Jace had heard everything that had just gone on in the outer office, and he was furious. He wanted to smash the cell door open to rescue Sammie from Pete.

He didn't want the filthy outlaws touching her in any way.

She was the woman he loved.

He wanted to protect her and keep her safe.

Trapped as he was, though, he had no way to save her.

Frustration didn't sit well with Jace. He was a man used to being in power and getting things done, and it was a true test of his will to bide his time and wait to see what happened next.

Sammie had said Grant and Walt were close by. She'd

said it was only a matter of minutes before he'd be released, but the thought of her in the back room with Pete was pure torment.

In the back room, Sammie drew Pete over to the bed. She became aware that he was getting unsteady on his feet and grew more and more hopeful that he would pass out.

"Come on, big guy," she said in a throaty voice. "This is where you belong."

"I know it," he said, grinning and leering at her.

"Are you going to take your gun belt off? I don't think you're going to need it right now, do you?"

He wasted no time in unbuckling his gun belt and throwing it aside.

Sammie's relief was great, but she didn't let it show as she put her hands on his shoulders and pushed him down to sit on the bed. It made her sick to think that this lowlife was going to be lying in Jace's bed. Disturbed, she knew her acting abilities were really going to be tested right now.

"Want to take your shirt off and get comfortable?" she asked.

"Yeah. Take my shirt off, woman."

She came closer and reached down to start unbuttoning the shirt. "Why don't you lie back and take it easy?"

Sammie gently urged him to stretch out.

Pete did, and though the mattress was hard, after spending the night in the chair at the desk, he found the bed incredibly comfortable. He was trying to keep his thoughts on Sugar, but he couldn't.

"There, that's good. That's real good," she murmured softly, hoping to lull him into an even more relaxed state.

Intimate contact with this outlaw was the last thing

Sammie wanted. She remained silent, fearing that even the slightest noise would rouse him, and she didn't want him roused or aroused.

She waited.

Sammie had no idea what Ned was doing in the outer office, and right then she didn't care. She just wanted him to believe that there was something going on back here. She could linger as long as she wanted, making sure Pete was truly out before going to deal with Ned.

Sammie waited a good ten minutes before lightly touching Pete on the shoulder. She cringed slightly, not knowing what kind of reaction she would get. It shocked and elated her when he did not respond in any way.

She had one down and one to go.

Opening the door a crack, she looked out into the office. Her relief was tremendous when she saw that Ned was sitting at the desk with his head down on the desktop. He appeared to be as out of it as Pete was; this was the moment to act.

Picking up Pete's gun belt, she took his gun with her as she crept out of the back room. Ned didn't stir as she opened the front door and signaled Grant and Walt that it was safe for them to come in. Grabbing up her whip, she left the door ajar and went over to the desk to find the key to the jail cell.

Grant and Walt came rushing in with their guns drawn, just as she picked up the key.

"Keep an eye on him. I'll get Jace," she told them, and she hurried back to the jail cell to set Jace free.

Chapter Twenty-eight

Jace had been pacing the jail cell in a rage since Sammie had disappeared into the back room with Pete. Each minute had seemed an eternity to him, and when he'd finally heard the sound of the door opening again, he'd tensed even more. He had been shocked and relieved when he'd caught a glimpse of Sammie in the outer office carrying a handgun. He'd wondered what had happened to Pete and how she'd gotten the gun away from him.

Jace had been expecting her to have a showdown with Ned, and he couldn't figure out why things were so quiet. He'd wanted to call out to Sammie, but didn't. She'd told him earlier that it was just a matter of time until they freed him, so he was going to trust that this was part of their plan and she knew what she was doing.

A moment later he heard the sound of someone entering the office and then Sammie appeared in the doorway, holding the gun and her whip.

"Sammie, get the key and get me out of here!"

"I've already got it!" She held it up for him to see. "Our plan worked! Grant and Walt are already here."

She handed him the gun through the bars and started to unlock the jail cell door.

Jace was tense as he asked, "Are you all right?"

Sammie looked up at him and smiled. "I'm fine. It just took a little longer than I thought."

"What took a little longer? How'd you get Pete's gun? And what happened to Ned?"

Sammie pulled open the cell door and watched as Jace stepped out, a free man.

"Ned and Pete are both out cold," she explained. "We put laudanum in their food. They're not going to be giving anybody any trouble for a while."

Jace looked at her with amazement. "You drugged them?"

"That's right. They didn't suspect a thing, and they didn't recognize me. Neither one of them!"

Jace paused, taking just a moment to appreciate how gorgeous and sexy she looked in her disguise.

"I recognized you," he told her, bending down to give her a quick kiss. "I'd know you anywhere."

Sammie realized it was crazy, but she knew she had to tell him right then and there: "I love you, Jace Madison. Don't you ever forget that."

"Don't worry. I won't," he assured her, grinning. "And don't you ever forget that I love you, too."

There was nothing either one of them wanted to do more than forget all about the real world and lose themselves in the glory of their newfound love, but it wasn't to be.

The danger around them was too pressing.

"Let's see what Walt and Grant are doing and get Ned and Pete locked up as fast as we can," Jace said, eager to take action.

He and Sammie went into the office to find Grant and Walt guarding Ned.

"It took you long enough to get here," Jace taunted them with a half grin.

"Some jobs are harder than others," Grant told him, genuinely relieved to see that Jace was out of the jail cell and obviously moving pretty well.

"Has there been any news about Hank?" he asked quickly.

"No, nothing. The reverend rode out to give your uncle the news," Grant told him grimly. Then he asked, "How's your head?"

"It hurts like hell, but I'm not going to let getting grazed by a bullet stop me. I came here to do a job, and I'm going to do it."

Grant nodded. He'd kept his concern about Jace's physical condition to himself all this time, but he had been worried about the seriousness of the head wound and any injuries he'd suffered from Harley's abuse. Listening to his friend now, though, he knew Jace was back in charge.

Sammie listened to their exchange, and she realized that Jace was the strongest, bravest man she'd ever known. He was in pain, but keeping the people of Lawless safe was more important to him than anything else.

Satisfied that Jace was going to be all right, Grant turned his attention to the outlaw asleep with his head resting on the desk. He eyed Ned carefully. "Right now, I think this office is going to be pretty easy to clean up. Maybe you really should have hired Sammie and Mary as your deputies when we first got here. They just brought Ned and Pete down without firing a shot."

"Yes, they did, and it would be real nice if we could take Harley the same way, but that's not going to happen," Jace said, already working on a plan to bring down the other gunmen.

"I know what you mean," Grant agreed, his mood growing dark.

"Let's get these two locked up," Jace directed. "Walt, keep your gun on Ned while we move him back to the cell."

Walt stood guard while Jace and Grant pushed Ned back in the chair. They were glad when he didn't stir at all. He just remained slumped there, his head hanging heavily on his chest. Satisfied that Ned would be out for some time, Jace and Grant hauled him up and out of the chair and dragged him back into the jail cell, where they dumped him on the cot. Jace stripped him of his gun belt and took it with them as they left the cell.

"Let's get Pete," Jace said, leading the way into the back room.

A short time later, Jace and Grant hauled the limp Pete through the office and laid him on the floor in the cell with Ned. After locking the two gunmen securely in the cell, they went out into the office to talk.

As they stood together in that moment of peace, Jace looked at Grant, Walt and Sammie. "Thanks."

Sammie couldn't help herself. She went straight to

him and embraced him. "I was so afraid we weren't going to be able to get to you out of here in time."

Jace could feel her trembling as he held her.

"But you did," he reassured her, giving her a quick kiss before looking at Grant and Walt. "And speaking of time, we don't have a lot of it. We've got to go after Harley and the other men as fast as we can."

"I spoke with some of the folks around town yesterday, and they're ready and willing to help us," Sammie told him. "We just have to let them know what we need them to do. I can go get them right now."

"Shouldn't you change out of that dress first?" Jace asked, worried about her being on the streets dressed so provocatively.

"There's no time," she protested.

"Sammie—"

"Jace, you don't know my sister very well if you think she's going to worry about what she's wearing around town. Besides, she's got her whip with her," Walt said confidently. "She'll be fine."

Jace told Sammie, "Tell whoever's planning to help us to bring their guns and meet us here at the office in half an hour."

Sammie rushed off. She was going to spread the word, but first, she was going to find Doc Malloy and send him to the jail to tend to Jace's wound.

Jace, Grant and Walt remained in the office. They were locked in a serious discussion when the doctor showed up.

"Thank God they got you out, Sheriff," he told Jace. "Let me take a look at your head wound and see what I can do for you."

Jace didn't offer any protest. He knew he needed the care.

The doc went to where Jace was sitting in the desk chair and carefully unwrapped the wound. He studied the graze mark left by the bullet and realized just how lucky Jace was to be alive. With the utmost care, he cleansed the wound and put a salve on it to aid healing. He knew the treatment must hurt and was impressed by the self-control Jace exhibited. He barely flinched as the wound was cleaned and rebandaged.

"There, you're all done, and you look better already," Doc Malloy said, admiring his own handiwork. "Do you know how close you came to meeting your maker?"

"I know," Jace said seriously. His head still hurt, but he had to admit it wasn't as bad as it had been.

"Do you have a plan for getting Harley behind bars?" the doc asked.

"We're just about ready."

"If you've got an extra gun, I'm with you."

Grant handed Doc Malloy Ned's gun belt. "Welcome to the posse, Doc."

Doc Malloy strapped on the gun belt and then checked the revolver to make sure it was loaded. Satisfied that it was, he shoved it back in the holster. "How soon are we going after the rest of the gang?"

"As soon as everybody shows up," Jace told him. "We don't have a lot of time if we're going to take Harley by surprise."

While they awaited the arrival of the other folks from town, Jace got his own gun from where Pete and Ned had stowed it. He knew then he was as ready as he'd ever be for his showdown with Harley, Al and the others.

* * *

Sammie came running into the kitchen of the Tumble-weed.

Mary and Lilly had been waiting in a frantic mood for some word of what was happening, and the sight of Sammie smiling left them joyous.

"What happened?" they asked. "We didn't hear any shots!"

"Your cooking did it!" she told Mary. "Jace is free, and Ned and Pete are both locked up!"

She gave them each a hug.

"Thank God!" Lilly exclaimed.

"What about Walt and Grant?" Mary asked.

"They're fine. They're working with Jace right now to come up with a plan for dealing with Harley. I just let Jim and some of the other men know their help is needed, and now I've got to get back to the sheriff's office."

Mary was worried. "Do you know how many men will show up?"

"No. I hope a lot, but it depends on who's brave enough to stand up with the sheriff and his deputies." She was worried that the men from town would all back out at the last minute, leaving Jace, Grant and Walt on their own.

"Dennis is here and a few of the boys have shown up in the saloon already. Should we tell them?" Lilly suggested.

"It can't hurt," Sammie agreed. "But first—where are my boots?"

"Here, why?" Mary went to get them from where Sammie had left her clothes.

"If I'm going to keep moving fast around town, I can't be wearing these," she said, kicking off Lilly's fancy shoes and quickly tugging on her boots.

"Did you want to change the dress, too?" Mary asked.

"There's not enough time. I have to get back and help them."

"Let's go talk to Dennis," Lilly said.

The three women went into the Tumbleweed and approached the bartender, telling him everything.

Dennis had trouble keeping his eyes off Sammie, but he knew he had to focus on apprehending Harley King and his gang.

"What do you think, Dennis? Can we get these men to go help or do you think they might warn Harley and cause trouble?"

"Let's find out," Dennis said, picking up his shotgun and laying it on the bar for the men to see as he called out, "Boys, I need your help."

The three men who were sitting together in the back of the saloon looked up at him.

"What is it?" one of them called back.

"Sheriff Madison is out of jail and about to go arrest Harley King and the rest of his gang. We need some more guns in the posse. You coming with me?"

"Madison broke out of jail?" the man asked.

"That's right. I told you he was the best lawman we ever had, and right now he needs our help."

"Will helping the sheriff get us a round of free drinks when we get back?" one of them asked, grinning at Dennis.

"Absolutely," the bartender guaranteed.

"What are we waiting for? Let's go meet up with Sheriff Madison. Where is he?"

The three stood up, ready for action.

"He's down at the sheriff's office," Dennis told them.

Then looking at Lilly, he told her, "You're in charge until I get back."

Lilly nodded. "You watch out for yourself, Dennis."

Dennis said no more. He picked up his shotgun and led the other men from the Tumbleweed.

Left alone in the saloon, Sammie turned to Mary and Lilly once more. "I couldn't have done any of this without you."

"We were glad to help. Now, let's hope everything goes as smoothly when they're facing down Harley," Mary told her.

"I have to get back there so I can help them," Sammie said, hugging each woman again.

"Let us know what happens," Lilly said.

"As soon as I know anything, I'll get word to you."

"And Sammie?" Mary drew her attention. "Tell Grant to be careful."

"I will."

They shared a look of understanding.

The men they loved were going to be in real danger.

Chapter Twenty-nine

Hank wasn't aware of much of anything except pain as he fought to stay in the saddle. Weakness and dizziness were overwhelming him, but he wouldn't give up. His mother had always teased him about being as stubborn as a mule, and he was proving her right.

He'd come too far to quit now.

He was going to make it home.

Ben was a driven man as he led the way along the stage-coach route. The miles seemed endless, but it didn't matter.

His son was out there somewhere.

He had to find him.

Ben kept telling himself Hank was still alive. He wouldn't allow himself even to consider any other possibility.

"Are you sure we're riding the right way?" Reverend Davidson asked as he came up alongside Ben.

"This is the way the stage would have come," Ben answered, not slowing his pace.

The preacher could tell Ben was in no mood to talk, so he fell silent. He turned his thoughts to what was going on in Lawless and hoped the deputies and Sammie had managed to break Sheriff Madison out of jail. The sheriff was a good man, and the minister believed he was smart enough and strong enough to bring an end to the senseless violence and killings that plagued the town.

Reverend Davidson looked up then, staring off at the distant landscape. He frowned as he thought he saw something moving.

"Ben, look!" He pointed in the direction of the movement.

Ben glanced over and saw what appeared to be a horse and rider in the distance, coming slowly their way.

"Oh, my God! That's Thunder!" Tumultuous emotions filled Ben as he spurred his horse to a gallop, leaving the others to follow. "Hank!"

Thunder grew nervous and shied a bit as the riders drew near. The unexpected movement unseated Hank, and he fell from his horse's back and collapsed on the ground.

Ben reached him first and all but threw himself from his saddle. He ran over to his son and dropped to his knees to take him up in his arms.

"Hank! Son, I've found you! I'm here now!"

Through a pain-filled haze, Hank heard the sound of his father's voice and managed to open his eyes. "Pa?"

"We're taking you home, boy. Hang on," Ben urged, realizing how badly Hank had been wounded.

Reverend Davidson and the ranch hands hurried over to join father and son.

"Get my saddlebags and the canteen," Ben directed.

One of the ranch hands rushed to retrieve them for him, and Ben quickly set to work cleaning Hank's gunshot wound. He'd brought along some bandages and medicine, just in case, and he was relieved now that he had.

"One of you ride into town and tell Doc Malloy that we need him at the ranch," he ordered as he continued to work on Hank's wound.

"I'll do it," the reverend said. "I'll send him out to you right away."

"Thanks, Reverend Davidson," Ben said.

Reverend Davidson mounted up and rode out.

It took a while, but Ben finally had Hank's wound tightly bandaged.

"Let's ride, boys. We've got to get him back to the ranch."

"Pa—" Hank was barely conscious, but he was still worried about Jace. He managed to reach out and grab his father's arm.

"What is it, son?"

"Jace— Did you find Jace? They shot him, too. I think he's dead."

Ben grasped his son's hand tightly and told him only a part of the truth. "Jace is alive, Hank."

At the news, relief swept through Hank. He managed only a faint "Good."

Weak as Hank was, Ben knew he couldn't make the ride to the ranch on his own. With help, Ben managed to get Hank on his horse and then he mounted behind him to provide support on the ride back. They wouldn't be able to travel as fast returning home, but at least he knew Hank wouldn't be in danger of falling off and injuring himself even more seriously. He wanted his son safe at home. He wanted Doc Malloy there tending to him. The bullet wound was grievous, and he knew it could worsen if they didn't get him help as soon as possible. With one of the other men leading Thunder, they began the return trek to the Circle M.

Sammie reached the sheriff's office shortly after Dennis and the other men. She found Jace already thanking them for coming to help.

"Jace, Jim Peters and Tom Harrison are coming for sure. I let Charlie Wilson know at the hotel and Lou down at the stage office, too," she told him.

"Thanks, Sammie. We've got to move fast."

Grant and Jace shared a look, appreciating that the odds were looking much better already.

It was only a few minutes later that Jim, Tom, Charlie and Lou all showed up with their gun belts strapped on and carrying their rifles.

"All right, Sheriff Madison, what do you want us to do?" Jim asked as they crowded into the office.

Jace was feeling a lot more confident. With the manpower they had now, they could cover all sides of the house while they were flushing the gunmen out.

"These are cold-blooded killers we're dealing with," Jace warned, looking around the room. "We all know they'll do anything to save themselves. We've already got Pete and Ned locked up, so there's only Harley, Ed, Ken and Al left. Right now, they're over at the old sheriff's house, sleeping off a real wild night of drinking. From what I understand, they usually don't start moving until early to midafternoon, so we've got to make our move on them now, while they're still sleeping and hung over."

"Good idea, Sheriff," Lou said.

"We'll see how good it is once we get into the house," Jace said seriously.

"You plan on actually going inside?" Charlie asked, a little unnerved at the prospect. He'd thought they might just surround the place and wait for the outlaws to come out.

"I want to get the drop on them. If this turns into a gun battle, it'll be deadly. We've got to catch them while they're still asleep."

"All right," they all agreed, but they were nervous.

"What do we know about the house itself?" Jace asked Walt. "How's it laid out?"

"There are four rooms—a parlor and a kitchen and two bedrooms. One opens off the kitchen, the other off the parlor."

"How many doors?"

"Two. The front door leads into the parlor and the back door is out of the kitchen," Walt answered.

"What we have to do is get inside without their hearing us and get the drop on them before they have any time to react and go for their guns," Jace explained. "Grant, Walt and I will go in. I want the rest of you to surround the house and keep watch, just in case one of them might get away from us or try to climb out a window."

"We can do that," Dennis said, his shotgun in hand. He wasn't the best shot, but with a shotgun, he didn't have to be.

"You boys ready?"

The men answered, "We're ready."

"Let's go."

They started from the office.

Jace looked over at Sammie, who was standing off to the side of the room.

"Here." Jace handed her the extra revolver. "I've got a job for you."

"What?" She was more than ready to help in any way she could.

"You're officially in charge of the jail while we're gone." He looked her in the eye as he handed her the key.

"I'll be right here waiting for you when you bring Harley and the other men back. Just be careful and don't turn your back on any of them."

"I won't."

Their gazes met, and Jace gave her one last quick kiss before going to lead the raid.

Sammie stood in the office doorway and watched them go.

The posse moved quietly through town, and when they got within a block of the house, Jace directed each of the men where to take up his watch outside the building.

"Grant, do you want to take the front door or the back?" Jace asked.

"I'll take the back, and Walt can go in with you. It's more likely one of them will be sleeping in the parlor than the kitchen. You might need the extra gun."

"Sounds like a plan. Let's do it."

They checked their guns one last time and then closed in. They all knew to be as quiet as possible. They had to surprise the outlaws to prevent a shootout.

The house was located at the far end of town on a decent-sized lot. Jace was glad, for he didn't want any of the neighbors getting caught up in what was to come. They looked around for places where the men could hide out and keep watch, but other than some low-growing bushes, there wasn't much cover. Walt spotted a buckboard down the block, and, with the help of Dennis and several others, they pushed it close enough to provide some protection in case gunfire did erupt.

When the men from town were in place, Jace, Grant and Walt split up and moved in. They were hoping that the doors were unlocked; if they weren't, the element of surprise would be lost. They timed their approach so they would enter the building at the same moment, and they were greatly relieved when the doors opened easily and didn't make a sound.

They went into the house with their guns drawn. Grant looked around the kitchen and spotted the door that led to the bedroom off to the side. It was closed, so he had no idea whether it was Harley bedded down in that room or some of the other men. Ever so cautiously, he started to cross the kitchen, planning to stay out of sight by the door to the parlor in case Jace and Walt needed him to back them up.

Jace pulled the front door open and moved silently into the parlor. He immediately spotted Ed asleep on the sofa. He noticed right away that the outlaw didn't have his gun belt on. Jace looked around, but didn't see a gun anywhere nearby, so he went to stand over the sofa. Walt followed him. Jace nodded toward the bedroom door on the far side of the room, and Walt turned to guard Jace's back as he confronted Ed.

Jace slowly and carefully pointed his gun straight at the outlaw's face and said in a voice just loud enough for him to hear, "Wake up, Ed. You're under arrest."

"What?" Ed jerked awake, opening his eyes to find himself staring down the barrel of the lawman's gun. He froze. In hungover confusion, he frowned, trying to figure out what was going on. The sheriff was supposed to be locked up over at the jail. What was he doing here?

"Don't say a word. Just get up and head out the front door. We're taking you in," Jace ordered.

Unsteady from the effects of his drinking the night before, Ed managed to lever himself up and off the sofa.

Jace backed up a few steps, still keeping his gun trained on the outlaw.

"I'm glad you know how to follow orders," Jace ground out. "Now, do exactly what I say and I won't have to shoot you. Get out of the house."

He jabbed the prisoner in the back with his gun, and Ed stumbled nervously out the front door. Jace signaled to the men outside and two of them rushed up to haul Ed away.

Harley had been sound asleep in the front bedroom when he woke up unexpectedly. He didn't know what had awakened him, but he wasn't worried about it. It wasn't noon yet, so he knew he could stay in bed for a couple more hours at the very least. He rolled over, wanting to get comfortable again, but then he heard the sound of someone walking around the house. He didn't know why any of the boys would be up and moving this early, and he didn't care. Instead of worrying about it, he put his pillow over his head and tried to go back to sleep.

Jace kept watch until he was certain Ed had been taken care of.

He went to speak with Grant. "Let's get this over with. Take Walt with you."

Grant looked at Walt. "Let's go."

Grant and Walt were ready to take care of whoever was in the back bedroom.

Grant and Walt moved in.

Jace strode purposefully toward the door of the front bedroom.

Chapter Thirty

Jace, Walt and Grant wasted no time. With their guns drawn, they charged into the bedrooms.

"You're under arrest!" Grant and Walt shouted at the two outlaws who were scrambling out of their beds in a panic. Grant saw a gun on the table nearby and ordered in a deadly voice, "Don't even think about going after your guns!"

Ken looked over at the two men holding their guns on him and knew it was useless to try to fight back.

Al, however, wasn't about to give up. Without a second thought, he threw himself out the window, crashing through the glass and cutting himself badly. He didn't care about the cuts. He just wanted to get away. He landed heavily on the ground and thought he was free until he looked up to find Dennis, the bartender, standing over him with his shotgun pointed straight at his head.

"I got him!" Dennis called out.

Two of the men who'd been drinking at the saloon ran up to Dennis's side to help him cover the bleeding outlaw.

Dennis ordered Al, "Get up. You're under arrest."

"But Dennis, I'll give you money to let me go!" Al offered.

"There ain't enough money in Lawless to make me let you go. Move!"

Dennis and the other men guarded him closely as they moved away from the house.

Inside, Grant and Walt kept their guns trained on Ken as gunfire erupted in the front bedroom.

Jace had charged into the other bedroom after kicking in the door and had been momentarily stunned to find the bed empty. He hadn't let his guard down for even a second, though, for he'd known whoever had been in that room was still there somewhere; the window was still shut and there was no other way out.

Harley had grabbed his gun and thrown himself off the far side of the bed when Jace had kicked in the door. He'd recognized the lawman's voice immediately and had been furious that he'd somehow broken out of jail.

Knowing Jace was after him, Harley had jumped up and had begun firing wildly in his direction, hoping to shoot his way out of the house and make a run for freedom.

But Jace had been ready for him.

Jace had reacted instantly, returning Harley's gunfire and ending his miserable life.

When it was over, Jace stood there in silence, staring at the fallen outlaw.

"Jace! Are you all right?" Grant shouted.

"I'm all right, and Harley's never going to hurt anyone again," Jace called back.

Grant and Walt brought Ken into the parlor and found Jace coming out of the bedroom.

"I've got a job for the undertaker back there," Jace said grimly. Then, noticing that Al was missing, he asked, "Where's Al?"

"He jumped out the window, but Dennis and a few of his boys got him," Grant explained.

They moved outside with Ken to find Dennis and the other volunteer deputies holding Al and Ed at gunpoint.

"What are we going to do with them?" Dennis asked.

"We're locking them up and sending for a judge," Jace told him. "There's going to be a real trial and real justice in Lawless."

A cheer went up from the posse.

"Jace?" Tom, the undertaker, approached him. "Do you want me to take care of Harley?"

"I'd appreciate it," Jace answered.

"I'll do it."

The rest of them started back to the sheriff's office to lock up the surviving members of the gang.

Sammie had been sitting in the sheriff's office, nervously awaiting their return, when she heard the sound of the gunfire. Not knowing what was going on left Sammie nearly hysterical. She wanted to leave the jail and go check on Jace and her brother, but she knew she had to stay. Unable to sit still any longer, she went outside to watch for some sign of what had happened, some sign that her brother and Jace were all right.

And then she saw them coming up the street.

Ken, Ed and Al were being herded along by the posse, and she could see Jace and Walt among them. She wondered where Harley was, but figured if he wasn't with the posse, Harley probably wouldn't be bothering anybody ever again.

The horrible terror that had gripped the town was over. Jace had saved them.

Unable to help herself, she ran down the street to meet the posse. She hugged her brother and then threw herself into Jace's arms.

"You did it!" she cried.

Jace hugged her close for a moment, and then kept her close to his side as they continued to the office.

"*We* did it," he said proudly, looking around at the men who'd helped him.

"Where's Harley?" she asked.

"The undertaker's seeing to him right now."

Sammie's guess had been right. The bad times were over.

When they reached the sheriff's office, Grant, Walt, Dennis and Jim took the outlaws inside the jail and locked them up with Pete and Ned. Jace remained outside to speak with the others.

"You've done a great job, Sheriff Madison," Lou told him.

"We couldn't have done it without your support," Jace replied. "From now on, with all of us working together, we're going to make sure Lawless isn't lawless anymore."

Peace truly had come to their town.

"Do you need any more help today?" Dennis asked.

"No, I think we've got things under control now. Thanks."

"No, Sheriff Madison, thank you," Lou said as the men from town began to move off and return to their normal daily routines.

Sammie stood there watching Jace, knowing how special he was.

"They're all locked up, good and tight," Grant reported as he came back outside with Walt and the others.

"And they're going to stay that way until we get a judge here," Jace said. "I'll send a telegram this afternoon, so we can set up the trial."

"The sooner, the better," Lou agreed.

"Dennis, could you tell Mary—" Sammie began.

Before she could finish, Grant interrupted her. "Don't worry about that, Dennis. I think I'll go tell her what happened myself. If that's okay with you, Jace?"

"I think Walt and I can handle things here while you're gone."

Grant had just started to leave to go to the Tumbleweed and give Mary the good news when he saw the reverend riding in. Grant called out to Jace to let him know Reverend Davidson was coming, and Jace and Sammie hurried out to talk to him.

"Reverend— Did you—?" Jace wanted to know how his uncle had taken the bad news.

"Hank's alive, Jace!" the reverend exclaimed excitedly. "He's alive!"

Everyone who heard his announcement was thrilled.

"What happened?" Jace asked.

Reverend Davidson explained how they'd found Hank riding in. "It was a miracle that he survived, that's for sure. I've got to send the doc out there right now!"

"He just left here a few minutes ago. You can probably

still find him on the street heading home," Jace said. "Make sure the doc lets them know we took down the gang tonight, and have him tell them I'll be out to see them as soon as I can."

"I will." With that, the reverend rode off to track down Doc Malloy.

When everyone had gone, Walt went back inside to guard the prisoners.

Jace and Sammie lingered in front of the sheriff's office.

"It truly is a miracle that everything turned out so well," Jace said. "Hank's alive, and we brought down Harley and his men."

"And you're safe—" Sammie added.

"You know, the more I look at you in that dress, the more I think you should wear it to work at the stable," Jace said thoughtfully, finally relaxing and allowing himself to enjoy the view.

"No," she declined with a grin, "I think I'll save this for special occasions."

"And today is special?" Jace asked, a knowing glint in his eyes.

Sammie couldn't help herself. She grabbed his hand and drew him around to the side of the building where they could steal a minute or two alone.

"Today is a very special day," she breathed, looking up at him and rejoicing in having him there with her, safe and sound.

"You're right. It is." He said no more, but gathered her close and kissed her deeply. When they broke apart, he smiled down at her. "I know Grant and I talked about hiring you on as another deputy, but I've got a better offer for you—if you're interested?"

She gave him a decidedly seductive smile. "I'm always interested in anything you have to offer, Sheriff."

"I thought maybe instead of being my deputy, you might want to be my wife." He waited for her answer, gazing down at her, loving her.

Sammie's heartbeat quickened and her breath caught in her throat. "That's one offer I can't refuse."

"I was hoping you'd say that," Jace murmured, and he kissed her once again, sealing the promise of their future together.

Epilogue

Three months later

Mary adjusted Sammie's veil for her and stepped back to look at the lovely picture she made in her wedding gown. The demure full-skirted lace and satin wedding gown was gorgeous on her.

"You look beautiful," Mary told her with a smile. "Take a look at yourself in the mirror."

Sammie turned to the mirror and smiled. "April did a wonderful job on this dress. I've never owned anything this pretty before."

"Oh, I don't know," Mary joked. "Lilly's red dress was pretty."

They both laughed, enjoying the wonder of the day.

"How much time do we have?"

"We'd better leave for church now. The ceremony's due to start in about ten minutes, so your brother's probably a nervous wreck waiting for you. Are you ready?"

"I've been ready and waiting for this moment my whole life," Sammie said with heartfelt emotion. "I'm getting married to the man I love."

"I know exactly how you're feeling," Mary agreed, looking down at the wedding band she wore. She and Grant had married the month before, and she was growing to love him more every day.

Both women knew their lives had never been better. Lawless was truly a peaceful town again. Justice had dealt with the deadly gunmen shortly after their arrests and trials, and no other outlaws had dared to set foot in town since.

Sammie glanced at herself in the mirror one more time and then said, "Let's go."

The two women left Sammie's house for the short walk to the church.

Reverend Davidson was standing with Walt in the greeting area of the church, keeping an eye out for Sammie and Mary.

"What's taking her so long?" Walt wondered, nervous over the big day.

"She'll be here. I have no doubt about that whatsoever," the reverend assured him.

The groom and his best man were already there, and the church was packed with their family and friends, all waiting to celebrate the joyous moment of their wedding with them.

Just as soon as the bride showed up.

Reverend Davidson saw them coming a moment later and relaxed. It was going to be a glorious day.

"It's that time, Walt."

Walt saw Sammie and Mary coming, and he could only stare at his sister. The beautiful woman in the wedding gown was a vision to behold. She was stunning and he went to the door to meet her, offering his arm. He greeted Mary and then turned his full attention to his sister.

"I love you, Sammie," Walt told her, smiling down at her.

She looked up at him, knowing how much he meant to her. "I love you, too. You're the best brother a girl could ever have."

They shared a look of love.

The music started then.

Mary saw Jace and Grant standing with the reverend at the end of the aisle and told Sammie, "There's a real handsome man waiting for you at the altar."

Sammie looked up at her brother. "I guess we'd better get down there. I don't want to keep Jace waiting."

Music played as Mary proceeded down the aisle. She wore a lovely green satin gown, and everyone was watching her as she reached the end of the aisle and then moved to stand off to the side. The tone of the music changed then and everyone looked toward the back of the church as Sammie appeared, escorted by her brother.

Sammie had eyes only for Jace as she made her way to the altar. Lifting her veil, she gave Walt a sweet kiss and then turned to stand at Jace's side. She glanced up at him and found his gaze warm and loving upon her.

Excitement filled her.

This was the day she'd been waiting for—their wedding day.

For a moment, the memory of what Jace had told her

about the death of his fiancée returned. It had broken her heart to learn what had happened to Sarah, but the story had only deepened her respect and love for Jace.

"Dearly beloved, we are gathered here today to unite this man and woman in holy matrimony," the reverend began.

A hush fell over the church as the ceremony continued and they took their vows to love and cherish each other for the rest of their lives.

"I now pronounce you man and wife," Reverend Davidson proclaimed. Then he looked at Jace and told him, "You may kiss your bride."

Jace smiled and took Sammie in his arms. "I've been waiting for this."

"So have I," she breathed.

He claimed her lips in a cherishing kiss that only hinted at the passion to come. When they broke apart, the music began again, and it was time for them to proceed back down the aisle.

Jace saw his aunt, uncle and Hank sitting in the first pew, along with Eloise close by Hank's side, and he smiled. The memory of Reverend Davidson riding back into town the day of the shootout with the news that Hank had been found alive would always be one of the most memorable moments of his life. Jace believed it had truly been a miracle that his cousin had survived the ambush. What had been a miracle, too, was the peace that now existed between the Madisons and the Prestons. During the struggle to reclaim their town, they'd realized they were on the same side, and had come to respect each other. Of course, his marriage to Sammie helped, too.

Jace looked down at her, thinking of how much he

loved her. He was looking forward to spending the rest of his life showing her that love.

Sammie was in heaven as they attended the reception. When it came time for them to lead off the first dance, she went eagerly into Jace's arms and practically floated around the dance floor while they moved as one to the music. The rest of the evening was magical but even so, she could hardly wait to finally be alone with Jace.

They slipped away to the new house the town had provided for Jace as sheriff, looking forward to their first night alone together as man and wife.

They reached the porch, and Jace stopped Sammie when she would have gone inside.

"What's wrong?" Sammie asked.

"Absolutely nothing," Jace answered, sweeping her up into his arms and carrying her across the threshold.

Sammie laughed in delight and linked her arms around his neck to hold on. She was surprised when he didn't put her down, but kept holding her as he kicked the door shut behind them and carried her straight off to the bedroom.

"I've been waiting for this a long time," Jace told her, kissing her hungrily as he set her on her feet beside the bed.

"So have I," she purred, returning his kiss.

They remained locked in each other's arms, sharing kiss after passionate kiss. When Jace let her go and moved away from her, she was confused. She wanted nothing more than to stay in his embrace.

"Jace?"

She stood there, feeling totally abandoned as he walked out of the bedroom.

And then she heard him lock the door.

When he returned, he'd already stripped off his jacket and tie and was unbuttoning his shirt.

"I didn't want any unexpected interruptions," he told her.

"Neither do I. Here, let me finish that for you."

Sammie went to him and slowly unbuttoned the rest of his shirt. What was a simple thing to do turned into a sensual, erotic moment. When she finished unfastening the last button, she slipped her hands inside the shirt to caress the hard-muscled width of his chest.

Jace kissed her hungrily and began to work at the tiny buttons on the back of her dress. He found to his frustration that they weren't easy to unfasten.

"Right now, I'm thinking about ripping this dress right off of you," he growled between kisses.

Sammie quickly turned her back to him so he could see what he was doing and it would go more easily for him. She felt the gown loosen and deliberately let the bodice fall away.

Jace was staring at the beauty of her bare neck and shoulders, and he bent to press sweet, hot kisses along the side of her throat.

Shivers of ecstasy raced through Sammie, and she leaned back against him, loving the feeling of being so intimate with him. When Jace reached out to turn her around, Sammie quickly pushed the gown off and stood before him clad only in her chemise and petticoats. Jace took off his shirt and tossed it aside, then looked over at Sammie. She didn't hesitate. She wanted only to be with him. She slipped off the rest of her garments, and though she was feeling a little shy, the look in his eyes erased any uneasiness she was feeling.

Jace stared at the glory of her beauty and picked her up to carry her to the bed and lay her upon it. He followed her down and Sammie welcomed him to her.

They came together in a torrent of passion, locked in each other's arms sharing kiss after devouring kiss. Jace began to caress her, and she responded eagerly, moving restlessly, wanting more, needing more. His lips traced patterns of fire over her silken flesh, and she arched against the heat of him in love's unspoken invitation.

Jace could wait no longer to make her his own.

They came together in a blaze of glory.

One in spirit, one in body.

When at last they reached the pinnacle of rapture together, they collapsed in each other's arms.

"I never knew—" Sammie began, thrilled by the glory of his lovemaking.

"You're perfect," Jace said as he drew her close to kiss her again.

"So are you," she murmured against his lips.

No more words were necessary.

Their passions flared anew, and they loved long into the night, celebrating the beginning of their life together.